BIG CHICKEN

A novel

Sijin Belle

Selwa Press

Copyright © 2012 Sijin Belle
Cover Illustration by Bodie Shaw
Art Copyright © 2012 Bodie Shaw

First Edition
ISBN: 978-0-9701157-7-5

Published by Selwa Press
1101 Portlola Street
Vista, CA 92084
www.SelwaPress.com
www.SelwaDigital.com

Printed in the USA

For Daddy and Mama,
Uncle Don and Aunt Gino,
rest them every one.

BIG CHICKEN

PROLOGUE

Under a yellow sky that could be dust sifting across the Panhandle or an incubating twister, Gus and Tubby played pirate, whacking at each other with yardsticks they stole from Gus's gramma's garage.

"Avast, ye lubber," Gus lunged.

"Wot yo...I'll run ye through, ye black card," Tubby said, not quite quick enough to dodge the blunt punch of the yardstick-sword to his pudgy, 6-year-old belly.

"Crimenee, Gus," Tubby whined, slapping back with the yardstick, landing it flat against the black card's ear.

"Ouch! Damn you, you fatso dummy...no fair," Gus said, throwing aside his weapon and landing a head butt into Tubby's smarting mid-section, taking him to the hard packed ground where they wrestled and sweated until Tubby's big brother, Pinky, banged out of the screen door, walked over and collared the boys upright.

"Quit it you little shits, or I'll turn y'all over t' the sheriff," Pinky growled. "Tubby, quit crying like a titty baby. You ain't hurt. Both y'all, dry up."

The boys watched Pinky stomp off around the spavined house, its past a palimpsest of chipped rose and lilac paint over cheap redwood. Tubby thought this was the main reason it took less than nothin' to get his brother spittin' mad. With squirrel red hair and a pink house, his friends, such as could be found at the edge of Dalhart, Texas, saddled Pinky with a fruity name and perpetual rage.

With an eye roll and sidewise look, Gus and Tubby contemplated how long to wait until they could forget they were mad at each other.

That's when they heard the shuffling under the tangle of cedar trees growing out of control in the remains of the backyard ranch-panel fence.

"Whatcha think it is?" Tubby looked at Gus.

"How do I know?" Gus pouted. "Them trees blowin' probly. I never hurt you, neither."

"Did so. It ain't wind. Air's too still, dummy."

"I never touched you a lick." Gus upped the ante: "My mama said it's fixin' to rain. Could be thunder."

Shuffle…skritch came the sound from the bushes.

"Or probly just a stupid cat," Gus allowed. "I'm gonna chunk somthin' at it." He picked up a knob of concrete from a pile by the garden shed and crept toward the noise.

Tubby hadn't bargained on real bloodshed in his yard, but he wasn't about to argue when Gus had a rock in his hand.

They tip-toed together toward the shuffling and scratching, sneaking the way they knew the Indians did creeping up on some dumb settler. Stooping, peering through the branches, the boys waited.

"Ouch, dammit, quit it, Fuckwad! That's my foot," said Gus in an eye-bulging whisper.

"I ain't nowhere near your foot," Tubby whispered back. "Dickweed."

They looked down and hollered at the same time, surprising the shuffle out of the little chicken pecking at Gus' shoe, sending her flapping upward and them running for Tubby's sissy-colored back door.

Tubby's daddy, washing up from work at the old-time pump sink, told him the chicken likely run away from the chicken plant down the alley, past the Dairy Queen and the Dustbowl Days Motel. Tubby got whipped once for staying out too late and getting too close to traffic, watching the farm trucks grind in and out of the plant parking lot.

His dad dried his neck and slipped on a clean cotton shirt. He handed Tubby the damp towel and told him to run fetch a peck basket from mama's canning hutch, then come on out back. "And don't dare tell your mama about the basket," his daddy said, holding the screen open for Gus.

When they found the chicken, it must not a been too scared, Tubby thought, still under the bushes, peckin' away. His daddy tossed it some potato peels and caught it under the basket when the little guy scrambled after the scraps. Then the bird started up a ruckus, like when the hamsters skittered against the glass tank at school, diggin' to get out.

His daddy went to sit on the porch step and eased the squawking chicken from the basket. He tucked its head under one wing, flipped it over on its back and gently rocked it back and forth, swaying his knees. Before Tubby could decide what was happening, his dad held the sleeping chicken toward his friend.

"Here, Gus, you can hold her. Just keep rocking her like this and she'll stay quiet."

When it was Tubby's turn, he gently pushed his fingers into the downy white feathers as he rocked. It was warm, and he could feel a little drum beating in among the feathers. Tubby cradled the bird like his baby sister Abby held her Betsy Wetsy doll, but he wasn't gonna sing to him. That'd be dumb. He lightly touched the very tips of its wing feathers. He smoothed the funny curling feet, like yellow fingers stuck in the air, twitching. Tubby couldn't say why it felt like his birthday.

"Can we keep it, Daddy?" Tubby asked, now stroking what he thought was the chicken's belly. Tubby asked his dad if they could keep every stray animal he came across. But the chicken was something special. Nobody Tubby knew had a chicken.

"No, buddy. We don't have a place or the time to keep chickens. Besides, it don't belong to us. It belongs to them folks at the chicken plant. You boys are gonna take her back. It'll be OK. They're fixed up to take care of chickens. They'll make sure she don't get run over or eat by a cat, or go hungry runnin' around in the alley."

Tubby's daddy lifted the chicken from the boy's lap, turned it over and shook it a little to wake it up then wrapped it in the towel.

He handed the bundle back, squeezing Tubby's hand for just a second.

"Now you and Gus walk on over to the plant and let it go up by the front. You watch now and wait for the trucks to pass. Then get on back here."

When the screen door slammed behind his daddy, Tubby sat where he was, hugging the chicken, feeling how warm it was, its beak open a crack, panting.

"C'mon, Tub," Gus jumped off the stoop. "Let's go on over to the plant. Yer dad says it's OK. I wanna see them trucks. C'mon."

Tubby tried to think of a way to hang onto the chicken. It was calm now, sitting on his lap, wrapped up. The chicken's eyes were half closed. Up close, Tubby could see little bumps around the eyelid the color of a frog's belly. He could see the shiny BB of an eye underneath the skin.

Tubby jumped when he heard a rumble aways out west. So, Gus's mama was right. It was thunder and it was liable to storm. It might get too wet and scary to take the chicken anywhere. Maybe, just to be safe and all, he should hide it in the garden shed. Then after the storm passed, and everyone forgot, he could keep it, sneak out to play with it and feed it and stuff.

Durn if he didn't wish Gus would just go on home. He was pretty fun most of the time, but never knew when to shut up. Not the kind of friend to trust with a secret. Tubby knew Gus would tell his daddy if he didn't take the chicken back and then stay to see him get a whippin' for not doin' what he was told.

He scooted off the porch to go after blabbermouth Gus, rubbing the chicken's neck where it poked out of the towel. Tubby knew he had to do what daddy said, but he didn't have to hurry.

* * * * *

"C'mon, Tubby, I gotta go. Let it down and let's go home."

The boys were sitting on a ledge by the glass door in the brick front of the chicken plant. Tubby was holding onto Swabby. He had scuffed his heels, going slow as he could down the alley row of dilapidated shotgun houses, past the Dairy Queen and the Dustbowl Days Motel, thinking of a name for his bird. Swabby, a pirate name.

"I will, I just wanna hold him a little more. You go on if you want to."

"OK, I'm going, if you ain't. What if yer dad sees me?"

"Say I'll be there in a minute." Tubby held the chicken closer. He sat pushing his nose into the feathers, smelling dust. He didn't feel too good, his stomach funny and his throat like it was hard to swallow. He looked up when lights from a car pulling into the parking lot swung past.

A lady in a gray uniform and with a white shower cap like his mama's climbed out.

"What you got there, honey? That one of ours?"

"Yes ma'am. I found him in my yard. My dad says it belongs to you all and I have to give it back. He says you'll make sure he's safe and don't get run over or somethin.'"

The woman put back her head and hooted. She was loud, standing with elbows out and her hands on her hips. Her eyes were pinched shut from laughing so hard, and her nose reminded Tubby of 22 caliber bullet holes in a STOP sign. "Oh, son," she said, still giggling at him. "Wait right here."

The glass door swooshed shut behind her. Tubby whispered, "They can't all be that bossy, Swabby. I promise. They'll take care of you. I wished I could, but daddy won't let me. But it'll be OK."

The door swung out again and this time the loud woman was with a giant man. Tubby stared up. He was way taller than Tubby's dad and had a head the size of a dodge ball. He was wearing a red bathrobe over his work clothes and had on a shower cap just like the woman.

"Son, this is Mr. Hatfield. He's the manager here at the plant. I told him you rescued one of our little birds," the lady grinned. She had a bunch of real big teeth.

Tubby held Swabby up toward the giant, who cradled the chicken in both hands as nice as you please.

"Boy, this is one of our very best chickens," he smiled at Tubby.

"We would have been real sad to lose her. I don't know what we would have done if she'd got hurt. When Sandra told me, I wanted to come here myself and tell you thanks and give you this."

He handed Tubby a toy chicken, white with black spots and a cartoon drumstick on its front like was on the plant door. The chicken was made of rubber and was smiling with pointy white teeth. Tubby didn't think Swabby had teeth.

"Thanks," he whispered. His daddy was right. Swabby was a she. "Will you take good care of her? She likes having her stomach rubbed some. It calms her right down."

The man with the dodge-ball head looked at the woman and now they both started laughing, so loud Tubby thought they would scare Swabby enough she could peck them and escape the giant's clutches. They finally stopped and stood over him, just grinning again.

"Son, I promise you, I won't let anything happen to this little hen, I'll see to it personally," Mr. Hatfield said. "Now you run on home."

"You need a ride, honey?" the woman said.

"No ma'am," Tubby said, straining to see Swabby until she was blocked by Mr. Joe Hatfield's broad back as he walked through the glass door that whispered and clicked shut.

That night from the top bunk, he told Pinky that the boss at the chicken plant promised to take good care of Swabby.

Pinky kicked Tubby through the mattress. "Tubby, you ignorant asshole. Don't you know nothin'?"

"I'm not a asshole and I know a lot. And quit kickin' me." His stomach felt funny like before. Tubby thought he might cry.

"You don't know squat, Doofus. What do you think they do with chickens over at that plant, anyway, dress 'em up like little dollies and play tea party?"

Pinky kicked the mattress again, every few rotten words. "They cut their heads off, is what they do. Slit their throats so the blood gushes everywhere. Cut their little chicken heads off then pull out all their feathers, cut out all their guts and poop and chop 'em into little pieces. Your precious Swabby is probably gettin' its head cut off right this minute, or somebody's yankin' his innards right out. And it's your own fault 'cause you took it back. They'll take good care of it all right. Ha ha ha! What a stupid asshole, stupid as yer stupid dead chicken. Asshole!"

Tubby was staring at the ceiling where he saw giant chicken people with big heads in shower caps laughing and grinning at him with creepy wet teeth. He cried so Pinky wouldn't hear and twisted the black spotted sponge chicken with both hands as hard as he could until it popped in two.

ONE

Julie Duwray hung over the john bowl after a deeply scouring heave. This purge was taking way too long. She shouldn't have eaten so many of the hot wings Lyle brought home from the new Right Wings and Taters over on Brookside.

She was so entirely not into watching football all Saturday afternoon with Lyle and his a-hole buddies. They were such idiots, the first time she called them Lyle and the Boozer Losers, they whooped and group hugged her, taking it as a sign from God and Jerry Jeff Walker that they should move right then to Belize and become ace country rockers. She listened to them now through the bathroom's accordion door, over the blab of halftime and in between her retches. A bunch of two-bit inbreeds who'd never get closer to the music business than stacking chairs at the high-school battle of the bands. Not Lyle, of course. He might be a shitkicker, but he had a good job down at the 51st Street Blockbuster, a company with a future.

Julie had to be at the call center early Sunday. She just wanted to throw up and go. She had things to get done, but felt she owed it to Lyle to pretend to be a big OU booster. It was a freakin' chore, though, and putting up with a den full of goofballs, four quarters of forced idleness and all the pretense drove her to eat.

It didn't help that the only food in the house besides beer was Right Wings Buffalo Blasters. Damn, the drumsticky things were so good, with the extra ball of white meat on the tip and the spicy hot, crispy breading. She just couldn't help it. She had worked her way through a 20-piece "Dwindling Herd" portion all by herself.

Really, it didn't matter how much she pigged out. Julie has been throwing up on purpose ever since she packed 35 pounds on her butt by the end of her first year at the University of Oklahoma. She had quickly lost the freshman fatness and been buliminating ever since. It was way easier than eating rabbit food and going to the gym to stay cute. In fact, Julie thought she had discovered the only real all-you-can-eat diet, and she was going to stick to it. "Haaa-ockk," Julie surged.

She was feeling righteous at the moment about her binge and purge two-step, staring into the nauseous corroded stool in Kyle's way-off campus rental. His landlady, a perennially untenured OU Tulsa professor of the aging hippy persuasion, was avid in an avocado-hued time warp of 70s appliances and matted shag carpet, sticking with them through decades of toke memories and party deposits. Layered with a stale smell of too many male undergrads under one iffy roof, the hovel was enough to put anyone off off-loading dinner. Still, Julie's clockwork upchucking was all-important to her plan for looking the part if she wanted to move out of the despond of call-center customer service into sales where all the money was, and no fat girls need apply.

Julie gulped again and tried to let fly. "Ukkgkkahahkg." She needed to finish up before halftime ended, get back to Lyle, before he and the Losers started humping throw pillows listening to some off-key girl band butcher "We Will Rock You," so bad but boob rich that it gave 'em a community boner.

She braced her feet against the extra Bud 24-packs lining the bathroom floor, put one hand on the rusted grab bar next to the crumbling shower surround. She sucked her lungs full, then pushed and panted from the bottom of her cute Little MissMatched socks all the way up to her eroded molars. "Ughahgggggukag!" Damn and triple damn. Not a morsel.

Frazzled, Julie swallowed and strained. Nothing doing but a little dribble of sour beer foam. Something had to be stuck fuckin' sideways. She spit and tried again, but whatever was down there wouldn't budge. Julie hooked her right middle finger down her throat all the way to her fist knuckles to move things along. "Gahag. Gulp ulp, gaa-hagaaaaaghhhs." Oh, right, okay, she yanked her finger out and here it came, sploosh, into the bowl. I definitely need to chew shit longer, Julie thought, clutching cold porcelain and panting, eyes swimming.

Through the blur Julie saw a long sliver of purplish red floating in the upchuck. OMG! She swiped her eyes and squinted. Double OMG! With one unsteady hand, she gave the bit of redness a poke, terrified that she'd finally hocked up her esophagus. The sliver submerged for a second among wing bits and sauce, popping back up like a tiny, shiny maroon pool noodle tipped with a teensy yellow rhinestone.

Rhinestone? Hmm. Julie forgot about her still half-full stomach and pondered the notion of a rhinestone on a hunk of chicken. Then her vision cleared, her brain kicked in and Julie imagined that she'd just barfed up a bright future, one that had nothing to do with acres of office cubies peopled by guys in short-sleeve white shirts, knit ties and ear buds, or with whiners complaining about how they got screwed by their insurance company. Or even better, with the occasional extra pint of Chunky Monkey on her ass.

The maroon floater was not a gout of her tortured insides, Julie realized, but an acrylic fingernail that some minimum-wage high-schooler must have lost in the chicken fryer at Right Wings. And here Julie was, a poor trusting customer, just trying to enjoy a quiet Saturday afternoon at home with her boyfriend, a ballgame and a big pile of hot wings. She was just a poor, unsuspecting, defenseless consumer who swallowed something horrible and who even now was suffering Lord knows what harmful bodily effects.

And, ooh, thought Julie, warming up, she wouldn't be able to stop thinking about her excruciating bout of killer food poisoning followed by hours of debilitating vomiting. She wouldn't be able to sleep for weeks, years maybe, recalling the horror of it all. Or maybe even ever mess around again with Lyle. Julie knew she would have to work to sell the downside of that last part, given the state of Lyle's litter-bag-cum-futon, but never mind, she felt the post-traumatic emotional distress start to build.

She wiped her damp hand across her jeans, pulled her phone out of its holster and snapped away at the offending fingernail as it eddied and bumped against a flap of chicken skin.

Yanking back the bathroom door, she screamed, "Help me, Lyle, I'm sick. Help! I'm liable to die!"

Julie grabbed a bag of cotton balls off the tank lid and dumped the contents on Lyle's Naconas as he lumbered to the door.

"Whatsamatter, hon? I heard you urpin.' Those wings do a number, did they? Want me to hold your hair back?"

So sweet, thought Julie, but didn't bother to answer. She shoved her hand in the cotton-ball bag and reached to pluck the nail from the ick. Tweezing it between her bagged fingertips, Julie saw that the nail was evilly long and ornate with decals and glitter, now trailing a flume of her sick. She gave it a quick shake to drain the excess but dreck clung stubbornly at the base of the acrylic. *I can't believe I ate the whole thing*, Julie grinned to herself. She shook it again and raised the runny mess so she and Lyle could get a closer look.

"Big whoop. What is it?" Lyle asked, not really all that interested in scrutinizing a gob of puke and beginning to think that Julie, red-headed, hot and ready as she was, was too high maintenance for an aggie from Beaver County.

Julie stared. Stuck to the back curve of the acrylic she saw another fingernail, pale and attached to a fleshy pouch wrapped around a knob of bone that was trailing stringy ligament. Julie felt the blood drain from her face right before she dropped her personal injury lotto ticket back into the greenish commode. Then, she experienced her first authentic hurl in five years, spewing up everything clear back to yesterday's breakfast, a geyser of sound and sick that splattered all over Lyle's lucky OU sweatshirt.

TWO

SKIATOOK, OKLAHOMA

Greta Greenberry sat in the dark at Poultry Xtra Corporate in a room full of Quality Control heavy hitters and twice as many lawyers. They were staring at DVD images of a bejeweled acrylic nail attached to what the plaintiffs' attorney was assuring them was the desiccated tip of a human thumb eaten and regurgitated by his client. The nail and tissue lay next to what was supposed to be a thumb bone that the young woman claimed she had gnawed along with an order of Right Wings Buffalo Blasters flats and drummies.

Greta had seen a lot in her 10 years with Poultry Xtra, and some stuff back at the Purdue University food science lab that would have turned a weaker stomach, but looking at the phone stills of the alleged thumb tip floating in a toilet bowl of unflushed vomit was more than she wanted to see in full HD color.

Usually in product contamination incidents, they got to see the real thing. Eventually they would have access to the severed digit. But the lawyer for the woman who'd apparently mistaken a human thumb for part of a chicken wing wasn't going to let go of his evidence this early in the negotiations.

"Well, that's the lot of them," said Greta's boss, Andy McCutcheon. "Somebody hit the lights." When the recessed, energy-inefficient incandescent glow shone again on the heavy silk waterfall drapes, exotic woods and illuminated law books in ceiling high, etched-glass cases, Greta was impressed as always that this lavish room was the control center of, it must be said, a chicken

12

plucking chicken pusher, albeit a big plucker in the poultry universe.

Staring at a paneled wall bearing a Bev Doolittle print of Pinto ponies turning into aspens, or some kind of high country tree, Greta half heard Andy explain, "It's no movie prop, it's human. But the docs won't swear conclusively. Assuming someone didn't lose a thumb at the restaurant, it was in a batch of wings we tracked by Julian date and plant number. It looks like they entered the product stream in Mississippi, at Malapee."

HR Operations VP Sol Collins groaned and pounded once on the conference table, forgetting its sacred origins as the flatbed bottom of their founder's first egg truck, veneered now with burl and brought to a mirrored shine, probably in some sweatshop in Mindanao.

"You've got to be shitting me! Malapee? They're in discovery on the Title VII nightmare down there because some yahoo supervisor is masturbating with chicken necks. You believe it? Flogging giblets out their flies? And now they're grilling up human thumbs? My God, the plaintiffs' bar will wet themselves over this, not to mention the freakin' food Nazis. Jesus Horatio Christ!"

"It shouldn't come to that if we can shut this down soon" said Corporate Attorney Cletus B. Field, unfolding slowly to his full 6 feet 6 inches, using his Tenth Circuit baritone, making sure everyone in the room knew that Legal Was On The Job. "We're very familiar with these attorneys, Hector & Chase. We've been on their deep-pockets list since that race case in North Alabama, so there's a relationship we can leverage. That blonde Chase cookie will listen to me. Right now they aren't filing anything, just trying this little pictorial salvo to see what we'll lob back."

"You mean zeros, don't you? How many zeros we'll lob?" Sol felt like weeping, but he shot his cuffs instead. Being able to see his monogrammed initials in the proper place always improved his sense of control, even though any payoffs would come out of his cost centers. Well, a few more settlements this year and they'd hit stop-loss and the reinsurer would get stuck with the tab. But his annual review could go directly down the toilet.

"In the meantime, folks, we need to nail down what happened at Malapee," Andy said, pulling at his nose, a holdover from a minor undergrad coke habit, along with a flashback tendency to go manic in a crisis.

"If it is a human thumb, and Right Wings isn't behind it, how did it get in the wings? Who the hell does it belong to, I'd like to know. We need to get on the horn with Truly Lovett and his crew and get some answers. Greta, I want you to take the lead on this," Andy said. "We need a whole lot more information before we can respond. Cletus, we need that thumb so we can make sure it's the real deal."

Greta nodded her assent, but remained silent. She felt a trip to Mississippi in her future over this thumb screw-up. She loathed Mississippi. She spent a couple of years at Chamber Maid Foods in Vicksburg right after getting her Master's in Food Science. She had her fill of the state whose only saving grace was the ratio of great writers and musicians to assholes. One Welty, Williams or Faulkner, Sam Cooke or Tammy Wynette for every 100,000 peckerheads pulled Mississippi from its slough of crackerness and political jobbery but just barely.

If people asked her about Mississippi, she told them to watch the film "Mississippi Burning." Mississippi then wasn't exactly Mississippi today, but it was damn close in too many ways to overlook and with an added veneer of "New South" pseudo-penance and self-congratulation. In her experience, it was still a racist, sexist, homophobic backwater and she had no particular desire to make a return visit.

The state's ol' boy poultry brotherhood didn't give a flip about her credentials and job history. What they did like was Greta's honey brown hair and Indiana farm-fed body, which her husband, Toby, compared to "R. Crumb's most pneumatic of teen babes." The guys wanted her at the dance, just not in the game. Who needed that kind of crap in this day and age?

When the thumb turned up, Greta had felt relatively safe because her territory as senior QC auditor was the U.S. Southwest

Division. But if they needed her in Mississippi, she'd have to go. In major contamination cases, you didn't get to pick the place. So she kept her mouth shut and hoped that the well-manicured thumb-whatsit still might end up some lamebrain's idea of a rubberized joke.

"Let's meet back here tomorrow at 10 sharp to update. I don't need to impress on you that, so far, this situation is off radar and needs to stay that way," Andy said. "Cletus, get me that thumb."

* * * * *

At Andy's summons, Greta arrived 30 minutes early to the meeting. She expected he wanted to brainstorm about her trip to Mississippi before the others arrived. She wished like crazy she could talk to Toby, but at this point, husbands weren't on the need-to-know list.

She was building up a little head of steam about the whole drama. She thought they were making a huge mistake not getting ahead of the news hounds, trying to massage the truth. One of Greta's biggest problems, being in this business: She had a conscience.

Her mentor at Poultry Xtra, rough old Charlie Casey, a hard-core operations VP, had first recognized that Greta's moral compass pointed away from production and toward quality assurance, and encouraged her to make career tracks straight in that direction. Toby kidded her that Charlie just wanted her out of his hair, which Greta deemed unlikely since he could easily pass for an aging skinhead. Charlie claimed it exempted him from wearing those granny-panty hair nets.

As much as Charlie believed in running production full tilt and steamrolling the competition, he also believed that right was ultimately more profitable than wrong. Greta was pretty sure if he hadn't retired after winning $12 million in the Missouri lottery after a lifetime buying one ticket a day on the way to work, he would be kicking up a ruckus about the decision not to go public with the severed thumb.

"Greta," she could hear Charlie growl, "People will go with you a long way if you're straight with 'em. But when folks start listening to lawyers tell them to circle the wagons to protect the business, the crook factor goes up ten-fold and so does the chance you'll end up shooting your own pecker off, present company excepted, of course."

She was planning to tell Andy just that as she walked into the conference room. She was surprised to see that Andy wasn't alone. He, Clete Field and Grant Wallace, the VP for Risk Management and Security sat in a line next to HR Operations VP Sol Collins. She would be forced to take a chair facing them across the expanse of gleaming redwood burl.

"Greta, glad you could make it," Andy grinned. "Sit down. Clete and Grant have come up with a terrific plan to ferret out whoever's behind the thumb fiasco at Malapee and keep everything under wraps. You're our ace in the hole so to speak, and once we run it down for you, I know you'll love it and embrace it wholeheartedly for the good of Poultry Xtra."

Andy was avoiding eye contact like a CIA shrink. It was such a rehearsed and insipid remark that Greta ignored it and stood looking at the three other men in the room, each wearing a pleased expression as glossy as the tasteful embroidery on their Countess Mara ties. She tried to reckon the odds for feigning sudden illness, scolded herself for being such a wimp and sat. For a second she thought she could hear old Charlie.

"You got some balls, Greta, but if I was facing that school of sharks, I'd be hauling ass."

* * * * *

When the suits finally left her alone with Andy, Greta stared at her boss, who studied the swirls in the tabletop. She had expected he would send her to Mississippi. She didn't expect to be railroaded into some idiotic sting operation. Finally, Andy met her eyes, looking as if he might have felt the flicker of a conscience buried deep in some limbic molecule.

"Greta, what do you want me to do?"

"Well, let's see, off the top of my head, you could tell them no. Tell them I'm not qualified to go "undercover" as they put it. Or at least you could've backed me up when I told them the whole idea is nuts and maybe dangerous..." Even though she was just winding up, Greta stopped abruptly. Andy was shaking his head, his adam's apple sliding around like an undecided oyster. She could tell he was working hard to swallow his own BS.

"Greta, you'll be surrounded by hundreds of people. Besides, they...we just want you to look around, mostly at Malapee's QC operation – you know that better than anyone. That's it. Just look and report to me and Grant every day, anything you see out of the way." Brightening, he concluded, "Hey, you can tweet to us in real time. And if anything gives you the least case of willies, you get out of there. I swear you'll be fine."

"Are you willing to swear to my husband and two small children?" Greta thought a sucker punch was in order.

"Greta, you can't tell them about this yet. You heard Clete. This is not about us screwing up our own process, this is way bigger. It's about somebody screwing it up for us. We don't have a clue, not how or who...not anything. There's no telling what is involved."

"So, you're making my argument for me," Greta said.

Andy frowned. "My point is, Greta, we have to give a reasonable response, something the press office can release that doesn't make us look like were in the middle of a John Carpenter movie. We can't just say, 'Oh, yeah, somebody's putting human body parts in our products and we'll let you know what's up as soon as we figure it out.' The decision has been made to handle it internally until we get some answers, and..."

"Andy, please..."

"And," Andy cut her off, making that church steeple thing with his porky fingers that he thought made him look imposing. "The decision has been made on how to proceed. I know you well enough to know you're going to get on board. It's an assignment we'll prepare you for, and with the people involved at this level of risk, you do not want to be seen as uncooperative. It's OK to raise your hand and air your opinions, but it's also time to get with the program."

Greta sat back. Andy had quite a sucker punch, himself.

THREE

Lowndes Henderson swung his legs out of bed and sat up, bracing his hands on the mattress either side of his bare thighs. He coughed and ran one hand over his short cropped hair and across his face. It was 4:00 a.m. and still raining. Four days of rain was good for some crops but not so good for the disposition. But he had to feed the chickens, slop the hog, get his grandson Danny's lunch ready and get to work.

Lowndes had been heading to work at the chicken plant in Malapee, Mississippi six days a week for 32 years. He'd worked at every job in the place from back-up killer to a-hole checker, a job he thought they must have made up on the spot when the man from personnel told him what he'd be doing. It was exactly what the name described: Using a finger to make sure the gut end was still attached to the butthole on hundreds of thousands of freshly killed birds.

As soon as he was allowed, he'd transferred to the live-hang dock, a nightmare of noise, dust and flailing, shit-covered chickens under murky blue light. They said blue calmed the birds, but you couldn't have proved it by Lowndes. The chickens crammed into the hang trough to be grabbed, upended and hung in metal shackles by their paws never impressed him as the least bit relaxed.

If a man could hang 25 birds a minute, it was a good job pay-wise. Of course, Lowndes wouldn't have expressed it right out, but he understood that good was relative.

For the last two years, Lowndes had been in charge of the offal trailers. The smell of rot would strip shellac, but he got used to it after a couple of months. It was fairly easy as jobs went. He dumped barrels, moved containers by fork lift and occasionally had to shovel the bloody, gagging slurry of condemned, rotting chicken fat, bones, skin and innards. But nobody messed with him. That was the best part, being allowed to work alone, put in his hours, clock out and go home to Danny.

Lowndes didn't pay much attention to what the years of toil had done to his body – tricky shoulders from live hang, lousy knees and back from endlessly twisting to dump 70-pound tubs of chicken; hands arthritic from cutting shoulders in debone, thick skinned from operating fiery ovens and fryers twice the size of flat cars and permanently numb from working in water chillers just as big. His hearing was lousy from constant noise, but he considered it something of a blessing when Danny played his rap music, or worse, Barney tapes.

Lowndes wore his ailments like his Dickies work clothes, everyday without too much thought except that lots of people had it worse. He only felt down about it when he saw some young tally whacker with his pants slung below his under drawers heading off to the nurse's station the first night on the job because of some puny-assed complaint about his hands being sore. Sore, my foot, Lowndes would tell his friends. That sorry little so-and-so won't last a week.

Lowndes didn't think a whole lot of most of the younger generation, especially the ones who worked a little bit here and there to get some playin' around money but still mostly lived off their mamas – or their daddies. Lowndes had to admit it. He let his youngest girl Sharay move back with her baby Danny in between bouts of true love with some freeloader playing dodge 'em with two or three other baby mamas. The last time Sharay disappeared with a man, she up and left Danny behind. Lowndes was fine with that. He loved having his grandson around. Though he had been giving some thought to retirement, with the boy to see after, that wouldn't be happening anytime soon.

By 5:30, morning chores done, the old man bundled Danny next door to Miss Patricia's to have his cereal and wait for the school bus. Lowndes rubbed the boy's head then ducked back through the downpour to his '72 Datsun pickup for the 20-mile trip to the plant along narrow blacktop corridors bunched with trees cloaked and bent under kudzu.

The rain fell hard and steady, making the windshield wipers whomp without much effect. Lowndes strained to see. He swiped the windshield over the steering wheel with the side of one large hand to clear the fog. Lights flickered ahead. Lowndes slowed and rolled to a stop behind several cars.

He saw a couple of folks huddled under umbrellas. One headed toward the Datsun, and Lowndes cracked his window. It was one of the men from the plant who worked upstairs in the management offices. Lowndes had seen him over the years, but honestly couldn't say he'd ever heard his name. "Hatchery bus slid into a tree, chicks slung all over" he hollered, "We called live haul and MDOT."

Not surprising thought Lowndes, what with so much rain. The way those hatchery boys drove, like hell hounds, it was no wonder when they come a cropper. He imagined the dark, wild growth around this stretch of the Trace. Heavy rain and loamy soil always made him a little nervous in the thick woods. He thought about trying to back out and go around by Tickfaw Road, but then decided just to light up and relax. Like the office guy, most of the people held up by the wreck were headed to the plant. They'd all be late for work, but maybe with so many, they wouldn't be docked for missing.

Lowndes had perfect attendance and he would hate to blemish that record. He'd not missed a day in 32 years unless it was vacation. He had been given a special jacket like high-school quarterbacks wore for working more than 50,000 hours without an unexcused absence. Perfect attendance: It was something to be proud of in a life of plain old hard down work. An achievement that showed a person's true character. Not showy, but steady, every day.

He settled back and thought about his mess of a daughter. He knew Sharay would be back. She always turned up, worse for wear, weepy, with her hand out. He'd always given in before, but next time, he'd insist that she straighten up and go to work. She skated from responsibility because he let her. She could easily get hired on at the chicken plant, if she could just stop with her weed jags long enough to pass the drug test. He would put his foot down.

Lowndes blew out rills of smoke. He considered asking the office guy to borrow his phone so he could call in, but he couldn't see how they'd hold this trouble on the road, an act of God and a sorry bus driver, against his attendance record.

Lowndes turned off the engine to save gas and listened to the rain dance across the truck. Over the tattoo of drops, he heard a slow grind and figured MDOT must have arrived with a chain saw crew. The grinding noise grew louder, and just when Lowndes realized it wasn't coming from chain saws after all, the Datsun roof began to shriek and buckle under the weight of a massive, toppling pine. Its skimpy roots, loosened by four days of rain, had lost their grip on the gruel of soil in the bar ditch. The Datsun cab crumpled like paper, slamming Lowndes forward, crushing his neck against the steering wheel, severing his head, once and for all sealing his perfect attendance record.

FOUR

MALAPEE, MISSISSIPPI

Maintenance chief Wayne Daylight mauled his cinnamon toothpick and gazed at a washed-out aerial photo of Malapee, Mississippi Poultry Xtra that covered one wall of his second floor office. The other three walls were half glass, overlooking sections of the main poultry operations: live, front and back-half cut-up and further processing, or, dumbed down for the marketing hustlers, chicken with racing stripes and fog lamps added.

He contemplated the old overhead shot that showed the massive plant set well off the highway, encircled by service roads, expanses of employee parking and truck lots, the water treatment facility to the south and acres of hilly, wooded campus surrounded by the dark canopy of the Mississippi mixed-wood forest.

The vantage was wide enough that a person who knew what to look for could see, a little behind the lagoon, the edge of an acreage of mounded red dirt and rocks. Wayne had dubbed it "The Dog Yard" back when old Mr. Hiram Otis owned Banty Roasters, Inc., and trusted him to run the whole shebang, including the occasional fund-raiser involving dog and cock fights.

That was before Poultry Xtra bought out the Otis family four years ago, closed two of the three Mississippi Banty Roaster plants and told Wayne he could stay but not in charge, except for maintenance. With the department's $50-million annual budget, give or take, the comedown hurt but not enough to walk. So Wayne curbed his general self-importance and stayed put. True, every time he thought much about what had been taken from him, the pile of spent toothpicks scattered under his desk got so deep, it looked like blowback from midget UFOs shearing circles in a tiny wheat field.

Wayne had no truck with self-pity and had spent his time since the buyout becoming indispensible to the Poultry Xtra college grads sent in to take the reins. Those boys might have been hot stuff back home, but were just so many ex-high-school halfbacks here, where their hometown heft didn't count for much. It had been like pulling wet puppies from a drownin' bag. Wayne laughed at the image, careful to spit his pick onto the pile below and not suck it down his windpipe, as he'd nearly done this morning when a process server ambushed him with a subpoena. He was going to have to talk to some lawyer about sex shenanigans at the plant. Well, if it wasn't one damn worry, it was a dozen. Like the freakin' debone department.

He swiveled his chair to see if things were rolling again. He couldn't hear through the glass wall or over the sound of NPR, tuned to The Gestalt Gardner. He liked that Felder guy. A little odd, but knew his Mississippi horticulture. Wayne was partial to Terry Gross, too, the way she'd grab some glib SOB by the privates and shake, right there on the air, in this uncanny baby girl voice. She was like "The Bad Seed" of public broadcasting.

At least he could see that his boys had things under control, not real smooth but not stopped dead like this morning, when ten lines were backed up like I-20 after a Mrs. Butterworth's tanker jack-knifed across all six lanes. Of all the processes, debone was the biggest cluster. Nothing like the old days. Now, there were too many bosses, too many overworked, barely trained workers who didn't give a rat's ass about anything but break time, payday and whose sister was dating her own brother-in-law.

And too many high-dollar machines with tolerances set too fine, way too ultra-tech for an old farm boy who loved pumps and hydraulics, but would give a week's wages to bust anything with a touch screen. And too many customers with too damn many special demands.

But did any Poultry Xtra poor excuse for Billy Mays, rest his soul, ever once tell a customer "No. No, ma'am, it's not possible to make every single piece of your 7-million pounds of breast tenders weigh exactly the same and in the shape of a Saturn 5 Rocket, unless of course we start growin' chickens in molds." No, the clueless sales bastard who'd never been within three states of an actual plant said, "Yes, ma'am! Absolutely, we can do that. Give us a week, no two. The rocket molds will take extra time."

It had been a sort of shock to Wayne that it was easier to help the Poultry Xtra probies survive their Mississippi immersion than it was to run chicken this new-fangled way. It wasn't complicated, like that dad-blasted computer neatly out of reach on his desk. No, this state was as simple as every other rural patch from Oklahoma to Georgia.

Whether it was cracker or all black backwoods, country folk weren't real different. The natives all knew it, all Mississippians knew it, never mind what screaming liberal preachers and knee-jerk politicians said. And forget the KFC-Taco Bell combo drive-throughs, the U-totem and Dollar Store franchises and the other emblems that hollered Modern America. When they ventured into the state of mind that was the wild piney woods, newcomers had a way to hoe before they got anywhere with locals. Maybe if you stayed more than a couple of years, they'd warm up. Maybe not. Probably not.

But the college boys had no intention of staying that long, and arrived with an itch to get promoted out of there before their wives packed up the kids and hiked back home to mama. Nearly all of them were rural boys with aggie or food science degrees and just enough sense to know how things worked in the Deep South: things didn't. Not worth a damn unless you knew the right way and the people who counted. Wayne knew the right way. Wayne counted.

He'd accumulated and doled out favors in his little corner of Beauswamp County before the college boys were born. And they sorely needed him to call in favors from time to time to keep the plant running. If it was the crack of midnight on New Year's Eve, nobody but Wayne had the stroke to get some ol' boy out of his party duds and up to the plant to dredge a mainline backed up with chicken offal and all the junk workers threw down the drains – whole birds, dirty socks, hair nets, wrenches, old saw blades, hanging shackles, feminine hygiene products, liquor bottles, whole rolls of paper towel and the occasional ice-house shovel. If the drains backed up, USDA shut you down. Every minute you couldn't run, the clog might not move, but you were flushing millions in profit.

Being helpful wasn't the ticket for Wayne. It was experience and local leverage that situated him at Malapee as long as he cared to stay. So if he sometimes was put out that he'd been passed over, his ability as a fixer kept the Company boys off his back. Plus, Mr. Otis had treated Wayne right, proof being his big place over in Delk County planted in soy, cotton and fine ornamentals. Wayne figured if the young pups ever really pissed him off, he could walk away and be just dandy. Without Wayne, they'd be up Old Man River in a leaky bass boat.

In a way, Wayne thought, as he slipped the cellophane from another cinnamon toothpick, he may not be in charge, but he was in control. He and his maintenance boys ran things his way, as if Poultry Xtra was just a bad dream after a dinner of tepid crawdads. Nope, he had no problem handling the Company newts.

Unfortunately, it was the Feds who would give you the biggest headaches. And Wayne thought he felt a doozy blooming, one that all the BC Powder in the county wouldn't touch.

FIVE

Beebe Dovey and Hoopdy Creavy were Poultry Xtra supervisors, each other's best friend and Metal Gear Solid gaming fanatics. Liquid Snake and Solid Snake. Like a buddy movie in real time, except when life threw them a sinking slider. Then their go-to response was flying off the handle. Like today, all because Beebe's daddy's Bobcat mini-loader was busted again.

"Shit, Hoopdy," Beebe looked at the distance from the hobbled loader to stacked piles of bagged chicken litter set to move for sale. "I toldja not to ride the dang piece a crap all the way to the plant. She can't take that kinda distance and push loads, too. How many times do I gotta go over this? Git the Penske and trailer, load the shit in the truck and the Bob on the trailer and haul it that way."

"I didn't think it'd hurt, just the loggin' road, the hill 'n back. 'Sides, I couldn't get the Penske, Beebe. Wayne had me be buryin' them old lockers, then Jerbel told me to plow 'em back up and load 'em all so the truck's been full, and anyways you said I gotta hurry 'n get these bags outta here."

Here was an abandoned breeder house on the back edge of the Dovey & Daylight broiler farm that Beebe and Hoopdy managed for Beebe's daddy Chaplain Deacon Maitland Dovey and his brother-in-law partner, Tuber Daylight. With 12 working growout buildings to see to, plus recycling chicken litter, plus their other gig at the Deacon's funeral parlor plus work at the chicken plant, the boys would be screwed as a hex nut without the Bobcat.

"Oh yeah, Beebe, yer daddy grabbed me in the break room this mornin' 'n asked me if we was gettin' behind a'tall. I never told 'im that, but he sounded like he knowed. Beebe, how's he know?"

"He don't know," Beebe shoved his face so close Hoopdy could smell cheese fries and Grizzly Dip. "Hear me? He knows nothin' unless you told. Didja?"

Hoopdy, losing hope that Beebe would wind down anytime soon, tried to dodge his friend's spit shower and resorted to whining and oaths of brotherhood. "No, Beebe, I never. I swear. I never told a single one. Swear on Solid Snake."

Beebe backed off a step. "Dammit all, we're screwed even if he don't know. The furnace conveyor's busted 'n now the Bobcat. Sonova effin' bitch!" Beebe snatched the stained and frayed Gather at the River Funeralization Tabernacle gimme hat off his shaved head and threw it at the idled Bobcat.

"I think I can git 'er runnin,' Beebe," Hoopdy said, close to tears. "I know it. I'll figger what's up 'n borry the parts offa one at work."

"Hoop, we can't keep doin' that. Wayne's gonna catch on. If he gets suspicious 'n starts snoopin' out back, it'll be all she wrote. Then everbody'll know. Shit!" Beebe kicked a scuff of dirt, walked to retrieve his hat and seated it on his head.

"Wayne won't," Hoopdy pleaded. "He's got me buryin' stuff out back ever week or so. The ground's always tore up. Plus with all the rain 'n mud, he won't think nothin's amiss."

"OK, let me know what you need to git her runnin'." Beebe was out of steam. "I'll get it somehow. But, dammit, Chaplain Deacon's gonna have to do somethin'. This ain't no way to make a livin'."

SIX

The rumors giving Wayne Daylight sleepless nights blew up last week during the AgriBuddies Poker 'til She Hollers Night at the Five Card Mulligan tournament to benefit the Malapee Middle School Boys Club.

A couple of the regular losers, trying to fuck with his concentration, mentioned that the head guy over at bi-county Water and Sewer was "somewhat disquieted" about reports of elevated levels of sulfur, lead and arsenic showing up in local groundwater. Mr. Milhouse said nothing was much out of line yet, but when the puffed-up little bastard threw the news out along with the lamest call east of Reno, it got everyone squawking about the water.

"Didn't I hear the nitrate levels are shooting up, too?" said the county's lone ecotard, a vegetarian diet doctor who owned Prius of Malapee.

Well, shit, that was like pasting a giant red Post-it pointing straight at the nearest big animal operation: Poultry Xtra. Pretending he hadn't heard, Wayne had studied the cards in his hand, and succeeded in changing the subject by making such an idiot play that everyone started talking about what a donk he was.

It chapped Wayne's butt that the first place town boys looked when anything was the least bit out of whack was the chicken plant. Hell, the plant scoured more water clean in a week than Malapee and Paola counties combined could use in a month, and returned it to the local system better than it was in the first place. But they never considered mama dumping gallons of blue enamel down the storm drain because she decided it didn't match her sofa after all, or Doc Spahn, who hosed at least an industrial drum full of chemicals onto four acres of bright green sod, year after toxic year.

Still, there could be some evil ground tea seeping from someplace around the plant, and that someplace would be "The Dog Yard." He reached for a toothpick, but noticed his real craving was for a lip full and a moonshine shooter in that order.

In addition to being the perfect semi-controlled site for some good clean bulldog and cock routs during the Banty Roaster decades, Wayne and his boys had routinely used a deep swale in the yard to dump and cover trash, construction debris, paint, motor oil sludge, old pumps and hydraulic lines, refrigeration units, air-conditioners, office equipment, decrepit furniture, worn-out smocks, health office waste, anything and everything that was used up, busted beyond repair or hopelessly outmoded.

For years, he'd charged his brother Tuber and his partner Maitland Dovey a fair rate to unload a shit load of chicken litter from the Daylight & Dovey broiler farm. 'Course all that was way before Poultry Xtra started treating water right there at the plant, way before the EPA got so high and mighty and the TV news tarts started chewing their lipstick off with teasers like "Thalidomide in Your Tap Water? Babies Born with Flippers? The Truth at Ten."

Of course the truth was, none of it was true, exactly. But people went nuts all because a handful of reformers figured out that some toxins could leach down and taint the water table from things like old electronics, refrigerator coolant, computers and chicken shit.

Wayne yanked open his liquor cabinet, otherwise known as his top drawer, and pulled out a pint of his homemade 'shine, dumped his pencil caddy and poured. This batch was good, enough under 200 proof that the little oil-slick rainbow on the surface wasn't apt to make a man go blind, at least not right away. Wayne took a long pull. He didn't feel any guilt about a snort at work or dumping in The Dog Yard all those years. That had been as logical and efficient as the hot trail now searing its way down his gullet and back up to his brain.

Only a dumbass would haul everything clear down across the Interstate to the landfill. Hell, Mr. Otis didn't give a good goddamn, even if he'd a known. Not one whit. That old man and Ms. Otis just wanted all the money Wayne could carry to roll right up that circular drive in front of their version of Tara. Otis invented don't ask don't tell. So Wayne never bothered Mr. Otis with day-to-day shit like getting rid of useless, old stinky stuff you couldn't even sell for walkin' around money.

In a hazy nod to a sympathetic Almighty, who Wayne learned back in Vacation Bible School kept a goatskin full of wine on hand for emergencies, Wayne prayed that in the four years since Poultry Xtra took over, any blighted ooze from The Dog Yard had eased its way out of Beauswamp County and into the wide, diluting embrace of Big Muddy.

He worried his boys might be stirring shit up burying the last couple thousand rusted out lockers ripped out of the break room. Until his superintendent, Jerbel Byrne, confessed he sold the busted up mess to some artsy professor from over in Oxford for a dollar a locker. The guy said people were paying millions for old medicine cabinets and vacuum cleaners boxed up in Plexiglas, so why not a bunch of junk in a trashed locker?

Wayne figured either the professor was drunk when he talked to Jerbel or Jerbel was drunk when he listened. Or maybe they both were drunk, unlike Wayne who was just flushed and sweaty. Anyway, Wayne didn't ask Jerbel how he ran into the artsy guy. He had an idea, but Poultry Xtra had a policy of not discriminating based on sexual deviation, and Jerbel was a damn good engineer. Plus he solved the locker problem.

Wayne's ulcer and another swallow told him something was bubbling up in The Dog Yard that was about to land them smack in the EPA's crosshairs. This might call for some horse-trading. He might be forced to call in a bunch of chits and good will, especially if Mr. Milhouse didn't win a few hands next Poker Holler night.

Even so, he was going to have to talk to Maitland and Tuber, damn it all. Wayne had trouble tolerating those two goobers anytime outside of Thanksgiving Day, when his mama and sisters could pretend all the boys got along and the boys would pretend they were there for something besides football, mama's ham and pineapple upside down cake.

Wayne took a final swig, reloaded the pencils and stashed the bottle. The water problem would have to wait. Wayne had an appointment to set Mert Ellis straight. She had poor little Jerbel huffin' three packs a day, bitchin' about her debone water blade making too many miscuts and tanking her butterfly breast yields.

It wasn't so long ago that Mert reported to Wayne, when he could put her in her place and she'd stay there. He still gave her fits, coaching his guys to make her wait whenever she and her girls paged maintenance. But that kinda fun would be more trouble now since Poultry Xtra got its corporate tit in a wringer over this sex lawsuit. Thinking about it made Wayne wish he'd taken one last calming slug. It just wasn't natural, having to tiptoe around all the women and minority stink bombs.

Wayne looked with longing at the photo of the place where once he held sway and thought that some things weren't meant to change. And then they went and changed anyway, one sacred thing after another. Maybe it was time to hang it up, leave it to the Poultry Xtra weenies to work shit out on their own—the water mess, this hostile sex nonsense. They could mop up the entire bleedin' shambles with their fancy sheepskins. Ha! If they even knew what a sheepskin was.

Hell, they probably thought it was the fake shearling inside the faker suede slippers their wives brought every Christmas at that hoity Anthropologie boutique over in Jackson. One more sign that life as he knew it was going in the shitter.

When had it happened, Wayne wanted to know, that a man could no longer expect to find a perfectly good pair of wooly house shoes under the tree, the thick sock kind with tire treads on the soles that itched like the devil. It just was not right.

SEVEN

Eulie Lacrosse stood outside the double-glass front doors and fluffed half-heartedly at the tired black funeral bows someone had stuffed away the last time a Poultry Xtra Posse Member died. Lord, why did it have to happen again so soon, and of all people to Lowndes Henderson. Out of a couple thousand employees, Lowndes was one of the two or three hundred who actually came to work every day, on time. Eulie had been at the Malapee plant for nine short months as HR Manager, but it didn't take that long to figure out who the real workers were. Lowndes had been the best.

Now, his daughter was on the way to find out how much her daddy's death was worth and that slimy part-time chaplain Deacon Maitland Dovey would be coming around to offer Sharay sympathy and a sky high funeral package. And here Eulie was, still hanging woebegotten crepe. A company as big as Poultry Xtra should be downright ashamed of such limp, graying funeral bunting. The big paper ribbon bows looked like they might have been fresh for Lincoln's funeral, although that was unlikely since this was Mississippi. Probably the only thing hung here to mark the Great Emancipator's passing was an effigy. Anyway, they were ratty way beyond any refluffing she tried. Every time she asked to buy new bows, her boss Junior Couch said "Remind me next time."

"Next time, what?" Eulie imagined saying to him. "Next time somebody dies? We've lost five employees in the last two months – three Posse Members in a head-on collision, one who collapsed in the parking lot with a coronary and now Lowndes felled by a tree. So let's definitely wait 'til next time, or the next. I'm sure we can get a bunch more uses out of these crappy bows, so you don't have to spend any money or call any attention to yourself. Then, someday when you feel like it, you can stop by Malapee Bloom & Balloons on your way to the casino and pick up a couple."

Eulie felt herself crushing the ribbons. Shoot. There was no percentage in ranting. She loosened her grip and taped the bows, one each to the front doors. Getting flustered wouldn't do any good, and besides, Eulie would never go off on anybody, no matter how irked she was. She'd been around long enough to know when righteous indignation worked, which was next to never at Poultry Xtra. They said ostriches buried their heads in the sand. Maybe they learned it from chickens. Or chicken processors. Dealing with Junior and his boss, Truly Lovett, and their "Ain't We Got Fun" routine, was like trying to conduct business in a clown car.

She could always count Junior on to smile at her and pretend to be interested, all the while tapping away at video poker on his laptop. Or Pop & Drop. He played that a lot. For a thirty-something, Junior had all the sophistication of a Happy Meal. And Truly, well, he would just shake her hand and tell her to keep on doing exactly what she was doing, neatly avoiding having to express an honest opinion, make a decision or answer a simple question. Oh, well, if the worst things about Junior and Truly were that they were respectively absent and ineffectual, she would just have to deal with it.

"Eulieeeeee." Eulie heard her clerk Daisy yell over the radio. "Sharay's fainted at the guard shack. I already sent the nurse." Eulie rested her head on the glass beside the bedraggled bow. This day was going to suck, no doubt about it. And probably suck downhill from there.

* * * * *

Poultry Xtra part-time chaplain Deacon Maitland Dovey sat facing Sharay Townsend in Eulie's office, holding one of her hands in both of his, leaning near, serious, concerned. Lowndes Henderson's daughter was flushed, her head rocking forward and back as she keened and trembled. Tears mingled with snot bubbled down to her upper lip then flew onto the Deacon's shirt front whenever her head stopped and restarted its orbit.

"Eulie, I believe Miss Sharay needs another hanky and a beverage. Could you see to it?"

Eulie didn't bother to object. The Deacon expected all bystanders to do his bidding. Daisy had the good sense to evaporate right after she and the nurse had helped Sharay limp up the front drive, the steep stairway, through the barnlike break room and into Personnel where she dropped outside Eulie's office door like a 100-pound sack of melons.

"I don't see why I can't have my daddy's check right now," Sharay cried. "Me and Danny got nothin' to tide us over. I don't have gas to get home, I need that check."

"Sharay, it will just be a week or two for the paperwork to go through," Eulie said. "You're Danny's mom, and he's the beneficiary, so it'll come to you. It just takes time."

"But that's not right," Sharay wailed, flinging gobbets at Deacon Dovey, who didn't flinch and remarkably scooted closer to Sharay, bracketing her knees with his.

"Deacon, can't you make them give me the money?" Sharay gurgled a sob behind a shredded tissue.

"Now, Sharay, honey, Eulie's right about these things, they always take some time," Deacon Dovey smiled, his buffed and rosy cheeks only a shade lighter than his signature pink tie. "But me and Ms. Dovey will help you take care of everything, don't you worry. We'll tide you and little Danny over if need be. You just get all these papers signed, and we'll go down to the Tabernacle and talk it all over. It's a terrible time, too much for you to bear all alone. My hand to my heart and petition in God's ear, I'll help you through it. You know I will."

You know he will, Eulie sighed. Help you and help himself. Eulie eyed the Chaplain's body language and Sharay's shapely legs. Well, somebody has to bury people, and Deacon Dovey's Gather at the River Funeralization Tabernacle was convenient if nothing else, located south of the plant, catty-corner across a couple of logging roads and past a big broiler farm, still twenty miles closer to Malapee than the next undertaker.

Advising people on funeral arrangements wasn't something Eulie should mess with, but her heartburn kicked up whenever anyone turned to Deacon Dovey in times of need. He mined his part-time chaplain gig at Poultry Xtra for end-of-life opportunities. He made the most of every hospitalization likely to end in death for any Posse Member or their relations. Eulie supposed he did bring people some comfort, even as he prepared to fleece them.

In his hand-stitched suits, tassel loafers and Necco thin gold watch, he was a swanky vulture preying on misfortune and trouble, seeming to revel in it. Offering solace and a listening heart, he sold jacked-up, tricked-out coffins and extravagant rites at a ridiculous price.

"I'll go get some Kleenex and a Pepsi," Eulie said, heading out the door, hoping her disgust didn't hang in the air behind her.

EIGHT

It was nearly impossible for Eulie to walk through the break room without being waylaid by someone with a question or complaint or both. She hadn't been at Malapee long, but she'd been walking the same gauntlet through a handful of other factory common rooms for a few years. In every one, she pulled out her Blackberry to take notes as she listened, nodded and promised to follow-up.

Sometimes, when people got wound up over some stick in the collective craw that she'd already answered a dozen times, her mind wandered. Often, it strayed to a perennial question: What would possess anyone to think it was a good idea to paint such a huge room, where people came to rest or eat, in the precise mustard shade of breastfed-newborn-shit, or in some variation of safety orange. Eulie's friend Lovey Tillman said it was the work of a "color psychologist" who had cornered the décor market in manufacturing America. This person was being paid millions to keep break time short, productivity up. Eulie thought it was because, in contrast, those shades made the cafeteria food look edible.

Right now, Eulie didn't have time to ponder the industrial psyche, she was doing the Chaplain's bidding. She tried a broken field run in and around the café seating, no easy task since they were bolted to the concrete floor. She would have made it but for the grip on her elbow of earnest, young Deputy Chumley Bucket, the off-duty officer who had helped fire-carry Sharay Townsend up the front walk.

He wanted to know how poor Mrs. Townsend was holding up. As he rambled, Eulie detected the beginnings of love-sickness in his shy smile. She thanked him for his concern, but said she could say only that the grieving daughter was in the good hands –well, hands anyway– of Chaplain Deacon. The deputy, with a polite nod, left almost as fast as the smile slid from his face.

Then, just as Eulie cleared the cash register, Mertricious Ellis, an assistant plant manager, blocked her path. Ignoring Eulie's full load of fountain drinks and a napkin dispenser for the bereaved, Mert shoved a wad of paper money at her.

"This is from the folks in debone for Sharay and Danny," Mert said, straight to the point as usual, "about $250 so far. I have to touch base with my people in packout and shipping, and check the bereavement jars up in admin, so there'll be more. Pretty good haul on a Tuesday before payday. Oh, and Maynard said he'd have donations from cut-up, live hang and evisceration tomorrow morning."

Eulie set aside the drinks and napkins, took the money and counted it where she stood in the middle of the break room. "OK, $256. I'll log it. Did you make a list of donors?"

Mert's radio crackled with a voice and summons Eulie couldn't make out. "Gotta go," Mert waved, her smock flapping behind as she went. "I'll bring you the rest as it comes in."

"OK, and bring the list," called Eulie.

"List my ass," hissed Mert, shoving through the swinging door and into the plant.

* * * * *

Eulie stood at the front of the mustard and orange orientation-training room watching as Stevie Speh, a supervisor who knew Lowndes, spoke to a room full of Posse Members there to pay respects. Stevie was a stem-winder class lay minister and was starting to rev up when Truly Lovett, the head man at the Malapee operation walked in. He clasped his hands in front of his belt, tilted his head down reverently and slipped around to stand by Eulie.

"Hey Eulie, how's everybody doing?"

"Hi, Truly," Eulie whispered. "OK, I guess. About what you'd expect. People really thought a lot of Lowndes."

"Yes, I imagine so...how long did you say Landers worked here?"

"Lown-des," she corrected. "Over 30 years."

"Well, now, what a shame, what a shame...horrible business...yes horrible." Truly knitted his brows and grinned weakly, trying to summon an appropriate expression. "Have you seen Junior? We're due at a Rotary meeting at three, and he's not texting me back."

Eulie longed to tell Truly that Junior had taken his customary long lunch at Glittering Sky Slots and Smokes in nearby Ofo, an extremely small town that first showed up on maps with the opening of the county's first and only purportedly Indian-owned gaming venue.

Sky Slots consisted of video poker and a handful of low-ball, glitter-flake slot machines crammed into a refurbished WWII troop Quonset, amenities including a convenience store cooler full of vodka cocktail six packs, canned espresso double shots and frozen Snickers. It had a hollow-core front door and a semi-restricted exit to a double-wide "dressing" trailer for staff. Assorted metal out-buildings offered fry bread and pulled pork, corn nuts, Slim Jims and tax-free cigarettes. It wasn't a big operation, but Eulie suspected that Junior's losses alone would help fund any planned expansion.

"Sorry, I haven't seen him since before lunch," Eulie said. "I think he said something about meeting with a union rep in town."

"Well, I guess I better say a few words. Introduce me..." Truly said, craning to see Stevie's name embroidered on his uniform shirt, "when, um, Stewie gets finished."

Listening to Truly, a lanky young man with a brownish bowl haircut wearing a Poultry Xtra uniform with extra heavy starch, Eulie marveled. Every member of management dressed the same: gas-pumper gray twill pants and button front shirts with the blood-red rooster comb Poultry Xtra logo and their first name embroidered over chest pockets. On Truly the plain work duds looked spruce and fresh, as professional as bespoke on a hedge fund boss.

Unfortunately, his personality was as repressed as the crease in his pants.

Company lore held that Truly wasn't always wrapped so tight, not before his rise among Poultry Xtra bright lights had come to an abrupt brownout a few years back. His then-pregnant then-wife somehow managed to sic a SWAT team and TV helicopters on Truly one summer evening when he was in a closed meeting with the new industrial health nurse in a motel in Godforgot, Alabama. Eulie didn't know Truly before his embarrassing turn of fortune but thought it might account for his head-down, tuck-tailed lack of grit and purpose. She didn't know how to explain his practice of saying one thing and doing another, but if the lore were true, it probably was part of his character all along.

Eulie cringed as Truly stumbled through a painfully long appreciation of Lowndes, a man he probably had never met and certainly hadn't known, mispronouncing his name twice, again forgetting how long he'd been with the company and having to stop in the middle to be reminded what his job had been. Eulie tried to give Truly the benefit of the doubt – there were 2300 people at the plant in any 24-hour period. But, damn, not very many of them had been here over three decades.

Eulie's boss Junior might be AWOL most of the time, but when he was here, he could talk the shine off a trailer hitch and rarely forgot a face or name. Of course, what he mastered in fact he lacked in sincerity. Short and fireplug stout, Junior wore his grays rump-sprung and wrinkled, as if his mama dressed him on the fly in a huge onesie and he was always hauling a seat load.

Eulie had come to think of Truly and Junior as two parts of a nearly whole person. They rode to and from work together, swapping cars –Audi Cabriolet one day, Dodge Ram 2500 Hemi the next– and spent most of their time locked up in each other's offices, or texting when they were apart to make sure they both knew what to think. When Junior was off gambling and refused to call or text anybody, Truly acted like a stranger in town whose OnStar was on the blink.

Eulie bowed her head as Stevie replaced Truly at the front of the classroom. "Let's join hands and ask the Lord's blessing on Lowndes, Sharay and little Danny," Stevie said.

Taking Stevie's hand on one side and Truly's, thin and clammy, on the other, Eulie said a silent prayer. "Dear Lord, cover Lowndes with your grace, watch over Danny, have mercy on Truly and please give everyone else what they deserve."

NINE

Mert leaned across her desk, where pens and pencils were aligned and papers were filed or trapped in clipboards hung in perfect ranks along the back wall. She was trying to make herself heard over the sound of a pitched argument outside her closed door. She handed two No. 10 envelopes of cash to her shift superintendent Honoria Black. "The top one is your split. Give the other one to Eulie before she leaves today. It's donations for Lowndes' daughter, the wide-assed twit."

"Oh, Mert, you're just mad because she juked your baby brother and then he dumped her," Honoria grinned, probably unwisely. "She's the lucky one now, alright, makin' off with her daddy's insurance 'n all. Hey, maybe Dion should sniff her up again, get some of that inheritance."

"Just make sure you get that to Eulie, and put her off if she asks about signatures. I'll get with her later. Now see who's killing who out there and then get all the supervisors in here. We got a boutique order to squeeze in, a half-pallet of 1830s. And we need to talk about the Thigh Steaks people."

"When is that happening?" Honoria groaned.

Mert didn't blame her. Nobody looked forward to customer visits, the Japanese least of all. They dogged every detail, down to the color inside a cooked thigh bone, breaking them open to lay alongside a perfect marrow color chart. Mr. Ogoni told her that chicken bone marrow was a delicacy in his country and had to be cooked just so. If the marrow wasn't deep maroon – not red, not brown, but maroon – it didn't matter if the meat was perfect, Mr.

Ogoni said, bowing so often he reminded her of mama's Famous Drinking Bird as Seen on TV. As far as the Japanese were concerned, we could go peddle the whole ruined mess of marrow somewhere else. Mr. Ogoni voted for mainland China.

Even worse than the influx of picky foreigners, customer visits meant that three or four days beforehand everyone ran around like loose broilers one step ahead of the catching crew. Aside from running regular orders, you had to juggle conflicting edicts from seven levels of management that had nothing to do with running chicken and everything to do with window dressing. Then, business as usual until the next invasion, when everyone would go berserk all over again.

"They'll be here a week from Wednesday through Friday," Mert said. "Now get going." Mert waited for the door to close, then opened her center drawer and consulted a list of supervisors' not-so-confidential computer passwords she finagled from her sister-in-law in Accounting, a serial cuckolder who wanted to keep Mert quiet and Mert's baby brother in the dark.

Mert signed on using the ID of one of Maynard's new supervisors. Anyone bothering to check the punch trail would see that supervisor Teresa Coppage printed off a list of employee data. Mert quickly cobbled the names and e-signatures she needed to manufacture a donor list to match the money she turned in to Eulie. There would be no record of money skimmed off the top on Mert's list. Eulie would never take the time to check; she just needed something to show in case the auditors ever did.

Compliance was an open joke to Mert and other managers who were delighted to learn that the hoops you had to jump through if you wanted to firewall the collective corporate ass were about the appearance of compliance. If you seemed to follow the rules and recorded it all on an endless variety of forms, you could do just about anything, rules be damned. Then, you just had to stick to your story, however bogus, and stay firmly up the right butts.

Mert hit the print button and sat back to wait. Some people might sniff at going to all this trouble to cover up filching from sympathy donations, but in a plant the size of a small city, sympathy added up fast. Mert started out too poor ever to overlook a windfall, however measly. But she had to be careful; she wasn't about to let anything jeopardize her main gig as Malapee's first woman assistant plant manager. But it wasn't about the title; you ended up doing the grunt work no matter what they called you. For Mert, who had many irons, the beauty of her position was access to the fire.

It took Mert 22 years to get where she was, years of grinding hard labor, forever having to be amenable. Good girl Mert, always ready to back down in the end to a long line of insufferable crackers and just the plain old dickheads who always seemed to end up in charge. She was doing pretty well for somebody with no college. She didn't make what her night-shift counterpart Maynard Travis did, with his college degree and six paltry years on the job. But he was a white male in the Deep South. Mert knew she would never draw even with or without a degree.

What the hell, there was more than one way to level the playing field, and as far as Mert was concerned, money was the only way. There was no achieving equality, and only fools believed there was. Just staying even was a huge win.

Still logged on as Teresa, Mert opened the timecard control and replaced a couple of clock-out times for Lamentatia and Levitica Taylor, twins who worked in the laundry- supply room and company store, one on days and the other nights. Mert erased the girls' punches and added a half-hour of overtime here and there, time they hadn't worked but would be paid. Tatia, Tica and the laundry and supply center figured in one of Mert's earliest and most profitable sidelines, and she made sure to keep the ladies in her pocket by lining theirs.

Years ago, Mert saw the bounty no other manager saw, and in fact one they avoided as beneath them. No question, washing dirty smocks and handing out hairnets and gloves was not likely to put an ambitious supervisor in line for a raise or promotion. And absolutely no one wanted to be responsible for the surly bunch of worker's comp malcontents who ended up on laundry duty because their lawyers insisted they be given sit-down jobs. But those other supervisors had lacked Mert's commitment to the main chance, her vision or patience.

She'd jumped at the offer to control the goose that would lay her golden egg. She curried the laundry ladies and finessed ways to tuck, roll and cadge inventory into cash flow. It was as neat and simple as shuffling numbers to divert an off-the-books supply of work boots, jackets, Poultry Xtra logo koozies, squeeze toys and everything else – including chicken seconds and overstock – the Company pimped to Posse Members, paid for of course through payroll deduction.

Mert picked up a foam rubber polka-dot Poultry Petie stress ball sitting next to her monitor. She grinned to equal Petie's anatomically incorrect toothy beak and squeezed. Who knew why people wanted this crap. But Mert had sold bushels of the stuff through a network of swap meets, flea markets and car trunk sales across the state.

The enterprise worked so well, after a couple of years she was able put together a nut big enough to finance short term loans to Posse Members, payable in installments, cash on the barrelhead every payday. From the first, the profits were breathtaking. Naturally, Mert worked even harder to pay off anyone necessary to grease the enterprise, including the supply room twins and her cousin, Richard T. Bass, who ran the Quickie Ricky's store near the plant entrance.

Posse Members trooped by the hundreds down the long entry driveway every payday Friday to cash their payroll checks, pay utility bills and cover the installments on loans they thought Quickie Ricky was bankrolling at a very attractive, easy to figure 10% interest. Unlike the big lenders, Mert knew that if you didn't totally screw low-income people on the vigorish, they actually paid you back and borrowed again.

Mert also made sure that no one could link her to any funny business because she knew how to point computer tracks at someone else, like hapless Teresa Coppage, fresh out of Old Miss, a crybaby who tuned up if someone looked at her sideways. If the twins' padded overtime ever surfaced, Teresa would have no explanation and would be gone before the tears dried. Too bad, but no big loss as a supervisor in Mert's opinion.

"Thanks, baby," Mert said to the flat screen as she logged Teresa off. "You better hope payroll stays asleep at the wheel."

Her focus immediately turned to a glitch with 16 pallets of underweight 20-pound boxes of chicken tenders that Quality Control had put on hold. Mert wanted the load to ship tonight and didn't much care what it took, as long as it was out of her cooler by the same time tomorrow morning.

She touched the radio button on her shoulder and paged "Bad Fruit" Purdy, the night shift evisceration superintendent. She could always badger him into doing her rework because he was hopeless at keeping the lid on his hook-ups with cute lady Posse Members or with the plant booze and drugs concession he ran on the side. BF loved crowing with his cronies, a bunch of blowhards who didn't know a thing about playing close to the vest.

The hook-ups and the users and the blowhards covered for BF. So would Mert, for a price. She knew more than enough to take him down. Of course, he might do the same to her, but not likely. BF wasn't ruthless enough to mess with her. She, on the other hand, would harvest human kidneys to fill a giblet order.

Honoria stuck her head in the door. "Mert, Miss Lydia is all upset again. She says one of the new shoulder cutters threatened to shove his steel glove down her throat, and he claims she's been calling him "boy" all morning and bumping him on purpose. I've got them writing statements, but they want to talk to you."

"You handle it or go find Eulie. I have to chase down Bad Fruit before he leaves," Mert left her office still trying to raise BF on the radio and wondering why some people, Miss Lydia for example, had their heads so far up their asses they couldn't get through a single work day without fighting like a bunch of school kids. Rounding the last cubicle in the supervisors' bullpen, she nearly plowed into Fano Alcides, one of the refrigeration technicians. He sidestepped Mert neatly.

"Oh, Fano, sorry, I almost clipped you there," said Mert, thinking she'd take the penalty for a little holding with such a fine looking guy. Mert didn't believe in fishing the company pond, but underneath her uniform and determination, she could not deny she was a full-blooded female.

"Oh, no problem, ma'am. No harm done," Fano touched his hard hat and winked, brushing past a little closer than was entirely necessary. "Don't give it another thought."

As if, Mert winked back.

TEN

Truly's canned but sunny demeanor seemed to be on hiatus this morning. He had called Eulie, Mert and Maynard Travis, the co-assistant plant manager, into his office for a command conference call from the head of Corporate Compliance, Darby Dummit, known not so fondly as Sgt. Doom. She and one of the legal hired guns would be weighing in on an upcoming EEOC mediation on a complaint by a fired supervisor, Betina Tripp.

Naturally, no sane person would be smiling at the prospect of a call from Sgt. Doom, who routinely reduced senior VPs to quivering sacks of tics and gibberish with her drill sergeant belligerence and intolerance for slow answers with too many qualifiers. Nobody doubted that she knew her stuff, but she made grown men with high six-figure incomes go to ground when shit surfaced in their territory. There was scant hope of keeping Doom Dummit in the dark, but at least they could cover their executive asses and roll the blame downhill.

"Good morning, Malapee," Doom barked from the tri-cornered meeting module on Truly's desk. "Sol Collins is here with me and Mike Tisdale from legal. Who's with you, Truly?"

"Mert and Maynard," Truly said. "Junior's out recruiting but should be calling in any time now. Eulie's here in the meantime."

Eulie sighed. On the hook again. She looked with little hope of sighting Junior's big red Dodge with its mud-bogger tires out the panoramic window overlooking the plant's several acres of sod, cars and blacktop. It was doubtful her boss would be checking in to do his job today. He probably wasn't at the casino this early but wherever he was, he would be distracted long enough to miss the call from Sgt. Doom.

"OK, unfortunately, we've got a mess of stuff to cover this morning. Emphasis on the mess, I might add," Doom said. "Let's get to it. Betina Tripp is claiming wrongful termination; that she was fired because she is pregnant and unwed, and further because she is engaged to an Hispanic Posse Member; that she's being discriminated against because of her condition and his national origin and retaliated against because she refused to stop seeing …let's see … his name is Fano, Mr. Alcides. She says that our claim that she destroyed QC hold tags and purposely relabeled product incorrectly to fill an order and falsified production documents is trumped up. She says she never did anything other than what she was instructed. So what's the deal and what are we going to mediation with? Don't everyone talk at once, folks," Sgt. Doom said into the staticy silence. "Speak up!"

"Uh, Doo…Darby, Truly here…I think it's all in the e-mail we sent."

"Great, and I can read that in all my spare time. Now somebody tell me what the hell happened with Betina and how we're supposed to counter it."

"OK, Darby, I think Mert can fill you in since she's the one who uncovered everything."

"Well, you know how I was so worried about the short-weight reports from Dairy Daisy, since I knew for certain that we were weighing out correctly at this end, and I told you how I set up a kind of a sting operation to see if I could figure where that weight was going."

Mert was the star of her own story for the next twenty minutes, detailing how in the course of trying to nose out the source of underweight drumstick bags, she had come across Betina relabeling 20-pound boxes of chicken tenders that had been run for one product to make up a rush load of another one. Except the rush product, No. 1318, Tasty Teriyaki Tenders, had a teriyaki coating and No. 1320, Salty Lemon Planks, were salty and lemony. Not a huge difference, Mert admitted, unless you tasted them. She said Betina ripped off the right labels and replaced them with the wrong ones to make up the order, then she fiddled the records to make everything come out even. Luckily, Mert discovered Betina trashing a bunch of Salty Lemon labels right when a USDA inspector walked into the area. Mert had no choice but to turn her in.

"You know that I hated to do that," Mert said, her voice shaky with the affront of it all. "I've known Betina for so many years and we go to church together. But you know, and I've told all my people this over and over, I cannot condone somebody doing anything dishonest like that, no matter how much pressure we are under. It's just not in my character, and people have to know whether we're friends or not they cannot expect me to just overlook something like that. I just will not do it."

"Thanks, Mert, we know how conscientious you are," Truly said. "It had to be very hard for you to turn in your own supervisor and friend. Eulie, anything to add?

Eulie jumped, deep in thought about Mert's self-affirmation. Eulie believed Mert was protesting a little too much and always had her doubts about the whole episode. She found it perplexing when she first investigated Mert's claims, that Betina refused to defend herself at all. She refused to speak or respond in any way other than to offer the non-denial denial that she only did what she was told. Beyond that, she was stubbornly mum. Mert connected all the dots on paper, giving them no choice but to terminate. According to Mert, it was a onetime deal for Betina that Mert suggested must have been triggered because the supervisor was beset by a slew of personal problems on top of the rough schedule at work. That seemed awfully pat to Eulie.

"Well, Ms. Dummit," Eulie said, "the claim that we fired her for being single and pregnant just flies in the face of reality. I'd guess on any given day, upwards of five percent of our women employees are pregnant, whether they know it yet or not. Most of them are single. If we fired people for that, we'd have to shut down half the debone floor. As far as her dating Fano, he didn't report to her and she wouldn't be giving him any work instructions. Betina had nothing to do with refrigeration. They weren't doing anything against policy. We did change Fano's schedule so he wouldn't be in her area at all. If anything, Fano could have complained about the schedule change, but they both agreed it was the best action at the time."

"OK, sounds like we've got her cold, so I say we don't offer her anything more than her travel cost to show up at the court house in Jackson and be done with it," Sol Collins interjected.

"Well, she is asking to settle pre-mediation," Mike Tisdale, the attorney, conceded. "Apparently she's dealing with health problems related to her pregnancy and wants this over. We can probably get her to go away for something in the teens."

Maynard signaled for Truly to mute the speaker. "Boss, can't we persecute her?

Eulie managed to keep from slapping her forehead or Maynard. "You mean prosecute, Maynard?"

Maynard paid no attention. "After all, Boss, she cost us a bundle for screwing up that rush order for Haiku Poultry. Isn't that felony fraud or something? Hell, her personal shit isn't our concern. Why should we pay her to walk away just because her hormones have her thong in a wad?"

While the Corporate fixers continued to iron out the details for Betina's hearing, Eulie waited in vain for Truly to tell Maynard to dummy up. To his credit, Truly did look vaguely abashed by Maynard's wife-beater mentality, but he wasn't about to mess with him. Maynard might be a mouth-breathing throwback but he ran chicken like a wide-open fire plug—full speed and high yield. In this business, that meant his philosophical lapses usually got a wink and a pass. Enduring the rank stupidity of some managers was simply a cost of doing business that didn't amount to squat next to billions of pounds of fast food chicken, packed and shipped. Sometimes the company had to spread around a little money here and there to deodorize the worst behavior, but that was small change, too.

Eulie blanched when she heard Doom say, "Let's move on to the sex case, Sol. Where are we on that?" Too bad the mute button wasn't on the fritz during Maynard's little fit, Eulie thought. Doom would have some inkling why the plant was smack in the middle of the biggest federal sex-harassment case in the history of Poultry Xtra.

She pulled out her Blackberry to check her e-mail. Eulie knew way more than most people about Leary v. Poultry Xtra. And with all the depositions she would have to endure as company rep, she had no stomach for a preview now. Lord only knew what The Bubbas were going to say. Or poor, dim Hoopdy.

ELEVEN

Fano walked the periphery of the break room trailing Mert, conscious of an uneasiness the earlier encounter stirred up, a feeling somewhere between reflux and revulsion. He intended to nurse it, hoping to build up his resistance. For what Fano had in mind, he would have to become immune. To get close to Mert, enough to hurt her, would be a tall order.

Since his first day on the job, he had seen Mert use people to further her career and line her pockets. Of course, Mert wasn't the only person on the take at Malapee by a long shot. Fano spent his first few months scouting the opportunities to be mined among thousands of laborers stuck miles from the nearest town. Mert had a lot to offer to a go-getter like Fano. But he also saw that her most lucrative pursuits were built on the whim of spendthrifts, blind loyalty of butt-boys and jacking around with computers. Too much risk, too paltry a payoff.

So Fano's original decision to pass on working for Mert was just good business. Instead, he joined Bad Fruit's crew – a couple of witless supervisors and dozens of maintenance and refrigeration techs – who together supplied the plant with weed and vodka, the drugs of choice among the majority of Posse Members. BF's boys had the right products in the perfect market.

Malapee was the ideal place to run drugs and hooch: High turnover provided a steady stream of buyers and willing runners pitted against a bevy of pretend security guards and off-duty cops, half of them chesting around playing DEA and the rest themselves half in the bag. Hiding the enterprise was simple. No one ever thought to question the off-the-clock visits Fano and the crew made around the plant.

They had access to every boiler room, storage room, utility and pump rooms, production area, box room, roof shed, outbuilding, tractor-trailer, cooler, freezer, dock, nook, cranny and forgotten alcove in the 300,000 square-foot plant 24/7. Every likely place to stash product or make a quick handoff.

Stocking Bad Fruit's inventory at just-in-time levels was a cinch, and kept the boys in plenty of cash. So did the outdoor concessions, the parade of vehicles that could deliver trunk loads of what's-your-poison within the maze of driveways and parking slots in the Poultry Xtra mall-size lot. BF's was a distribution system that even Jeff Bezos might envy.

Even better from a risk management perspective, when stumbling drunk or stoned Posse Members were busted for "reasonable suspicion" nobody got fired anymore because being continuously shitfaced was classified as curtailing one or more Major Life Functions under the Americans with Disabilities Act. Like getting a forkful of food to your mouth, or making it to the throne instead of taking a dump in your baby sister's new Ariel backpack, or not being able to sleep without drowning in your own drunken gorge. Or, say you needed psychological help after your third DUI when you wiped out a Dodge Caravan full of teen-age Mormon missionaries.

And if that didn't get an addict off, Poultry Xtra supervisors weren't above fudging the impairment checklist, or hiding a particularly prized imbiber in a bathroom stall until enough time and force-fed Midol-laced Gatorade diluted the problem. That coupled with a fast hook-up between the supervisor and the duty nurse would make the test panels turn out all nice and negative. Worst case, people who botched the drug test or cracked the breathalyzer, or the ones nobody wanted to save, agreed to "self-detox" for a period of their choosing and were off work only as long as it took to get clean enough to pass the return-to-work re-test.

Posse Members who couldn't rely on managers – friendly or family – to help in their cause found other means to stay lit and employed. Mythic ways to get around the tests were legion: pee scrubbers like Urine Luck sold online and sucking down cranberry juice, vinegar or multiple liters of sports drinks were said to sufficiently dilute the substances of interest.

Fano was most intrigued and not a little disgusted with the people who bought baggies of clean urine over the Internet supposedly from the pristine wee-wees of Sunday school toddlers. Since drug panels didn't track levels of SunnyD and Ovaltine, kiddy samples were quite in demand. Posse Members carried the piss of innocents in a zipbag tucked in a bra cup or pocket in case they were nabbed for a drug test. Then, they either microwaved the bag or stuffed it between molars and cheek hoping the ringer pee they dumped in the cup was the right warmish temperature to fool the tester. (Fano made it a rule never to nuke anything in the break room microwaves).

It was pointless to ask the ones who tested positive to give up a supplier because everyone knew no one would. Even non-smokers and teetotalers called in as witnesses in the mandatory drug sweeps after an accident could be counted on to heed the unwritten rule against rolling over: When authority called, people didn't see anything, hear anything or know anything, even if they were standing beside a guy who stuck a knife in another guy's gizzard because he short-sold him.

Fano had no illusions that his wrongdoing was for any higher purpose than Mert's hustle, but he looked at trafficking in the plant as a simple matter of claiming the best corner in the neighborhood. These people would be buying some kinda juice from some dude somewhere to help them withstand the deadly monotony and nagging pain of working in a line factory that, depending on the job, was too cold or too hot and always wet.

But Mert used people, threw them away, yet always came out ahead. BF was just helping provide a quality product and good service for fair return. There was give and take in his operation.

Mert was all about take. Still, Fano always followed BF's lead and gave Mert a wide berth. She had her deal, they had theirs, and everything had been just fine until she messed with Betina.

When Mert maneuvered his fiancé out of her job, he was not about to let it go. Betina had worked at Malapee as long as Mert, but hadn't risen as far because, in Fano's opinion, she had wasted herself carrying Mert's water. Mert was a master at attracting lap dogs to pet and spoil into doing her bidding, no questions asked. Exactly like Betina until the day USDA showed up at the wrong time and someone in QC woke up long enough to discover a paperwork juggling act that Mert employed to bump production numbers on high-dollar Haiku Poultry breast tenders. As usual, Mert made sure that her pets had done all the fudging. The juggled numbers couldn't be traced to her.

Fano and Betina had a killer row when all the questions started. He hadn't come close to persuading her to finger Mert. Betina said Mert wouldn't let anything happen to her if she just kept her mouth shut, that she owed Mert everything: her promotion to supervisor, her annual bonus and for a sizeable personal loan when Betina's teenage daughter was chucked in jail for criminal child neglect and her grandbaby was yanked by DHS.

Betina had to go to court to be declared legal guardian of Tarrian, and Mert had fronted money to get a decent lawyer. So, when the set-up came, Betina kept her mouth shut, refusing to say anything in her own defense, refusing to believe she'd been back-doored by her best friend.

Mert made damn certain Betina took the fall. Now Betina was trying to get her job back by telling the EEOC she was fired for getting pregnant with a Cuban daddy. To Fano, it was a stretch. She might get a little money out of Poultry Xtra, but only to shut up and go away. She could forget getting her old job back. Mert had enough stroke to prevent that.

Fano hurried through the bullpen and exited into a cavernous area of trashed metal lockers off the main break room. The 3-foot-tall lockers stacked two high in long rows had been so vandalized and neglected only a few hundred actually had padlocks attached. The rusted out, barely usable remaining 1500, originally, twice that number, were so crammed with garbage and crusty, foul smocks, that the sanitation folks had to unload and hose them out with industrial solvents every other Saturday to keep armies of water bugs, roaches and furrier vermin on the run.

Of course, Bad Fruit's marketing crew and their customers didn't object to the bugs and trash because the rabbit warren of metal walls was great cover for handing off pints or baggies. Fano had set up many an exchange in the area. Foam plates of leftovers in randomly selected lockers provided the perfect stash for bindles or vials among the half-eaten remains of powdered eggs and turkey sausage.

Tonight, drug deals were the last thing Fano needed to think about, and he took the quickest route through the maze to the debone floor. Fano intended to keep close tabs on Mert. Coming on to her was no fun, well, maybe a little, but either way a necessary part of the plan.

He knew she had an itch for him and he wanted to play it, to play her, stay on her good side. Fano wanted everyone to know the real Mert. He had an angle working and he promised himself to see it through. It was complicated, but Fano was nursing a combination of unbridled love, bad blood and a brooding taste for vengeance. Everything he needed to do the right thing for Betina and the baby. And to Mert.

TWELVE

Normally, Mert kept her head, but right now she was fuming. Maintenance techs and supervisors routinely ignored pages from female managers. If Mert or her women supervisors complained, the response rate dipped further. The solution was to snag a passing male production supervisor and make him summon help.

But Bad Fruit knew better than to ignore Mert without a seamless explanation.

Just inside the evisceration dock, she clicked through the channels, asking if anyone had a sightline to BF and received a chorus of "No, ma'ams." No one could see him, or would admit it if they did. Mert was grinding her expensive new veneers. She forced herself to slow down, to breathe. Where to look?

"I believe he's on the yard, ma'am…some accident with a cage." Mert jumped at the voice so close she felt a puff on her hairnet. She turned and took a step back. Fano was tight against her, no smile or wink this time. He looked serious.

"I believe Clarence got pinned. BF is on the loader while the old man's in the infirmary."

"Oh, OK, thanks, Fano," Mert said, unnerved that she hadn't noticed him and because he was still so close she felt something like a static shower arcing at her. "I'll head out back, then. Thanks again."

There came the smile, slow and wide. "Anytime, ma'am. For you, anything, anytime."

Mert blinked at the obvious come-on. She turned quickly away so Fano couldn't see her knowing grin and headed for the live dock.

First she'd get the short weight problem out of the way and then figure out what to think about Fano.

* * * * *

Mert found Bad Fruit in his closet of an office in back of the evisceration bullpen, holding forth on his favorite topic: the "good old days" in the chicken business, when men were in charge, women weren't and PETA was a gleam in the eye of some overeducated pansy.

"You don't like factory farms?" BF blew a bolus of tobacco juice into his Super Swoller spit cup. "Well, I say, get off your Kentucky Fried Ass 'n raise your own damn free-range, goose-liver-stuffed chicken nuggets. Or pay some poor unsubsidized, beat-down farm family to do it for you. Like that'll ever happen."

BF's boys yukked like wise guys at a Capone family picnic. Mert pushed through so BF had to acknowledge her.

"What, Mert?" Bad Fruit said, his massive upper body hiding the chair he creaked forward and back, cradling his spit cup. "I heard you was in a fuss to find me. 'Course that's my usual condition, bein' chased by one woman or another."

Hoopdy Creavy, perched on the front corner of BF's desk, whooped and put up his palm to high five his boss. BF grinned at Mert, ignoring Hoopdy.

"What happened with Clarence," Mert asked.

"That lucky ol' fucker, he should be dead," BF said, leaning to pull off his right boot and then sock. While Mert stood watching, he crossed an ankle over a hefty thigh and used the sock like a rag, pulling it back and forth between his toes, one after the other.

"What happened with Clarence," Mert repeated, finding it hard to ignore the cascade of flakes the sock unearthed.

"The cage fell, is what happened," Hoopdy said. "Them things weighs 500 pounds, ya know. It was empty a'course, wasn't no birds in it. Pinned 'im up agin' the truck. If ol' Clarence woulda been one blame inch either side, it woulda lain'm flat. Ol' Clarence'd be history, ain't that so, BF?"

"Yep. Lucky fucker for sure, likely to be sore tomorrow is all," BF concluded, pulling on his sock, his itch apparently scratched. "Now, what can I do you for, Mert?"

"You can get your boot on and follow me. I've got a chore for you." Mert left the office.

"Damn," BF said, shoving into his boot, "I hate it when she's peevish. Hoop, while I see what she's got up her craw, get them last tweaker orders bagged for Fano and the guys and I'll be back in a jiffy."

"Yeah, see what she got shoved up 'er onion, BF, 'n up 'er hush puppy while yer at it," Hoopdy said, his voice the timbre of a playground challenge.

"Dammit, Hoop. Wha'd I tell you about that? You gotta watch it. Stop talking about girl parts. Those lawyers might be sniffin' around, hear me?"

"Yeah, BF. I fergot." Hoopdy looked contrite, watching BF go after Mert. Then as quickly as his brow clouded, it cleared. He giggled. "Yeah, see what she got stuck up 'r ol' panty hamster."

* * * * *

"Mert, I don't think I got the people to get 16 pallets reweighed tonight. That's a helluva bunch of product to mess around with. I can get 'em done over a couple of nights, but 16 tonight, no way," BF said.

"BF, I'm not telling you to reweigh them, I'm telling you to get them shipped." Mert couldn't believe he thought she was trying to negotiate. "You get someone to get it done tonight. I need that cooler space," Mert said, turning to go.

"I could shut down the paw room and liver table to pull people, but Maynard's gonna be unholy pissed." BF argued.

"Look, BF, if you think that's what you need to do to get the job out the door by morning, then that's what you do." Mert said. "Personally, I'd figure out how to distract QC, move those boxes to new pallets, rewrap them, get one of your baby girls to make the hold tag disappear and be done with it."

"Dammit, Mert, that's a lot a boxes to pretend to weigh without gettin' busted."

Mert stared at BF. She loved it when grown men whined. "You know, BF, I'm supposed to give a deposition in this sex harassment case. That's just like being in court, you know, under oath and all. Do you suppose that means I'll have to tell them the truth if they ask me about your trips to the truck yard with that data collector from shipping?"

She waited, but BF knew when to shut up.

"You suppose that means I'll have to tell them about how you got your nick name and how all your girls know the story. The whole story?

Bad Fruit's lips were clamped so tight they formed a line as thin as his pencil moustache.

"Good," Mert said, patting BF on the shoulder as she walked past. "I'll be sure to let Maynard know how much I appreciate your help."

BF was pissed but had only himself to blame. He never could resist bragging how he got drunk in that titty bar in Bahrain and ended up with a magnificent curved banana etched on his chest under the legend "Bad Fruit." It had been a present from a cutie pie MP with a dangerous sense of humor and a stash of date-rape pills who had developed a crush on BF as soon as she'd clapped the cuffs on him for conduct unbecoming.

When he came to, he couldn't remember much but figured if the worst thing that happened to him was an awesome tat, he was OK with it. Until he saw squiggles scrawled in Arabic inching up the angle of his pecker. At first he had been afraid to ask what it meant but found an Egyptian doctor with an office near the gold souk where he got a blood test just in case and a loose translation.

The doc told him it said, more or less, "What the fuck? Get that bleepin' boomerang outta my face!" He would have had it removed except he didn't think he could get drunk enough to stand that kind of pain. Having a tool with an ID, well, it was not a good idea. Just ask the King of Pop, God rest him.

BF was moderately sure Mert wouldn't dime on him. She had her own skeletons and she knew he knew most of them. The shit was, he didn't think he could prove any of it. He was stuck with moving her pallets, like it or not.

BF didn't believe in hitting women, at least not very often and only then if he was truly provoked. But he was tempted to go after Mert right now and slap her sideways. Instead he turned back to his office. He was so busy picturing Mert's hair net flying off when his hand landed, he didn't see Fano step from behind a yellow barrel of USDA-condemned chicken and go after Mert.

THIRTEEN

Quality Tech Elvis Ridenour watched Fano watch Mert and wondered what it meant. No telling in this place. Elvis had other stuff hanging at the moment, but Fano stalking a plant manager was something to file for future use. Or maybe he should be checking Mert himself. She was always up to something, usually shady.

Elvis wasn't all that surprised at the extent these Poultry Xtra crooks gamed the system. Whatever policy or SOP stood in the way, they figured out how to bypass it. A lot like the Corps – so many regs, you had to memorize a manual to cross the street. Elvis felt their pain, he did. And he firmly believed you could jimmy things up some and still stay on the right side of the line between good and bad. But some days, these people were on a whole other grid.

Mert, for example, jiggered production reports and QA records to get chicken out the door and conned, bribed or strong-armed anyone in the way. Elvis also knew something about a few other, more lucrative deals, activities he classified as low-rent: peddling trinkets and payday loans. Still, Elvis had to admire her as much as he did BF with his bantam-weight cartel. They both believed in themselves and the principle of low-hanging fruit, just as Elvis believed in himself and his cause. Of course, Mert and BF were out to feather their own nests. What Elvis did – earn extra cash pushing booze and drugs – was for the good of the mission.

Elvis had weighed the risk of turning Mert in for quality violations. He knew he could have her job for the most blatant cover-ups, but to what end? It might be his responsibility, but it wouldn't advance his cause. And he wasn't about to flip on BF. Either move would draw attention to him and the quiet, purposeful life he led.

He glanced at the break room clock and headed toward the evisceration coolers for another temperature check, practically in awe at the free rein he had as a QC tech. He was almost as unfettered as the maintenance guys, although he couldn't go as many places.

His only job tonight was to temp and record six birds per hour on three adjacent lines, which took about 15 minutes total. The other 45 minutes each hour were his, as long as he made a pretense of monitoring the process every so often.

Forget Mert's scams and Bad Fruit's dope service. This QC job was the real racket

FOURTEEN

"Damn, I'm too fuckin' big to be meetin' you guys in this rabbit hole," Regis "Bad Fruit" Purdy groused, squeezing past condensers and stacked belt sections into the center compartment of a hulking unused freezer.

"But you need to see it. It'll be the best place yet," Fano said. "I heard Daylight say it would be offline for at least six months, maybe longer if they don't OK the money to overhaul it. This'll be perfect – no cameras, pretty soundproof, out of the way, consolidate storage, minimize the risk."

BF hefted his bulk up a couple of tiny stairs and flipped open a folding metal chair. "Who's usin' it now? Did the rats bring in a table and two chairs?"

"No, it's just those two day-shift bozos from building and grounds. They come in here to play dominos on their break since Daylight told 'em they can't play in the break room or people will think they're goofin' off," Beebe Dovey said. "They just carry around a buncha zip ties to replace the lockout tag every time."

"So how do we get them to give up their little club house?"

"No need, BF," said Fano. "Lopeter and Tarn are two of our distributors. They can work while they play."

"Well, looks OK to me. Guess we wouldn't have to be movin' the inventory around so much." BF often worried that his dealers could easily get caught stashing their small stockpiles around the plant, the pints of vodka and sloe gin, weed, some pills and a lot of crank.

"Set it up. But make sure you keep your ears peeled if Daylight finds out the freezer's gonna come back on line. And the boys better remember to replace the zip tag better than they normally keep up with lock-out tag-out or somebody'll be in here raidin' the merchandise."

"No problem, BF," Fano told his Boss. "Before you go, me and Beebe are gonna make a run to Jackson tonight, so we'll need cash."

"Whyn't you guys go during the week? You're gonna get knifed or somethin' goin' there on the weekend." BF said "I worry about you boys, with all them hardcore peddlers."

"Nah, we got plenty of weed. We're still getting it from the doc over in Malapee. Cooker's bringing in crystal first thing tomorrow," Fano said. "Tonight we're just going to Sam's Club to get vodka. I've had the trash guys collecting all the empties they can find every morning and a couple of the girls are refilling them with the bulk booze."

"Fano, you're a goddamn environmentalist. A downright green sonovabitch, that's what you are."

"Thanks, BF, I do what I can."

FIFTEEN

After Beebe left all mad over the Bobcat, Hoopdy was so upset he had a hard time remembering what all set him off. Everything wrong at the Tabernacle and broiler farm, all the work piled up, plus all the new do's and don'ts about how to act at work ricocheted around his brain.

When he returned to the yard, he stood rooted next to the disabled Bobcat. He was frantic to fix things to make sure Beebe was still his friend, unable to think straight. He was feeling one of his headaches coming on and before it got too bad, he knew he had to get home. And that's when it hit him: WWSSD? What would Solid Snake do?

Hoopdy had walked straight home and taken up his post underneath the big cardboard box he saved from one of his sister Geneva's Big Lots binges and hid in his Pepaw's shed. It worked just like the box Solid used to camouflage his whereabouts in the middle of a terrorist attack. It worked like that for Hoopdy, shielding him from too many sensations he couldn't explain much less escape. Sitting curled in the quiet and closeness of the box, Hoopdy began to order his thoughts, rerunning levels of the game across a little screen he could see on the inside of his forehead.

Slowly, Hoopdy saw that Solid Snake always prevailed because he did something unexpected. He solved the problem that nobody had thought of yet. That's what Hoopdy would do for Beebe. Fix a problem he didn't know he had yet, make him glad before he had a chance to be mad. Of course, Hoopdy didn't have the wherewithal to recognize the simple brilliance of this revelation, or he might have left Malapee for Madison Avenue. Instead, he headed for the plant.

Hoopdy found Beebe in the supervisor cubicles, pounding at a computer that evidently wasn't cooperating. He looked at Hoopdy briefly, then slapped the top of the boxy monitor and cursed. "Piece of shit!"

"Beebe, lookie here." Hoopdy spread the handles of a white plastic grocery bag, sagging full of grainy powder the color of a pee trail in old snow.

"Dammit, Hoop, wha'd you bring that here for. You crazy?" Beebe jumped up, grabbed the sack, spun it closed and shoved it in a file drawer, looking around to make sure no one saw.

"It's OK, Beebe, I just took a little bit from off the top. Them boys won't even know any's gone."

"But what for, Hoopdy? Why'd you take a chance like that?"

Hoopdy was starting to sag. "I thought you'd be happy, Beebe. It fixes a big problem we got ourselves."

Beebe sighed. Half the time he had no idea what was going on in Hoopdy's head. The other half, he knew and wondered how the poor guy was able to walk upright.

"Hoop, what problem? The only problem we got now is gettin' it back before BF finds out it's pilfered. What problem?"

"Well, your daddy don't know how backed up we are right? But we hafta give him somthin' or he'll know fer sure somthin's wrong."

Beebe shook his head, at a loss. Hoopdy just kept looking at him with his hair flopped over his eyes and a goofy grin.

"He's gotta have ashes to hand over to all them loved ones," Hoopdy was nearly wiggling with excitement.

It occurred to Beebe that he might the slow one.

He put his hand on Hoopdy's shoulder and squeezed. "Boy, you took a real chance, but all I got to say is, you done good. You done real good. Don't take no more of BF's stash, though."

Hoopdy's face fell. "You said I done good."

"You did, man. We need to make a couple of adjustments is all, but this is a damn fine idea," Beebe grinned.

If he were a pup, Hoopdy would have rolled over and piddled in submission and ecstasy.

SIXTEEN

Early morning at shift change and the boys were holed up in Dwight Butts' tiny office off the supervisors' bullpen, lounging in seat-sprung task chairs, boots covered in chicken gunk propped on desk drawers and trash cans, outlaw cigarettes fouling the air and making the twitchy overhead fluorescence even grimmer. This Band of Bubbas, first so-called by Eulie, included Bad Fruit, who ran slaughter and evisceration, and his two third-shift live-hang supervisors, Beebe and Hoopdy; BF's day shift counterpart, superintendent Dwight Butts and his evis supervisor Perkins Cantwell.

The group was loosely aligned in its determination to run off any more female managers who had the bad sense to accept a position in the slaughter end of the operation. They didn't believe women managers had any business in their territory, primarily because it was traditionally the preserve of men looking for a little extra slap and tickle.

You might not take the women from the production line home to mama, but they were just fine for flirting and occasional flings in The Old Box Room or out between the trailers on stand-by in the truck yard. Hook-ups helped to pass the long work night for the men, and the women sure as hell didn't object to the extra breaks, added time on their time sheets and the cushier jobs that came their way. Like, say getting a sit-down job cleaning gravel out of raw gizzards, which the boys liked, too, ever since Perkins Cantwell pointed out it looked a lot like the girls sorting the organs were rubbing plump little purply poontang.

In the effort to keep the lid on their baser thoughts and extracurricular activities, the Bubbas had successfully frozen out the last three women who either thought they were a match for the shenanigans or who just didn't know what they were getting into. Dwight was working on a new supervisor trainee who so far had been unmoved by his campaign to unseat her. Bad Fruit didn't have any girl supervisors, but his run-in with Mert had renewed his resolve to avoid them like mall shopping with his wife.

BF reported to Mert's counterpart, Maynard Travis. Still, he couldn't defy her outright. She would hang him by the short curlies if he tried. And as long as Mert didn't need a body to clean up a mess, like the 16 pallets of skimped weights she blackmailed him to ship, she stayed hands off.

This was a good trait in a woman boss, BF believed, unless there was romance involved. Unfortunately this was an unlikely prospect with Mert. He knew because he once took a shot during a company sponsored team exercise at Malapee's eight-lane AlleyOops and Abstract. No joy, there. Her nose had been as far in the air as her butt was nicely rounded. Flirt with Mert, feel the hurt, BF told the boys.

The irritations of dealing with Mert were the least of the Bubbas' worries these days, because some pissed-off former employee filed an EEOC charge and won the right to sue Poultry Xtra for fostering a sexually hostile environment, a term the boys had always sneered at during annual training they were forced to attend. BF had told Eulie the first time he laid eyes on her that the environment wasn't hostile toward sex. No, by damn, it was "hospitable. We welcome sex, anywhere, anytime."

BF remembered the laughter and ripple of applause from the other guys in the room, but Eulie didn't grin even a little. Made him feel a foot tall. Well, so fuckin' what? HR didn't run his operation, he did. And what his boys did when HR wasn't watching was just fine, as long as they got the work done. Still, the lawsuit had everyone acting wall-eyed crazy. Ever since Karen Jones Leary's attorneys had showed up at the plant to go through files, he and the boys had been acting like BF's hounds when they got caught digging nap holes in mama's begonias. They tucked tail and got real small, real fast.

The shit of it was that he didn't even remember this Leary bitch. No one did. But she remembered them, especially Hoopdy, poor dumbass cracker. BF's mama always shook her head and said, "Bless his heart," when the subject of Hoopdy came up. It was her southern PC way of calling him a retard.

But even though Hoopdy was backward as all get out and had no earthly idea how to act in polite company, he was a savant when it came to getting people to work in the hellish atmosphere of the live hang pen. Anyone who could accomplish that was Grade-A supervisor material in the poultry business.

The key was to contain Hoopdy's more antisocial, adolescent tendencies. That was no cakewalk because Hoopdy's main goal in life besides hanging chickens and playing video games was to make the guys at work laugh. His judgment about what constituted funny was often as illegal as it was accurate: The Bubbas always laughed and egged him on to ever more outrageous antics.

That some woman had been offended when Hoopdy stood behind her on the line, poked a chicken neck out his fly and pretended to masturbate was a surprise since nobody including this Karen woman complained until she left and hired a lawyer. Now, it wasn't just Hoopdy in a pickle. Everyone even remotely involved with the evisceration department when Karen worked there was liable to suffer in the upcoming trial. If the lawyers pulled the string hard enough on the chicken neck prank, it could unravel into revelations about all the activities the Bubbas had worked so hard to keep quiet.

Which was the real reason for this morning's confab in Dwight's office: He had been first to be deposed by Karen's attorneys. BF for one hoped to benefit from the experience; he could tell just looking at Dwight, who was an awful pale green around his mouth, it couldn't have been too good.

* * * * *

In fact, it had been so dismal, Dwight was still sweating sheets. The nightmare came back to him in a rising funk of fear, even after dousing himself with half a bottle of Jade East. He knew he was in a tight spot worse than any he could remember. Worse than flipping his truck during his senior year at Bayou Fatigue Longhaul High, plowing donuts among the headstones in the Jewish cemetery south of town. Worse than when he was homecoming king and had to wear a smelly cape and fuckin' crown during halftime to walk Madonna Entwhistle across the turf and up a cheesy stage made of stock tanks and Kleenex flowers to stand there in his cleats and choke through a fuckin' speech about Longhaul pride being invincible even after 17 fuckin' losing seasons. That was bad, but it was high-school bad. This whole court case deal was the real deal bad. Just thinking about yesterday made him want to weep like a little bitty girl.

Dwight had tried to look all calm and churchified before the tiny, shiny balding man across the table, his skin taut and polished, his suit silvery and his eyes the color of new dimes. Either he's stoned or I am, Dwight thought, absorbed in watching the light reflect off the reading glasses on the man's glimmering nose.

"Mr. Butts, you can answer the question anytime," said Braswell Boone Hockentrump, of Pylon, Foch, Takim and Goetz, the firm representing Karen Leary.

"Could you repeat the question, please?" Dwight squeaked out, amazed at how far away his voice sounded. He looked sideways down the table to see if Eulie noticed how anxious he was, but she was scooched back in her chair and blocked from view by the Company's lawyer, Dade Jones, a big guy who hadn't said much the whole time the squirt lawyer had been picking at him.

Hockentrump turned to the court reporter who sat tapping silently at the head of a glass-topped conference table in the offices of Pylon Foch in downtown Vicksburg.

"Ms. Moore, Mr. Butts said please, so let's oblige him."

The lady stopped tapping and contemplated her pale green steno screen. She read in a voice entirely devoid of expression: "Mr.

Butts, do you sit here before me today and tell me that you didn't know anything was wrong in pulling your male member out of your trousers and comparing its length with the length of the male member of Poultry Xtra supervisor Alfonso Creavy, called "Hoopdy," as all the while barely three feet away both male and female employees were engaged in hanging live chickens on the line on…what do you call it…the live dock hanging pen, and which action both you and Mr. Creavy proceeded to discuss actively, and I emphasize the word actively in that you were both manipulating your members at the time, discuss actively with Beebe Dovey and Perkins Cantwell, actually importuning them to "vote" by contributing dollar bills for the male member of their choice. As you sit here today, are you saying you didn't know that these actions were against the rules of man, country, God and Poultry Xtra?" The woman poised her fingers ready to record Dwight's answer.

Dwight swallowed and leaned toward Dade. "What does in poor tuning mean?"

"It means asked, Mr. Butts, you asked people to give money to vote on whose dick was the longest, did you not?" Hockentrump broke in, eyes a glare behind his lenses.

Dwight sat back and regarded Hockentrump. The lawyer sure sounded put out, but looked as if he was about to grin. He's just a guy after all, Dwight thought, breathing a little easier.

"Well, not the longest so much, just whichever one they thought was best. But I guess it was kind of gambling. I know that's against Company rules."

"So you knew it was against the rules to gamble and you were gambling on the outcome. OK. Did you see anything else wrong with it?"

"Well…not really…it was sorta like Bingo is for a good cause…it's gambling but everybody does it for fund raisers and doin' unto others. Hoopdy come up with the idea that we could put out empty mayonnaise jars and ask people to take a look at us and put a dollar in the jar for the one they believed was, you know, the best, winner take all except we was gonna give some of the money to

Chaplain Deacon's Youth YeeHaw Yahweh Night…we're always taking up donations for some poor soul…we take a lot of pride in doing stuff for our Posse Members in need. That's why I agreed to compete. Plus it's dark back there – you can't see much anyway."

Dwight stopped. No question about it, the lawyer was grinning for all he was worth and seemed even shinier than before.

"Sort of like Bingo is for a good cause, you say?" Hockentrump glistened.

"Yes," Dwight said, remembering what the company lawyer had said about keeping his answers short.

"Who won?" Hockentrump grinned even wider, and as Dade Jones jumped to his feet to object, said "Never mind, Mr. Butts, you don't have to answer that."

Dwight ducked that bullet gladly. He didn't want it in some court record that Hoopdy had won, for heaven's sake, even though Dwight knew that it was just a popularity contest. Because for sure Hoopdy did not have no prize winning roger. It was just that, ignorant as he was, people really liked Hoopdy.

"All right, let's move on." Hockentrump said. "I'd like for you to tell me about an incident, if you know about it, that happened during Ms. Eulie LaCrosse's first visit to the live hang area when Perkins Cantwell openly fondled her buttocks – that is placed his outspread hand on her left butt cheek and squeezed firmly twice while calling 'Honk, honk, slap that ho, get up front, there you go!' loud enough to be heard over the cage dumper. Do you recall hearing about that incident, Mr. Butts?"

Eulie's gasp dissolved in a fit of coughing. This guy is a piece of work, Dwight thought, bringing that up with her in the room.

"Mr. Butts?"

Dwight pulled his bandana from his back pocket, mopped at the sweat trails down his face and wished he was somewhere out in the deer woods as far away from this stifling room and glowing little fucker as a body could get.

"Yeah, I heard."

SEVENTEEN

Hoopdy Creavy sat on little rise behind one of Deacon Dovey's chicken houses holding his stomach, laughing at a bunch of drunk chickens flap and stagger trying to peck up the surprise he brought.

After mucking chicken litter out of two Dovey & Daylight broiler houses for Beebe, Hoopdy hauled four hand grabs of birds out of a full house and set them on a batch of slimy beer hops Geneva asked him to dump. Then he climbed the little slope and sat down to lunch on ribs, a potato pancake and some Spicy Hot V-8.

The chickens didn't like being outside at first. Once the hatchery boys slung chicks by the tray-full into a broiler house, the babies would run around in a little square space right at the spot they first landed, trying their durndest never to stray an inch further. This bunch was near full-grown, but they'd never been outside and ran scared for a spell 'til they came across the hops.

Boy howdy, Hoopdy thought, clapping his hands, if they wasn't goin' after the slop, now. It wouldn't hurt 'em and nobody'd know 'cept Beebe when Hoopdy told. The main thing was, Beebe's daddy and Mr. Tuber Daylight wouldn't know. They mostly never showed up even though it was their farm. Hoopdy and Beebe handled it.

He hugged himself laughin'. He couldn't wait to tell Dwight and BF. They'd bust a gut. He wiped tears. Chickens was funny, and he liked 'em a lot. Spend any time around 'em and you knew what they was gonna do. Not like people who keep you twisted up, tryin' to keep 'em happy. When people smiled and they was happy, Hoopdy knew he was in the clear. So he always did his best to make everbody smile.

'Cept his sister. He give up on her. Geneva never smiled even when he took her his check on Friday. He never remembered her ever smile at nobody. Maybe she didn't see the need, since she didn't go out all that much and never could keep a job. She told Memaw people was too stupid and she wasn't workin' for no stupid people. So she kept house for Memaw after Pepaw died, spendin' granny's monthly check to run things and tend what was left of Pepaw's home brew business. When Memaw died last year, Geneva and Hoopdy stayed on at Memaw's and kept up the beer business. It didn't pay too good, and most of it turned stinky and exploded. Geneva drunk off what didn't. It all worked out even, Hoopdy thought. Geneva needed his money and he needed somebody to do for him like Memaw.

Hoopdy was hopeless at stuff like rememberin' bath day and clean underwear and socks, or fixin' his dinner bucket. So Geneva took over, took his paycheck and helped 'im out with what his 6th-grade teacher had once called his daily personal needs and responsibilities. She told him so many times about personal bathroom responsibilities it made his head hurt. He'd left school the year when the headaches got so bad he couldn't get outta bed. That same year, the school told Memaw he had to go on the short bus and Memaw told the school they could rim her exhaust pipe.

The headaches stopped after while but he never went back to school, and anyway he could read some and do his times tables. He took odd jobs 'til he was 18 and could hire on at the chicken plant, back in Mr. Otis's time when they called it Banty Roasters. He and Mr. Otis found out how good he was with chickens at about the same time, when Hoopdy was hangin' 31 birds a minute and had all the hangers workin' to hang the most. Mr. Otis made him a supervisor on the spot. Hoopdy was never prouder of any smile than Memaw's when he told her he was a boss.

Hoopdy sure didn't need Geneva or nobody else when he turned into Solid Snake. When he was in his room with the console in his lap, it was real life for Hoopdy only better. Bad characters and terrorists and shit was all around, but all you needed to fight 'em was in yer own head. You couldn't always tell who was who or where they was comin' from. Sometimes friends or even brothers turned out to be enemies. But Beebe said that didn't matter, friend or enemy, you did what you was told and stayed loyal to the soldier's code. A terrorist was a terrorist, false friend or foe, Hoopdy could spot a terrorist when he seen one and turn 'em to table scraps for hungry hogs.

In real, real life, though, about all Hoopdy did real good was fixin' stuff and workin' with chickens. His boss BF said he was a dyin' chicken's best friend. And he was good at runnin' the live hang pen. Hoopdy loved it on the line, showin' new folks how to grab, flip and slot paws in the shackles. He couldn't tell how to do it, but he showed the way you had to move and listen to the birds. After awhile, all the noise, shit and dust disappeared and it was peaceful. Hoopdy could hang and hang for hours and never give a care what anybody else wished he was.

Lookin' at the big pitcher, like Beebe said, Hoopdy had it pretty good. 'Course, livin' with Geneva was like a big, mean dog is fixin' to grab onto you the minute you look away. But, mostly he didn't have to mess with her, 'cause he was usually at work.

Beebe and Beebe's dad and uncle, Mr. Tuber Daylight, always acted happy to see Hoopdy and always give him a job to do. He helped Beebe out at the Tabernacle furnace to avoid what Chaplain Deacon called a bottleneck and Beebe called a fuckin' nightmare. Or he was here at the chicken farm. Plus, he did extra stuff at the plant when Wayne or BF said. All of his jobs but hangin' was stuff people wanted done but they didn't want him talkin' about. No matter, as long as they paid you and smiled when you was finished. Hoopdy thought he had it pretty good. He liked work plus his old room at Memaw's where Geneva hardly ever came and nobody dared mess with Solid Snake. Pretty durn good.

Hoopdy hooted at a hen that flopped down in the middle of the soppy mash and tucked her head under a wing, too drunk to move. Some of the others still pumped their heads, flapped and pecked at the wind.

"You'uns a riot!" Hoopdy hollered, bent double until he rolled sideways. The drunk chickens was ever bit as funny as he ever was. BF always swore Hoopdy was born funny, that he come out his mama poppin' a wheelie on a Schwinn Stingray with streamers flyin' so even his mama had to laugh.

"Hoopdy, boy, you a goddamn laugh riot," BF had bragged when Hoopdy showed him a article on how beavers was a boon to all mankind. The hunting magazine he found in a stack back in Pepaw's shed had a pitcher of a girl with her Daisy Dukes showin' part of her butt and unzipped to show way down to her other main parts, what the girls at work called their vajayjays. Just above the girlie's belly button it said "Miss Beaver. Damn! 1999." BF, Dwight and Beebe all laughed and punched each other 'til they teared up, like a bunch of friends would.

The chickens was all asleep now or peckin' over the last of the hops, kinda mopey. Like Hoopdy started to feel when he remembered Miss Beaver didn't make BF happy for very long. BF had called him to the office later and said he wasn't to bring pitchers like that to work no more because of the trial. Hoopdy knew about the trial because he had to talk to some lawyers from the main office.

He still wasn't sure what he done that was so bad. They asked him if was trained on how to act around old people, soldiers, women, regular African coloreds and brightskins, plus, Mexicans, crippled folks, and homos, and how you couldn't tell jokes about 'em. He told the suits he didn't remember exactly. He went to meetings and signed a sheet to prove he was there, but he couldn't really say what they were yappin' about. But he'd always trusted BF to know what was what and keep Hoopdy in line. BF always laughed the loudest at his jokes, him and Dwight did. So it was okay to joke 'cept when it wasn't. It had Hoopdy all mixed up.

They told him some woman he never met told 'em Hoopdy harassed her and done somthin' she thought was nasty. How could he do that and not know her? They said it happened when he taken the neck of a six-pound bird and stuck it through the pocket slot in his smock and out through the flap, whalin' on it like it was his peter, beatin' off, playlike. Well, sure, he did that – all the guys did that sometimes. And the girls, they took whole birds off the line, pinched up the neck end like flat, fat lips and went around makin' smoochy sounds while they shoved it up in some guy's face. It was all just to have fun and pass the time.

Now, BF said all that was against the rules. No playin' with chickens or chicken parts. 'Specially chicken necks. It was too bad. The chicken neck joke was a good one to spring on new supervisors, 'specially women. When Hoopdy pulled that trick, BF said those girls didn't know to shit or go blind. Now BF told him he had to stop. Plus he said to quit checkin' his business all the time. Hoopdy didn't know what that meant, and BF said when Hoopdy got to talkin' around the girls, he would go to shiftin' his self ever ten words. Hoopdy told him for sure he'd quit it, but durn it, how could he stop if he didn't even know he was doin' it?

Well, at least out here, behind the chicken houses, things was different. Hoopdy leaned back on the patchy grass and squinted. He reached down and slipped his right hand inside his drawers. Out in the open like this he was glad he was skinny enough he had lots of room without strippin' off. He rearranged his steak 'n eggs, played a little bit, then a little bit more. Solid Snake, he breathed.

When Hoopdy finished, he lay gettin' his air back, his hand still warm in his shorts. He wasn't thinkin' about much, 'cept how he felt fine. And about the time his Uncle Kevin caught him messin' with his self when he was a squirt. He'd showed him some tricks, like how to wiggle his ears and whistle real loud with just lips and no fingers. And his favorite, the trick for dicks, Uncle Kevin said and winked at him. That was the one Memaw slapped him for when he showed off, and Geneva hollered and took after Uncle Kevin with a fly swatter. Well Memaw was dead and Geneva couldn't see him now.

Hoopdy pushed against his fly, workin' his right thumb through the space between two buttons. He raised his head to see how it looked. He wiggled his thumb just like Uncle Kevin showed 'im.

Hell, it'd work as good as a chicken neck stuck out his britches. It'd be so slick. Just hangin' it out while everbody was yappin,' payin' no mind. When they finally seen what you was up to, it'd be a goddamn laugh riot, like BF said.

Hoopdy wiggled his thumb again and stared for a long time at blue sky. He would do it, but if he put his hands down his pants at work QC and USDA would go crazy. And the lawyers. Dwight told him they'd been all over him about the day he and Hoopdy pulled their peckers out to see who was biggest. He couldn't put his thumb in his drawers, and he couldn't do no tricks with chicken necks.

He grinned, then laughed loud enough that a stinkin' drunk hen shot up, squawked and keeled back over. Hoopdy clapped his extra hand over his mouth to stifle giggles. He believed he just come up with a trick to call his own.

* * * *

Hoopdy went by the house to take Geneva's garden shears before he met up with Beebe at the crematory to do some work that was stacked up since the furnace belt busted. He hurried to get there early, before Beebe came with the Bobcat. He went right to the furnace room to pull on his waders and work gloves.

He was surprised when he walked out the back door at how big the pile was. Him and Beebe was gonna be durn busy.

Hoopdy kicked rocks off the edge of the tarp, and pulled out Geneva's garden shears. He wasn't hurtin' nobody. Nobody would even know. He only needed one or two.

EIGHTEEN

Psalm kinds of Love
Play on life's tape,
Sing Psalm at life's end
Oh, leave us agape.

Eulie stood in agony at the back of the knotty pine and red-ruched velvet Gather at the River Tabernacle Home Going Sanctuary as Chaplain Deacon Maitland Dovey's three nieces from Baton Rouge sang The Deacon's own composition, "Psalm Kinds of Love," to the full house of mourners crowding the service for Lowndes Henderson.

She wished like the devil that she could kick off her blue snake knife-toed spikes and wiggle her crumpled toes but was afraid she'd never be able to wedge them on again. In fairness though, almost an hour into Lowndes' rites, she figured that enduring screaming feet was fit retribution for not having done more to steer Sharay away from the path of the Dovey family marketing juggernaut. If she had known the size of the bill of goods Sharay bought, Eulie would have taken off one killer blue shoe and chunked it at Dovey's bowed head.

* * * * *

The Chaplain Deacon was in an ecclesiastical and fiscal happy place, standing suited in a shell pink Nehru jacket and tuxedo pants the color of blue dawn over The Glittering Sky Slots and & Smokes

Casino. Similarly dressed Beebe Dovey, not so comfortable in prom duds, squirmed at his father's side on the rostrum.

Ignoring his itchy offspring, Deacon Dovey prayerfully calculated that with funerary non-negotiables plus all the add-ons and furbelows, Lowndes' send-off was fast approaching a $20K sweet spot. Dovey's cheeks blossomed in rosy sworls at the prospect that the Henderson windfall, no disrespect intended, was turning to gold loaves and silver fishes. Well, wealth untold anyway.

The service would be the talk from Malapee to Atlanta for its unparalleled high style and entertainment value. It was such a cavalcade of talent, Dovey wished he had considered selling tickets to non-family members. But no, it was perfect as it was. Such good advertising to so many arrayed before him. So dignified and sweet, Dovey smiled affectionately at his little singing sunbeams, Deirdre, Danita and Doreen Dovey, whose daddy Toliver Dovey would take home a nice emolument for their rendition.

Sharay had wanted every last member of her daddy's family to arrive with their bereavement offerings in hand before holding the service, so it had been nearly two weeks since the tree felled Lowndes. This required Dovey's state-of-the art albeit more costly pickling of Lowndes with Balm of Everlasting Gefilte, a concoction heavy on salt, short on formaldehyde and long on shelf-life. Dovey was gracious in giving credit to his Jews for Jesus cohorts, and forgave them the Balm's origins during their former state of disgrace. In any event, Balm Gefilte gave Dovey ample time to work on Sharay, so that Chaplain Deacon Dovey and Mrs. Dovey had persuaded her to foot the bill for the finest funeral money could buy at a mere 1500% markup.

Dovey was able to offer Sharay a deal on a top-of-the-line casket because the family of an earlier expired client balked at the $6,000 price tag. Dovey had all his caskets drop-shipped from an e-Bay Super Seller out of Texas and never paid more than $400 a unit, even for the exotic wood models with gold-tone grips. But he sometimes had to unload the custom jobs people requested in the throes of grief.

So Lowndes (who Dovey speculated to Sharay had a lifelong wish to putt his way beyond the heavenly water hazard to the well-raked and sandy shore) rested before them in a lily-laden casket entirely and exquisitely imprinted with the photo image of the 18th green at Pebble Beach and labeled in silvery script "The Ultimate Hole," all at the rock bottom price of $5700.

The gravy of the deal was, the Deacon would ultimately be able to resell the casket because Lowndes "burial" today would be ceremonial. Dovey had persuaded Sharay that a fine figure of a man like her daddy would have chosen cremation if he had lived to see what a powerful number the tree had done on his severed head. Dovey and Mrs. Dovey had described the difficulty in significant detail, generously admitting that not even their expert ministrations could have prepared her father for an open casket visitation and home going.

But Dovey assured Sharay that Lowndes would still want to take his place in the Tabernacle's adjacent Heaven's Rest Memory Garden. Even though the Doveys ran the only cremation retort in six counties, they did so mostly in service to that misdirected set of believers who had faith that Jesus could find them during the rapture no matter how far and wide their ashes were cast.

But of course, Dovey had explained, Lowndes being more traditional in his beliefs would have wanted a full burial, dust or not, with an upright monument and statuary that left no doubt as to where he would arise and reconstitute on Judgment Day or as to how much Sharay loved her daddy. After the showcase service with the glorious but empty casket, it would a matter of neatly sliding the Cadillac coffin back into inventory and returning in a day or two to bury a very nice particle board box holding the residue of Lowndes Henderson after Sharay took her share. All with no one the wiser.

Sharay, who had taken to bed for three days after having to identify her dad's body, was of no mind to argue with such complexities. Her expressed wishes, coming as they did between bouts of tears and swooning fits, were simple.

First, she said, whether anyone saw him or not, she wanted her daddy to look good going to his Earthly end. So Mrs. Dovey had arranged to dress Lowndes in his own favorite double-breasted church suit with wide, light blue chalk stripes on navy, but added all brand new blue picked cotton dress shirt, pima undershirt and satin boxers, striped silk hose and a fine pair of the Deacon's own slightly dated cordovan and cream wingtips. And Sharay insisted that they should not forget her daddy's Poultry Xtra logo tie just because his neck and head was out of commission.

When Mrs. Dovey gently revealed the added cost for the extra finery, Sharay waved her hand, dismissing all consideration of expense. She might have many questionable traits, but she was not stingy when it came to her family, even the deceased. Especially since she found out how much was in the pipeline from her daddy's life insurance.

Interpreting her wave for continuing carte blanch to put on the best for Lowndes, and disinclined to wait for every last distant Henderson family members to show up and volunteer, Dovey pulled out the stops, putting Doveys and Doveys by marriage on the program, each for a small honorarium, on the whole not all that big a hit on the Deacon's final take.

The flower girls, somewhat long in the tooth at 26 and 31 were Dovey's girls Demeter and Desdemona from his second marriage to the late Minnie Dovey nee' Slocum. The dozen ushers and usherettes in white gloves, straight-backed and austere as they hand-signaled mourners to their seats, were Dovey nieces, nephews and cousins of quite some remove, but relations nonetheless.

He hired his aunts Tisbee and Clothilde to be official keeners, since he wasn't sure that Sharay had any moaning left in her. Just in case, one of Mrs. Dovey's sisters, who was a home health aide, was ready to revive anyone overcome by the expected public show of grief with amyl nitrate poppers and ice water.

The HalleOoorah Trumpet and Trombone Band, a couple of musical ex-Marines turned out in camo tuxedos and spats, would lead the recessional of flowers and the Jazz Funeral march to the cemetery. The boys mostly stuck to martial music, but they came recommended by Mrs. Dovey's daddy, a bird colonel in the reserves. Deacon Dovey thought they were the image of Mrs. Dovey in drag, although Lydia swore they were just friends of the family, not kin.

Dovey was forced to hire a couple of gospel soloists and an organist from the community college music program at a higher rate than he might have preferred, but he was certain he could sell at least one of them a pre-paid funeral before they could pack their sheet music and start for the car.

The rest of the choir was made up of Dovey's sister, Prell Dovey Daylight, and her teen-aged brood: three baritones, a tenor, an alto and three sopranos.

And after Dovey's inspiring eulogy and altar call (15 saved and signed up for his "God's Plan for Renubial Bliss – The Secret to Marriage Resurrection" DVD) and the even more awe inspiring round of gospels and the recessional, there was no telling what Sharay might spring for next. She and Danny would need emotional support and advice for contending with Henderson's Poultry Xtra Life, Voluntary Life, Accidental Death and Dismemberment and 401K payouts. She'd needed an experienced adviser with the horse sense to secure and protect those assets. And Chaplain Deacon Dovey was just the horse poor Sharay could ride. He grinned at the mildly racy image, not nearly so backslidden a fantasy as his fallen idol Jimmy Swaggart must have harbored.

Dovey figured he could start things rolling by asking Poultry Xtra to grant Sharay's second request, which she had decided was her father's dying wish: To have a portion of his ashes strewn among the offal trailers at the Malapee plant.

"Chaplain Deacon," Sharay had sobbed. "He went to work every damn day. That's all he ever did. He was on his way to work when the Lord whacked him with that pine tree. I prayed and prayed, and I think since we have his ashes and all and they can be kinda divided, that it's what he'd want...for a couple of tablespoons or so to end up at work."

Of course, it would be a difficult negotiation, but he knew it was God's will that he make every effort to see that Sharay's wish came true.

Dovey sighed, and nudged Beebe to quit fidgeting, thinking what a blessing had been the life and death of Lowndes Henderson. He watched Sharay and Danny in the front family pew, both arrayed in lamentation white and looking bewildered. He was somewhat irked to see Deputy Sheriff Chumley Bucket seated in the family section, and vowed to keep an eye on this development. Still, confident of his powers of persuasion, Dovey swelled with contentment, secure that he was in covenant with his calling, helping those adrift in grief and uncommitted funds.

As the organist pumped up chords for a closing hymn, young Rooster Daylight, a Dovey by marriage, began to sing "He Looked Beyond My Fault" in a sharp tenor that sliced through most listeners like a good conscience but missed Deacon by a mile.

NINETEEN

As the HalleOoorah Boys swung into the strains of "In the Sweet By and By," and people assembled under a tent over Lowndes' next to last resting place, Beebe Dovey thought it might be a good time to get a quick word with the Deacon, who stood at the head of "The Last Hole" all sober and preacherly.

"Deacon, a word?" Beebe said, sidling up behind his father.

"Not now, boy," the Deacon said, nodding as mourners passed.

"But, Deacon, it's about Hoopdy. Trouble with the Bobcat and everthin' else, the shitty conveyor and fertilizer stackin' up.

"What trouble? I thought you boys got all that fixed. You'd think between the two of you, you could handle it," the Deacon frowned and actually looked at his first-born. "Son, really. Use your heads. I don't have time for this now. You and Hoopdy figure it out, OK? Just git 'er done. And no more screw-ups."

Beebe nodded and backed away from the Deacon. Figures, Beebe thought. The Deacon didn't like to deal with the dirty, earth-moving end of the business. Ever since Beebe had been old enough to pop a clutch, he'd been tapped as the Tabernacle's hired man. Only he wasn't hired, he just did the work and got room and board. Until he met Rachel.

She was an LPN at the Malapee Quick Fix Clinic when Beebe came in with a strawberry he got on his right butt cheek playing left tackle for the Malapee Antlers. After a half season of seeping misery, Rachel took one look at the jarringly large pustule on his hairy rear, lanced it, scraped it clean and soaked it in astringent all without batting an eye, even when Beebe had screamed like a goat having its kabobs skewered live. But the strawberry dried up, and Beebe moved in with Rachel the following week. Because he loved her as much as he could, he'd felt obligated to get a job, which is how he ended up at the chicken plant.

The Deacon and his mom said they could live with it but they still expected him to work for the Tabernacle pretty much for free. The only concession the Deacon made was to let him hire his own crew, which consisted of five or six illegals in constant turnover and Hoopdy Creavy. Hoopdy would do anything for Beebe, so great was the poor ignorant soul's desire to be part of any group that would have him.

Beebe pocketed most of what the Deacon advanced as pay and he didn't feel great about it, but hell, there was always another Mexican ready to work off the books and Hoopdy didn't know the difference. Plus he'd just turn around and buy some trinket trying to impress some girl at the plant, which everybody knew was going to be his downfall. Maybe everybody's downfall if what they were saying about the big lawsuit was true. Course, Hoopdy wasn't the only supervisor at the plant that was hornier than a three-peckered billy goat. Just the stupidest.

What they all ought to do was to find a nice girl like Rachel. So what if she was homely. She could slap down a plate of fried chicken, greens, roastin' ears and mashed potatoes any time he wanted plus stitch him up if he was to happen to get bested in a bar fight. She didn't even bitch that if he hadn't stopped off at a beer joint, he wouldn't have been stove up. Most amazing of all to Beebe: Rachel didn't seem to mind the hours Beebe and Hoopdy spent in their twin recliners playing the latest version of Metal Gear. All in all, Rachel was a way better way to scratch the itch than hooking up with the plant ladies, who didn't necessarily have a fellow's best interests at heart, much less keep shut about what a guy did in his spare time.

Beebe might be fixed for wick dippin' but he was fresh out of enough money to pay all his hands and get the Bobcat runnin'. Parts don't grow on freakin' trees. Even the Deacon ought to know that much. He'd have to figure some way to fiddle Hoopdy's pay, or get the part ordered on the sly through the parts room at the plant. Or maybe tell the Deacon he was going to have to charge extra from now on if he and Mama expected him to wear one of these fuckin' pastel monkey suits to another funeral.

Or maybe he and Hoopdy would just go directly to Plan B if they could come up with one. Only thing certain, they needed to get something done hurrier rather than later or they were going to be up to their armpits in chicken shit and cadavers.

TWENTY

It was 8 a.m. on a Friday. Debone was running like a million bucks: long enough after start-up that the kinks had been worked out, a pretty straightforward product mix – just wings and bone-in half breasts, tenders – no fancy portion-controlled cuts for boutique restaurants. No big no-show holes on the line. Attendance was always good on payday at Malapee, at least until first break when the supervisors handed out checks and a good number of Posse Members caught payday flu and didn't make it back to the line.

But right now, things were on a roll. The delivery conveyor running above and perpendicular to the front of all ten cone lines was dumping cascades of front halves with syncopated ease to each line as weight sensors in the load tote automatically detected the line loaders pulling out front-halves to place over cone-topped rods. The continuous parade of pale broiler front halves looked more like pot-bellied torsos, miniature guillotined potentates with wingtips splayed and ready for cutters to grab and score the perfect shoulder cut. Shoulder cutters were the MVPs of deboning. The right cut was crucial to release the wing shoulder so the carcass would give up the highest-dollar drapes of flesh to breast and tender pullers, who could then strip them clean down to rib and keel bone.

The whole department was humming along in concert, a din of shouted conversation among nearly 300 workers intent on being heard. Talk about this baby's asthma or that son's graduation, or some daddy's deployment or grandmama's run-in with the cops, all layered over the reverberation of an amphitheater full of chugging pumps and motors, blades and track chains. Smooth and routine, noisy enough that it was a second or two before anyone reacted to the commotion at the end of Line 3.

Three tender pullers each were pulling with one hand, scissor trimming with the other. Like all the other tender pullers on all the other lines, working side-by-side on 4-foot-long sections of raised platform, stomachs pressed to the conveyor rim, backs to a stainless rail. They had enough room to pivot with the passing cones, but were packed tight enough there was no extra space for the floor guy from evis who thought he'd take his break time to come into debone and confront the woman in the middle.

The little bitch was one of his exes, who his mama said she knew for a fact from a friend who worked with his cousin in dayshift debone that the punk-ass little two-timer was the one who keyed his Camaro the day before in the parking lot. His mama told him he'd put up with enough of her shit when they were married, and he was a pussy if he let her get away with messing with his vehicle.

He'd had all night to work up steam and the morning to knock back a pint of vodka he bought off one of the maintenance guys. Thus fortified, and with his mama's crude map of the debone maze in his hip pocket, he stomped through the double doors, swerved around hand jacks and giant totes of breast meat until he located Line 3. Undeterred by the tight squeeze, he forced his way onto the work stand. Beyond calling the key-wielding vandal out and maybe roughing her up a little, his plan wasn't exactly thought out, so it didn't go all that great.

His ex saw him as soon as he mounted the stand, lurched away but with a nimble stab at his eye with her trim scissors, screamed, "Step off, Bradley!" It was that lurch, the bump into the little tender puller on the end, then a shriek and a really odd gurgling yelp that started heads turning. Then came a horrible scream and a broad, misty spray of blood and the rush of people leaving their lines to converge on the trouble. A few thought to hit the emergency stops on some of the lines, but either people on Line 3 were too new on the job to know where the e-stop was, or they just weren't thinking when the little woman caught between the rampaging floor guy and his ex lost her footing and fell against the line track.

In the second it took for her booted feet to slip off the edge of the stand, a carcass clip snagged her hairnet and the tight bump of her pony tail, dragging her down the line. Co-workers tried to pull her by the smock away from the track chain. The beleaguered ex now used her debone scissors snipping frantically to hack away the woman's hair before her head bumped to a resounding stop against the gear housing at the line return. As the track chain moved on, the tiny woman's scalp peeled away from her skull as easy as if it had been chicken skin from boneless breast meat.

By the time the madness had peaked in debone, moved into the break room toward the health office, the evis floor guy had hidden in plain sight. Forgotten in the immediate uproar, barely sober, he had enough sense to linger behind to untangle the pelt of hair from the underpinnings of the line. He wrapped it around a scoop of ice from a tub of graded tenders and carried it like Galahad with a garland to the woman in the infirmary, who was barely conscious and being held by the weeping industrial health nurse until the ambulance arrived. Which was probably why she, the tragically hairless victim, not the drunken dickwad who caused the disaster, was the only Posse Member tested for drugs or alcohol in the wake of the Company's first ever industrial scalping.

Once the woman had been transported, Lines 1-6 debone were roped off for investigation, all product from Line 2, 3 and 4 condemned back through start-up, witnesses were rounded up for interviews, debone restarted after the lengthy break with just four lines running and limped on to shift's end with a skeleton crew and two supervisors borrowed from cut up and evis.

Debone managers gathered in pockets to decide what they had seen and when. The Line 3 supervisor would be responsible for delivering the main accident investigation, but would not start until the automated system triggered by the nurse's report alerted him to begin some days later, so he had plenty of time to come up with a story. Since his line was down and his checks delivered, he left Mert a voice mail that he was not feeling at all well and left the plant.

The first half-hour of the post-accident management pow-wow consisted of Eulie, Mert, Maynard and Truly sitting in the conference room as Truly's administrative assistant attempted to locate the plant safety manager, who had not yet arrived at work, having stopped at the Malapee McDonald's for his ritual Big Breakfast and McDoubleshot.

Nor was Eulie able to rouse Junior Couch quickly. He finally responded in text after three voice mail messages, not revealing his whereabouts but reckoned he'd reach the plant within 20 minutes, about what it would take for somebody to make the drive from Glittering Sky Slots and Smokes.

With nothing to do but wait for the quorum, the four sat in a funk of unfocused guilt. The dismal silence was more than Maynard could stand. Shifting in his seat he drew a breath signaling his intention to hold forth. But Eulie, shocked and sick at heart as she was, stared him down with an intensity that prickled his neck hairs. For once, Maynard held his tongue.

With the eventual arrival of the two tardy managers, and the marshaling of early information, the dreaded calls to Corporate commenced.

Mert listened as Truly and his safety manager tried to lob back the occasional answer to the questions pounding down from various risk managers at corporate. As usual during the first conference call, verbal brickbats were slung all around, but, the people up the food chain from Malapee ended up arguing with each other about the disaster of the moment, rarely letting the locals get a fact or excuse in edgewise.

Mert always kept her counsel during such bloodlettings unless somebody asked a direct question. What could anyone say, really? They were sorry it happened. They'd find out how it happened so it wouldn't happen again. Did the folks in the Big House really think the people in the field were so stupid they couldn't proceed without a thirty-minute call for everyone to state the obvious? Of course they did. So while the VPs from HQ were shouting everyone down, Mert was content to play dumb while she contemplated the opportunities invariably presented to her when all hell broke loose as it had this morning.

With all eyes – those honestly concerned or just idly curious – following the crowds surrounding the injured Posse Member, and all tongues wagging in all directions thereafter, Mert had been able to pick up the skim envelope left for her by the vending contractor known fondly as Mr. Chips. She usually sent a minion, but with such commotion, she felt safe slipping into the storage closet off the laundry that Mert let Chips use for a small consideration.

He sometimes liked to catch a nap or a quickie there or in the kitchen pantry with his current cafeteria cashier of choice before he headed back to Jackson each day. When she found Mr. Chips unloading a case of corn nuts, she had taken the opportunity to suggest a better deal on the closet rental and her cut off the snack machines he tended at Quickie Ricky's.

Mert had been disappointed that he seemed reluctant to increase her take, but hadn't pressed it today. Mert had been weighing her reliance on Quickie Ricky. But as long as that arrangement worked, she figured threatening Chip's concessions at the store and the plant would eventually pay off. Her term on the cafeteria committee during contract renewal was a revelation to Mert, that vending profits at a mega-plant like Malapee were sizeable, and in fact, vendors only ran full food service cafeterias if they got the vending concession in the deal.

So, there was a fortune to play with, plenty rich for vendor profits and payola for Mert. If everyone cooperated. If not, let Chips fall where he may. Mert nearly laughed aloud, until she remembered where she was and the poor injured Posse Member lying in the hospital in Jackson probably praying Worker's Comp would pop for a total hair transplant. Mert decided to listen to the conference call long enough to get the woman's name so she could send flowers.

TWENTY-ONE

Fano Alcides stood arms crossed, hard hat tipped low over his eyes, watching the eviscerated chickens weave along three intricate production line of curves, rises, switchbacks and plunges, past a few workers and USDA inspectors, eventually dropping sans giblets, feet, oil sacs and necks into the giant chillers that Fano kept running.

Old timers in the union complained to him that the chicken business was getting too automated, taking too many jobs, just like the Mexicans.

Conflicts among Mexicans and blacks were routine at Malapee with occasional major flare-ups. The crews were multi-racial, like the plant, but the blacks slightly outnumbered their co-workers.

Almost all the Mexicans worked a couple of other jobs during the day to earn money to support family back home. Sanitation, a comparatively short overnight shift fit their schedules. But with only four hours allowed to clean and de-grease all production areas, sanitation was among the hardest, most dangerous work at Malapee, putting the workers in a rush lugging stiff, heavy hoses, up and down ladders, over and under huge hunks of disassembled machinery in a horribly hot, wet, chemical steam bath.

So when an agitated group of Hispanic workers staged a march on HR to lodge a formal complaint that the black workers were lazy, given to standing around calling them stinking, union-hating Nachos and job thieves, while the Nachos did all the work, the racial pot boiled for weeks. It involved multiple crew changes and hours – long mutual slur tossing meetings, complete with full translation, among union reps, plant management, local clergy and a contingent each from the warring sides.

Fano was amused, but considered such sparring beneath him. As a Cuban, he believed all sides were justified in the poor opinions of one another. Since he was paid to keep sophisticated machines running, he didn't really give a shit that the old timers hated the Mexicans, or yearned for the good old days. And neither did Poultry Xtra really. It was way easier to fix machines than people.

Fano nodded at Elvis Ridenour, a QC tech walking to the chiller spout for his hourly temperature check. He watched Elvis check six birds and record the temperature, just as he did every night at this time.

And just as he did every night at this time, Elvis walked to Fano's side and handed him his clipboard. Fano scanned the first page of figures, flipped the page and quickly palmed the piece of lined notebook paper folded between the sheets. Fano handed the clipboard back to Elvis and pocketed the paper, orders from Elvis's runners and their regular customers.

Business done, they watched the chickens glide past.

Elvis leaned in close to be heard over the constant 80 decibel roar. "My friend, what's up with you and the formidable Ms. Ellis? Anything?"

"Oh, she's sniffin' around. Maybe a little something," Fano's expression gave nothing away.

"Mert. Huh. The last woman the last man of us would dare go for, and you're after a little something. Huh." Elvis nudged Fano's shoulder with a gloved fist. "You got stones, man."

"I got business, is all. Just some business on the side, you know." Fano clapped Elvis on the shoulder and smiled. "Not everyone knows it, but Mert is a very deserving person."

"I'm sure you're right. From what I see, she deserves plenty," Elvis agreed, thinking Fano took his meaning.

"See Bad Fruit before you leave Friday," Fano said.

"Will do," Elvis said. "Hey, what's Hoopdy think he's doing?"

Fano saw the little supervisor slam through the swinging door from the feather picking room still wearing his red live dock smock patterned with chicken shit and feathers, without his hairnet and carrying a six-pack cooler. He rushed hell-bent for the evis supervisors' bullpen. Once inside, they saw through the office glass, that he put the cooler behind some fat notebooks on top of a filing cabinet. He struggled out of his filthy smock and tossed it over the cooler and notebooks. He rushed back out the door and came toward Fano and Elvis at a gallop.

"Hoopdy," Elvis said, "Your hairnet!"

Hoopdy, eyes down, still walking at a clip and shaking open a plastic sack, wasn't listening.

Fano caught Hoopdy by his shirtsleeve, jerking him to a stop. Hoopdy let out a whoop and jumped straight into a low-hanging line of chickens twirling out of a wash carousel and landed on his butt in the trench drain.

Fano and Elvis ran to help him up, but Hoopdy had pushed his scrawny hindquarters up over the drain with a kind of mitered backbend and slowly teetered to his feet, dripping with chicken water.

"Are you OK?" Fano hollered.

"Huh?" Hoopdy yelped, "OK, yessiree Bob, I'm OK."

"You forgot your hairnet, Hoopdy," Elvis reminded him, pointing to Hoopdy's bare head.

"No, my rear end's a little tender, but my noggin's OK," Hoopdy grinned and sprinted off.

Elvis looked at Fano, who shook his head.

"I'll flip you for it," Elvis said. "One of us needs to go tell him before USDA finds out and shuts us down."

* * * * *

Hoopdy hurried back to the bullpen with a bag of ice he'd scooped out of a tote in leg quarter cutup, glad he hadn't had to run all the way to the ice room. He pulled the dirty smock off his lunch bucket and was about to crack the lid.

"Hoopdy, what the hell are you thinking?"

Hoopdy whooped for the second time in 10 minutes and whirled, knocking the cooler tumbling, flinging its contents right to the boot caps of the man standing in the bullpen staring from the floor to Hoopdy's stricken face.

After what seemed forever to Hoopdy, he smiled.

"Hoopdy, you forgot your hairnet. You've been wandering through the plant without your hairnet," he said.

Hoopdy inched one hand up to his forehead and probed, feeling for the fold of papery cloth head covering and finding the pomaded strands of his dislodged Jerry Lee Lewis cascade. He didn't take his eyes off the yellow hardhat of the man looking down at him.

Hoopdy lowered his hand, which had started to shake. "Boy, howdy! I sure did plumb forget. It won't happen again, I swear...you ain't gonna tell BF are ya? I was gonna show 'im, but he ain't seen it yet."

Elvis held Hoopdy's frightened gaze, then looked once more at the curiosity lying on the floor, nudging the near edge with his boot.

"I don't know, Hoopdy. This looks bad," he said, turning to leave. "Right now, you better scoop it back in the cooler and get yourself a hairnet before USDA pulls the plug. Then come find me and we'll talk, maybe work something out so we can both stay out of trouble."

Hoopdy gaped, nodding as the office door eased shut until he remembered to breathe.

TWENTY-TWO

Pinky Ridenour kicked Elvis through the slats of the top bunk for a couple more years after he told his little brother the truth about Swabby, until the night everything came unhinged and collapsed in a triple sandwich of ripe boys and bedding.

That was only a couple years before their mama had run off, then daddy fell off a roofing platform and broke both hips and his back. He finally cured his bedwetting and open sores by marinating his kidneys into an early grave along with his pining heart and broken carcass.

Pinky called Elvis Tubby right up until he climbed on the bus for Camp LeJeune. Pinky was an asshole and not all that bright, but he made sure Elvis had a place and stayed in school. So, Elvis followed him to the North Carolina. Miserable he might be, Pinky was all he had. Him and the Marines.

A couple years later, lying pinned and choked under the rubble in Beirut, Elvis remembered that crashed bed. Pinky had bucked and cursed until he'd thrown Elvis, his covers and the whole ruined top bunk into the far wall.

Trapped under what used to be part of the roof of the bombed-out U.S. troop barracks, Elvis heard Pinky screaming at him to get the fuck off, get up or he was going to beat the living shit out of him if he didn't fuckin' move. Elvis never hated Pinky more and swore over and over, drowning out the fear and screams through the maddening hours, that he'd never take shit off Pinky ever again, and if he got out alive, he would pay back every single punch, wedgie or insult his stinking brother had ever dealt.

When they flew Pinky in to see him at the hospital in Germany, Elvis told his older brother the reason he'd survived. Pinky had hugged him until they both cried.

It had been good for a while until Pinky had gone back to his unit and Elvis was left with nightmares that didn't get better. He relived the dread of fighting men detailed as peacekeepers in a place where peace was the reward for violent death, and the crippling disbelief that Marines had been ordered to carry unloaded weapons to appease locals, that barbed wire was their best defense.

He could still hear voices of the wounded and dying trapped around him back in Beirut. He would wake up shaking from dreams so violent, he knew he'd always sleep alone, on the floor and close to a doorway if he could. Of course, such spells interfered with the Corp's mission. Elvis learned everything is Semper Fi until it isn't.

He left the Corp in 1985 on a medical discharge, rejected and angry, ashamed to be alive. He knocked around for the next decade, living on disability, mac and cheese, fighting headaches and flashbacks. Pain followed him, clouded every waking hour and the few he managed to sleep. The anguish began to sear his outlook, sharpen his focus. A stonier Elvis emerged, righteous with the conviction that in any situation, he knew what was right. And when he acted, whatever he did would be right. He devoted time to this obsession, polishing the fury he felt for people he met everywhere who chose wrong.

On one of a thousand nights when he was afraid to sleep, Elvis walked into the Midnight Horrorfest in Louisville featuring "Land of a Thousand Corpses," "Planet of the Apes," and a short feature produced by some animal rights wing nuts showing doomed cows, pigs and chickens dragged, beaten and otherwise tortured on the way to the dinner table.

The next morning, Elvis set out to join the wing nuts, going back to the beginning to do the right thing.

TWENTY-THREE

PITTSBURGH, PENNSYLVANIA

Bitsy and Patience Povc grew up working for their dad, Mutt Povc, in his bar in Pittsburgh. Their mom had up and left when the fraternal twins were still in diapers, so it wasn't clear why Mom had gotten top billing at the little east end pub known as Mom 'n' 'em's Wings 'n' @.

When Mutt finally had enough of the stinking Pirates and Pittsburgh winters, he'd handed over the keys and inventory and headed to Key West where he hoped to emulate Jimmy Buffet, except for the music part, and eat some decent seafood for a change.

Bitsy, big and mouthy, took over the front of the house. Patience, bony and quiet, handled the cooking, not all that hard because you couldn't serve too much food in Pittsburgh or they made you send your smokers to purgatory on the sidewalk. Bitsy, a three-pack-a-day toker, kept close watch to make sure they didn't sell too many wings. She'd let some boozer slug back shots all night long, but ask for an order of wings that put receipts over 15 per cent of income and she'd cut you off like a rip saw.

Bitsy had just finished lighting one cigarette off another and started with her pre-rush prep when "Movie" Mike Ponder sauntered in with a satisfied look on his face.

"Heya, Bitsy, gimme a draw and somma the cheesy wings."

Bitsy stopped wiping down booze bottles and nodded at Mom's most faithful patron. Mike came in every day at the same time, claiming the same stool he'd co-opted when he moved to the neighborhood back in the '70s, and ordered the same thing.

But hell's bells, most of Mom's regulars were creatures of habit, like Bitsy herself, with the half-pack of Luckys stuck in the rolled cuff of her 3XL white T-shirt. At least Mike talked about different stuff every day, even though it was always something about movies, except when it was about crossword puzzles. But being a master of movie trivia and word games came in handy in a neighborhood bar. And it was Mike who told her a few years back that she should replace the 'at' with '@' on the pub sign to attract the younger, prosperous techie crowd. Yeah, Movie Mike was all right.

"Sure, we gotcha, Mike," Bitsy called. She turned to holler the order at Patience over the bar back transom. "Pee, Mike wants the usual."

Patience, as thin as Bitsy was fat and as taciturn as Bitsy was talkative said as much as she ever did, which was to repeat the last two words of whatever anyone said to her: "The usual."

Mike's usual was Black Gold Wings, pre-battered pieces first slathered in black strap molasses, hand-dredged in coarse pepper and crushed Cheetos then deep fried until they floated. With every big mess of Black Golds, Bitsy's patrons paid homage to the periodically World Damn Champion Pittsburgh Steelers and significantly hastened the accumulation of their arterial plaque, but it was for the Steelers, for god's sake.

Bitsy topped Mike's beer and maneuvered her bulk down the bar to his corner seat under the flat screen. "Here's yer beer, Bub," Bitsy said. "So, yins going out tonight to watch the Pens er what?"

"Nah, I just got premium box set remaster of "Peewee Herman's Greatest Skits"," Mike grinned, took a deep pull on his cold beer and neatened the foam from his lip with a paper coaster. "It has the director's cut of "Peewee's Big Adventure" and, get this, video extras from Paul Ruben's arraignment on public indecency for whacking off in that peepster theater in Florida."

Bitsy nodded. Jeez, it must be like winning the trifecta for a flicker junkie like Mike to own a movie starring a guy who ended up in a movie about being arrested for overly enjoying himself at a movie.

"Tight," allowed Bitsy. "Wings'll be up in a jif."

Then the improbable happened. Patience gasped loudly and spoke a complete sentence. "Bitsy, you better c'mere right now!"

Bitsy grabbed her chest. Whatever it was must be something for Patience to go on so. She steadied herself and looked beseechingly at Movie Mike. Mike took a quick swallow of his beer and walked around the bar to Bitsy's side. Together they pushed through the swinging door, crowding into the tiny kitchen.

Patience, sweating from the heat of the fryer, looked close to fainting. She pointed slowly to the marble lip on the griddle at a pile of chicken wings ready to dip, dredge and fry. Bitsy and Mike shuffled the two steps from the door to Patience's side.

"My Christ," Bitsy said, clutching at her bicep, fumbling for a smoke, which she clawed from the pack and lit with a shaking dimpled hand. She took a deep drag then laid the cigarette lit end out on the bar transom and poked aside a couple of the wing pieces. Sitting propped on its base like it was hitching a ride on Truck 19 was a thumb, nail and all, dark skin showing through the breading plain as day.

"Wow," breathed Mike. "It's like this movie I saw where a guy is eating a sandwich at a fast food joint and he takes a big bite and pulls out somebody's finger with a ring on it. Oh, man."

"More like 'Oh, shit'," said Bitsy.

"Oh, shit," said Patience

* * * * *

PipeSnark.com
What's backed up in the 'Burgh by Resaca Toomey, pipefitter and investigative blogger
ON SEPT. 23, 20XX, 4:08 AM
Disposable digit?

One of our Pub Crawl Correspondents reports that an East Side pilsner palace almost served up a new unappetizer with a side of wings a couple weeks back, battered, breaded and nearly deep-fried: Some poor soul's severed thumb.

Ace Correspondent says the pub owners aren't talking to anyone right now except their lawyers, and their lawyers are talking to the folks from some big purveyor of poultry, as yet unnamed. However, AC confirms the sighting, as he clapped his own headlamps on the horses de ovaries horribilious. (That's Latin for crudités that make you spit up in your mouth without even tasting.)

AC hastens to add it seemed to be one of a kind, so don't let's get too excited and stop eating on the East Side or screaming past hapless hitchhikers. RT plans to keep the goggles on this, though. I mean, it does rank a full five Plungers on the eeeesh scale. Stay tuned.

Today's Horoscope

If it's your birthday today, show a little common sense. Avoid varying your routine unless you routinely bar-hop on the anniversary of your birth for a celebratory basket of Buffalo wings or two. Be leery of the chicken tenders, too. Fill up on beer, and don't drive. This will pretty much rule out picking up hitchhikers or other serial killers who may deposit their Dahmer nuggets in the odd eatery.

TWENTY-FOUR

To get to the office of Poultry Xtra Senior Counsel for Corporate Affairs, Gable Chancey, you had to pass from the relatively ho-hum business environs of Company HQ in Skiatook, Oklahoma, into the deep carpet mystique of its storied past. Past an end-zone wide wall paneled entirely in gilt painted papier mache, mid-20th century egg flats, through hallways punctuated with paintings, sculpture and craft objects that ranged from high-end to hideous, past the open doors of executive offices, some of them shrines to deceased members of the founding family. Such as old Horace Hicksum, whose person in bronze – dressed in bronze overalls and with a bronze rooster tucked under one bronze arm – peers from beneath the cupped bill of a bronze gimme hat.

Assorted youngish executive assistants – all blonde – communicate in suitably reverent whispers if necessary, but mostly tap quietly away at their keypads, catch the phones before they ring, and totter about on impossibly high heels to hand deliver messages to the executive staff on old-fashioned While You Were Out pink slips.

Beyond the past and present Poultry Xtra Pantheon – Boudreaux Fallis is the current CEO and President – visitors arrive at the Corporate law offices, a comparatively raucous cul-de-sac where legions of attorneys toil, keeping Poultry Xtra powder dry. In an office marked for its leather and wormwood opulence and the sheer number of leaning towers of yellow legal pads, a group of suits sits at a conference table the approximate dimensions of an H3 convertible.

"What the hell is this?" Grable Chancey tapped the buffed nail of his right forefinger smartly on a screen capture of the blog PipeSnark and waited for someone to answer.

Associate corporate mouthpiece for various shit-storms, Cletus B. Field sat mute. Ditto VP for Media Relations, Mike Vole. Senior VP for Operations Sol Collins felt exempt from the senior counsel's obvious irritation; he didn't have an answer anyway.

Chancey turned his attention to the PR flak. "Vole, tell me anything you know."

"Sorry, Grable. Not much, I'm afraid. Our online crawler alerted us, but I'm not sure what the hit was, since there's no direct mention of Poultry Xtra."

"I thought we were tracking anything that tagged chicken and thumb," Cletus Field said.

"So you're saying this is about us?" Vole said. "First I heard of any severed thumb, guys."

"You didn't need to hear, Vole, until now," Chancey said testily. Let some folks past the gold egg flats and they started to put on airs. "But so you're not completely ignorant, this thumb in Pennsylvania makes the second one we've had handed to us on a platter by plaintiff's attorneys. Those Yinzer yahoos took their time coming forward, but it actually was the first thumb to make it to a consumer. So far, they've gone along with us on keeping it quiet until we get some answers."

"Yeah, maybe they'll use that Blitzburgh Terrible Towel for something useful, like a ball gag," Vole said, miffed at being out of the loop.

Chancey took a moment to pin his underlings with his trademark stare, used with much success in his last job as a take-no-prisoners litigator with a big box Big Apple firm, but perfected back when he was working his way through Panhandle A & M & L as a bail bondsman. It was a look that told local yokels, whatever their status, to grab their ankles and get braced.

"Obviously, they hope to leverage any settlement into the stratosphere by agreeing to a press embargo. It's a risky strategy, but gives us a measure of control. Gave, I should say. Since we have no fucking earthly idea how the butchered remains of dead people ended up in our best-selling food service wing pack! Dammit, people, how did some loon in Pittsburgh get hold of this?"

"Grabe, it had to come from one of the Povcs and it had to be against counsel's advice," Field said, almost immediately regretting he'd opened his mouth.

"Well, you were supposed to make sure that didn't happen. You said you had the ambulance chasers in the bag. Obviously, you were wrong. If we need to go back to Bounderby, et.al. to shut those two women up, do whatever you didn't do right the first time. Just get it done. And while you're at it, you better make damn sure we're still hanging tight with Hector and Chase, and our Ms. Duwray."

"I swear, Grabe, yesterday we were fine. Ms. Duwray is proving to be surprisingly patient." Field put up his hand to counter Chancey's evil eye. "But I'll put in a call just to check the temperature."

"Grabe," ventured Sol, "Should we dig a little bit on this Resaca Toomey? As you say, she sounds mental. I mean, a pipefitter with an investigative horoscope blog? And she's a damn union stooge to boot."

"Can't hurt, Sol. Clete, get somebody on it, but don't spook her. Vole, why don't you give him a hand? Maybe together you can manage not to screw it up. Just keep tabs on her, in case we have to bargain for a little prior restraint."

"Damn," Cletus Field said. "There's never a Stamp Act around when you need one."

"Clete," Chancey called, already on his feet and on to the next ass-kicking, "you're in some deep kimchi here. Shove the Ivy League lawyer jokes and get busy."

TWENTY-FIVE

Greta was in a funk. For one thing, she was certain that Andy sending her undercover in Malapee was the stupidest effing idea to come out of Corporate since R&D introduced shamrock-shaped chicken nuggets for St. Patrick's Day dyed the same moldy blue-green as a wedge of stinky cheese. Stupid and maybe dangerous.

For another thing, she couldn't figure out why, if you wanted to get anywhere in the South, you had to go three hours past your destination and then fly back two hours to get there. Nothing about air travel made a lick of sense. For a third thing, she was on her way to Mississippi. Having a four-hour layover in the Atlanta airport only prolonged the agony.

She scooted lower in the seat, plopped her feet on her bag and considered re-reading The Tale of Two Thumbs, but decided against it. They weren't any closer to figuring out where the thumbs came from. The only thing for sure: They came from one of the Poultry Xtra plants. The food-service pack used by Right Wings in Oklahoma and Mom 'n' 'ems Wings 'n' @ in Pittsburgh both were sold battered and breaded, ready to plunge into hot oil. The chance that someone at one of the restaurants had thrown a thumb in the order was slim to none.

Greta was even more certain of this after she learned about Pittsburgh, where there were three solid witnesses that the quick-frozen thumb came out of a Poultry Xtra date stamped plastic portion bag. Greta figured Pittsburgh had its share of characters, but the interviews with the Povc sisters and their customer persuaded her that they were your salt-of-the-Earth types with no interest in kicking up a media fire-storm to profit from their surprise encounter with a dismembered thumb.

Oklahoma's own Julie Duwray, though, was itching for a Jerry Springer moment, all Daisy Dukes and outthrust lower lip. Yep, that young woman was going to mine her windfall like a Mother Lode. Greta was not sure how much longer they could keep a lid on something like this, although the lawyers were sure that offering enough money and assurances they'd fixed the problem would do the trick. But it wasn't fixed, and no one knew if or when another thumb – or worse – might show up. What a cluster.

Greta wished she were home with Toby and the boys. Toby ran a small R&D cook plant in Skiatook, where Greta once worked. It was one of the more exciting places to be, overseen jointly by left brain QC Nazis and left-field foodies in Product Development.

Toby, who came out of plant operations, came down somewhere in the middle, practical but not hidebound, imaginative with an empirical bent. The kind of guy most people said had a good head on his shoulders. Some other people said that Toby wasn't the shiniest spoon on the table, but Greta thought that was just because of his imposing size and measured pace. Not slow exactly. More deliberate, like he didn't see any reason to get all riled up about things. Equanimity, thy name is Toby, Greta laughed to herself, and flipped the phone open.

"Babe," Toby answered.

"Hi, bud. How're the wild men?"

"Mikey's at practice and Rudy...well, while mom's away, Gameboy's in play."

"Toby, now..."

"I know, babe, I'll pull his chain in a bit. How're you? Where are you?"

"Stuck in Atlanta...darn, I am not looking forward to this."

"What's the latest? Anything major?"

"Well, not a lot more, but what I can tell you is that Andy says I have to work undercover as a security guard with the plant rent-a-cops. Like I'm some kind of spy or something. It's just nuts. Why didn't they just hire an investigator? I'm not Mata Hari for Pete's sake. I can't do this."

"Sure you can. Heck, you QC storm troopers are nothing more than a bunch of spies in plain sight. Besides, the boys claim you can see around corners or they'd get away with way more nonsense."

"Here I called you for moral support, and what do I get but insults? Anyway, we still haven't pinned down the plant where the you-know-what was found. It's probably Malapee, but that's not for sure since they had some kind of glitch where a mess of uncooked wings from Otto Avenue got mixed up with Malapee wings, and they all got processed together."

"Mess of wings is right, babe."

"Yeah, no one seems to know how that whole screw-up happened, and the QC and shipping documents are royally fouled-up or nonexistent, which is a whole nother kind of scary, never mind stray body parts. But enough. The more I talk about it, the more I wish I could just take a whippin' instead and come on home. What're you guys having for dinner?"

"Steak, eggs, biscuits and gravy. You know: man food."

"Man food, my foot. When did I ever turn down a meal like that?"

"Never. You the man, babe."

TWENTY-SIX

It had been a fairly quiet day for Eulie so far, no big fights to contend with, no competing baby mamas, no one collapsed on the plant floor with spiking high blood pressure. No nightmarish amputations. She'd made it through the weekly "Feedbag and Feedback" for Posse Members celebrating birthdays without having to spin any overly offensive comments from Maynard.

Mert had been tied up with some problem in laundry-supply, and as usual, Junior and Truly, in the name of community relations, ducked out of actual contact with the employees by going out for lunch with Deacon Dovey to the Malapee-Paola Chamber of Commerce & Moose Lodge.

Their mutual crack-up sessions after the weekly buffet made it clear that Junior and Truly went to eat free food, roll their eyes at each other and collect anecdotes about the bunch of service club rubes wearing wet-look Corfam loafers and big-buckled belts along with what the boys considered a thoroughly misplaced pride of place.

Not unexpected, Eulie believed, in such a sophisticated pair of Aggies. Eulie didn't recall any conversations between Truly and Junior that didn't involve video game tactics, college football or their favorite quotes from the latest hapless-horny-guys-finally-get-porked movie with occasional references to other shared totems of their Cartoon Network and Web-based upbringing. Oh, and they loved to share how idiotic their wives could be. Yeah, Eulie agreed, like when they married their husbands. Eulie often asked herself why she gave a hoot when Junior and Truly went AWOL. She didn't have a good answer.

It was almost 3 p.m., time for her night shift HR wrangler, Goodman Owens, to wander in. Eulie was trying to finish a weekly staffing report when a sharp knock on the door barely preceded the appearance of Union Steward Lovey Tillman.

"Eulie, you have to do something about Mr. Mizzle."

"Which one is he?" Eulie asked. She tried her best but couldn't keep track of everyone.

"You know, Marcus Wynn, the new guy they call Mr. Mizzle. I hate like fire to rat out potential dues payers, but he's a mess, literally."

"Booze or drugs?" Eulie asked.

"No," Lovey said. "Brainless."

Eulie saw the fairly quiet day start to circle the drain.

"What's he done?"

* * * * *

Eulie looked at Marcus Wynn picking at the baggy knees of his soppy, stained sweatpants, at his wide dark eyes caroming from her gaze around the office like a rogue Foosball ball. When he did make eye contact, she had to wonder if anyone was home. It was a marvel that such an incredibly handsome young man could be so limited. Shit, how was that for being open-minded, Eulie scolded herself. Working in a chicken plant could sure blow your biases right back in your face.

Marcus had been at Poultry Xtra about two months, and as far as Eulie could tell, he seemed to be an OK guy. Despite the uncanny angelic looks, it was his extremely poor personal hygiene that people first noticed, and which caused many complaints and one hemorrhagic nose bleed among Posse Members who had to stand next to him on the line.

She had counseled him about it and these days he smelled less like skunk sail cat and more like her little brother's sweat clothes when he left them in is gym bag over a three-day weekend, all in all a big improvement, considering. And Dwight had moved Marcus to a job walking around the evis department picking up birds that fell off the line. This helped disperse his essence so no one was subjected to Marcus unplugged for too long.

Now, it seemed he had developed some unfettered bathroom habits.

"Marcus, do you know why I called you in?"

"No, ma'am. Am I going to lose my job?" Marcus's pinwheeling eyes bounced briefly off Lovey, who was back in the office to witness the write-up and had on what she called her "Frowned-up Union Face."

"Marcus, one of your co-workers said they saw you relieving yourself in the drain in evis today during wash down. Did you do that?"

"No, I didn't do that. What is that?"

"Did you pee in the drain during wash down?"

"Oh, yes, ma'am. I was using the sanitizer hose at the time, so I just washed it right on down the drain."

"Marcus, why would you think that's OK? Don't you remember training in orientation about bathroom breaks and the talks we've had about cleanliness and hygiene? I have the papers you signed showing you were in class when these things were discussed. We can't use any place in the plant as a bathroom except the bathrooms, do you understand that?"

"I don't know about signing nothing. I don't think I signed it. I can't read or write anyways. Am I gonna get fired? Please, I need my job. My girlfriend's pregnant."

Oh great. He's producing offspring. Again, Eulie recognized her baser self reacting and tried to focus.

"Marcus, I have to write you up for it, and it will be what we call a serious warning. If you get two more write-ups like that, you could be fired. You need to learn and remember the rules we've talked about or I won't have any choice but to let you go. Do you understand?"

"Yes ma'am, I do and I'm sorry," he said to Eulie, then turned his big bouncy eyes on Lovey. "I'm really sorry. It's just I couldn't help it because Mr. Dwight asked me to start 15 minutes early to help set up clean tubs, and then I have to work straight through washing down when everyone else is at break before I can get a break, so I tried to hold my water today, but, well, it was like holdin' back a toad in a whip snake. I just couldn't."

He eyes careened back to Eulie. "I can't lose my job, ma'am. Mr. Dwight said as long as I'm on probation he can fire me for no reason and if I didn't finish wash down in 25 minutes, I should just go home."

"Mr. Dwight said that?"

"Yes, ma'am, and it sure was a surprise when he done it. He's been real friendly to me so far, letting me come in early for overtime, giving me a nick-name and all."

"What nick-name?"

Marcus sat straighter and smiled. His teeth were as white and perfect as his eyes were black and berserk, Eulie noted.

"He said he was gonna call me P-Drizzle, cause of how good I use my hose. Now everybody calls me that."

Eulie looked at Lovey, raised her eyebrows. Lovey shrugged.

"Mr. Dwight say anything else that stuck with you, Marcus?"

"Nothing special. He never told me not to be taking a piss when he seen me go out in the truck yard that one time, except he said I better hurry and shake it off and git it back in my drawers."

Eulie tried not to flinch, but failed. Lovey frowned harder.

"Did anyone else see you that time, Marcus?"

"I guess they could have, but I only seen Mr. Dwight and that great big supervisor with him, the one with the banana tattoo on his chest. Least, that's what I heard some girls saying."

"OK, Marcus, you're not fired, but you could be if you do something like this again. Let's go over the rules one more time. Then you'll know just what you should do and there won't have to be a next time, OK?"

"Yes ma'am, no next time. I promise."

* * * * *

Eulie, as frowned as up as Lovey had been, scowled at her monitor, reading the latest in what was turning out to be a long string of ass-covers:

Note to the file by Eulalena LaCrosse, Day Shift HR Manager, Malapee MS, Re: statements made to Marcus Wynn by supervisor Dwight Butts. I reported to HR Manager Junior Couch about counseling Marcus Wynn, and his claim that Dwight threatened his job but failed to counsel him formally for relieving himself on plant grounds. Also told Junior that Mr. Wynn had referred to a "big guy" with a banana tattoo – Regis Purdy known as Bad Fruit is rumored to have same – who was with Dwight when the incident supposedly occurred in the truck yard.

Junior laughed and said "Maynard told me about that nimrod. The folks are calling him Mr. Mizzle and P-Drizzle. Maynard said they've caught him whizzing all over the place, from the back dock to the flower urn outside the USDA entrance. He just can't seem to make it to the men's room."

I told Junior that it seemed under those circumstances there should be a record that Maynard or some other supervisor had counseled Mr. Wynn about the problem but that I hadn't found it in the file. I related Mr. Wynn's remarks about how he got his nick-name and asked Junior if he wanted me to follow up with Maynard, Dwight and Regis.

Junior said he would handle it and to e-mail my interview notes to him, that he would look into it as soon as he came back from the Malapee Rotary meeting tomorrow.

Eulie saved the note and signed off for the day, bone tired. It was hard enough keeping notes on everything that did happen. Nowadays she spent half her time writing memos on things that should have happened but didn't after she had reported something that started the whole circle jerk of documentation. Anyone in management not prepared to participate in the smoke-screen risked having someone else side-step responsibility by reporting you for not reporting that your first report was totally ignored.

No wonder everyone gobbled Advil.

Maybe she would start carrying one of those nifty little digital recorders in her pocket, permanently switched on. She knew from professional chat boards that there were HR folks out there who swore by them. The downside was the likelihood that the last thing you'd ever want committed to tape surely would be, and the first time you'd know it was when a plaintiff's attorney played it on the way to a jury trial. Nope. That was a potential problem way worse than the nifty little solution.

TWENTY-SEVEN

Excerpt from recording of Poultry Xtra Malapee Weekly Staff Meeting – Sept. 24, 20XX. Attending: Plant Manager Truly Lovett; Assistant Plant Manager, Maynard Travis, Assistant Plant Manager Mertricious Ellis, QC Manager Roy McKnight; Wastewater Manager Kris Kirchoff; Safety/Health Manager, Ardel Patrick; Maintenance Manager Wayne Daylight; Plant Accountant Jen Malcolm; HR Manager Junior Couch; Day Shift HR Manager Eulalena LaCrosse.

Roy: I haven't been notified officially yet, but the Corporate QC squeal is that either Malapee or Otto Avenue had a thumb amputation that got shipped out with a batch of wings.

Maynard: Well, at least they can't say we got our thumbs up our ass.

Wayne: Hell, if we did, we could tell them we're on top of it!

Junior: Hey, are they accusing us of giving folks the finger?

Roy: Wow. You people are comic geniuses. Just for the record, I think it's somewhat serious that somebody ate a human thumb under our brand.

Truly: Uh...now, let's stay on track. Thumbs you say? They must be joking. How'd they figure it's between us and Otto Avenue?

Roy: Somehow part of an Otto wing shipment was off-loaded here for restaging and ended up mixed up with some hold pallets for having the wrong box liner. Apparently they were reprocessed but we can't say for sure. No one is on record as having done the rework, although we have a tag release. Anyway, it's either Otto or us. At this point my boss just wants a look at our OSHA logs.

Maynard: How the fuckin' fuck did your people release holds if no one did the work?

Roy: Good question, Maynard. I could ask you the same thing. In the meantime, they want to know if somebody screwed up an accident investigation, somehow lost an amputated thumb and didn't stop the exposed product or record the incident. I mean, I know it's not likely, but Corporate wants us to cover all the bases before some ex-employee shows up without a thumb and claims we did it.

Ardel: You saw my graphs. You all know everything that I know – the foot amputation in November, but that was surgical from the crush injury in the dock door; the two fingertip evulsions and the scalping in debone. There weren't any pieces to find, other than some extra skin patches and tufts of hair on the scalp; the evulsions were so much paste after being shoved through the steel mesh glove. Definitely no whole thumbs, not that anyone reported anyway. How do we know if something happened and didn't get reported?

Jen: Jeez, Ardel, use your head for something besides a hat rack. You think something like somebody losing a thumb, much less two, wouldn't get out? Folks in the plant know when I need to use the john before I do. There's no way we wouldn't have heard about something like that.

Mert: Yeah, there's no way. My people know somebody's been fired before they hit the front door, much less somebody losing a finger.

Roy: You're both right. But I need to ask these questions. And for now, it can't go outside this room. We can only hope that if it's not us and it's not Otto, it entered the product stream somewhere else.

Kris: Maybe someone did it on purpose.

Maynard: Are you nuts? Who would cut off their own thumb?

Kris: Nobody I know, but they might cut off someone else's.

Maynard: Kris, you need to get out more; you been breathing too many microbe fumes.

Truly: Maynard, glad you brought that up. Kris, what's up with the water department audit?

Kris: I haven't heard any more than the e-mail I sent you. The city says they're finding elevated levels of lead, mercury and arsenic in groundwater. And nitrates. But there's absolutely no way that's coming from us. Our tests at the holding pond are clear. We'll be inviting them out to check for themselves.

Truly: OK, keep me posted. Junior, what's up with HR?

Junior: Well, as you know, I've been pretty busy with campus recruiting and we're in the home stretch on the organizing committee for Malapeelooza Daze, so Eulie should be able to bring you up to speed on our big ticket items. Eulie?

Eulie: OK. Can you take notes for me while I talk?

Junior: Uh, my handwriting's not so good. Jen?

Jen: Sure, OK. Thanks, Eulie.

Eulie: I guess you all saw the alert from Sgt. Doom, uhm, Ms. Dummit, that her friends at Immigration have tipped her to a possible raid in this division. No information that it's Malapee or even Mississippi for sure, but she says to make sure we've got our stuff in the right piles. Then, there's the sex harassment case. Sgt. Doom, I mean Darby says the depositions are on hold because Dwight gave Braswell Boone Hockentrump so much ammunition they want to expand the list and make another visit to dig through our files. I also heard Hockentrump has set up shop at the BBQ joint next to the Malapee Job Center, buying lunch or dinner for everyone we terminate who registers for unemployment. No telling what that means.

Maynard: It means we can worry about running chicken for a change and not have to answer questions about some pissed-off man-hating ex-paw sorter and her freakin' fantasy life. That little tender puller who had the top of her head yanked off, now she has something to bitch about. Worse than any bad conk job, huh, Mert? At least she don't have to be all ate up with hair issues, right, girl?

Wayne: Yeah, talk about a bad hair day. We need to make sure she gets a lifetime supply of hairnets.

Eulie: Jen, I'll take the notebook back now.

Sound of paper rattling

Maynard: And I heard she's another pregnant one, right? I still say we shouldn't be lettin' them work when they're expectin.' It's too dangerous to their ovaries. Stuff like this is bound to happen. And like my wife – her brain turns to mush ever time she's pregnant. I have to watch her ever minute or she'll burn the house down or go the wrong damn way on the Interstate. Just turns plain stupid.

Eulie: Jen, I can do it now.

Jen: Jeez, Eulie, OK, already. Give me a sec…the spiral's caught on my ring.

Sound of pages flipping…a gasp.

Junior: Yeah, I know what you mean. Jenetta can't string two thoughts together…it's like she's PM-essin' the whole time. She's gonna have to do better next time or Lennie's gonna be an only child.

Kris: Junior, that makes no sense.

Eulie: 'Scuse me, I've got an interview.

Sound of chair scooting, footsteps, door opening and closing.

Wayne: Man, Eulie liked to ripped your finger off gettin' that notebook, Jen. That'd be something, an amputation in the conference room. What's her problem?

Junior: No tellin.' Hey, maybe she's OTR.

TWENTY-EIGHT

Wayne Daylight waited in front of the Malapee Wonder Burger as his brother Tuber Daylight and brother-in-law Deacon Maitland Dovey pulled into the lot and rolled out either side of the Deacon's yam colored Chrysler 300.

"What color is that submarine, Deacon?" Wayne asked as he filed through the hazy glass door of the WB.

"It's custom. Sunset Pearl," the Deacon beamed. "It bespeaks my mission of seeing people off at the close of their Earthly day, don't you know. Glad you like it."

Wayne led the trio to a Formica table in the back, near the bathroom. Every table in the tiny diner was near the bathroom.

"Didn't say I liked it. It looks like you ran into the south end of a pack of wormy Beagles headed north," Wayne grinned.

The Deacon plopped down next to Tuber, all business.

"OK, Wayne, you said we have a problem. So get to it. I got appointments and I'm sure Tuber has duties at the farm."

"No, I'm good," Tuber said, eyeing the teen waitress's bare midriff as she slapped the menu flip cards down and pulled out her order pad. "Beebe and his crew got it under control. I'm gonna have a triple meat, double cheese stack on steak toast with chili fries. And a large vanilla malt."

Wayne ordered black coffee and the Deacon ordered the house salad, a half-wedge of iceberg lettuce soaked in Thousand Island.

After the waitress finished serving the boys their food along with a close up of the fine blond hairs on her youthful belly, Wayne got down to business.

"We got problems with Malapee-Paola water district. They're showing lead and arsenic in well water, and nitrogen's up, too. Naturally, they're pointing the finger at the plant first."

"What's that got to do with me and Maitland?" Tuber asked before he took a gargantuan bite of his triple double.

Wayne wondered how his brother managed it. Must be his jaws unhinged like a pit viper. "Well, the wastewater girl at the plant says it's not from what we're treating. So, I ask myself where else it could be coming from and The Dog Yard comes up every time."

The Deacon raised a hand. "I still don't get what we got to do with it. We haven't hauled anything back there since we started selling our litter for fertilizer, what, two years ago?"

"Yeah, but I'm still burying some stuff, nothing that would obviously leach arsenic or lead, and for sure nothing to add nitrogen. I'm just afraid that even that little bit of dozing has stirred some of the old shit up and it's getting into the water table. If that's the case, you two are in it up to your necks. Before you stopped dumping, you shoveled ten year's worth of litter and fuckin' dead birds."

"We paid for that already. You oughta know, you collected for that tight old sphincter Otis you worked for," Tuber smacked, using his tongue to mine the remains of a recent mouthful. "Besides, what about all the junk you hid back there? What about alla that? Bound to be crawling with crud."

Wayne chose to ignore the awful truth of Tuber's question. Instead, he clarified his threat. "You paid squat for dumping back there and you both know it. If the Dog Yard is the problem, it's gotta be fixed, cleaned up, maybe put a landfill liner down. That's gonna cost way more than I can fiddle outta my budget. I don't want the Company looking too close. This is federal crap, and I can tell you who'd take the fall if those boys get involved. It sure as shit wouldn't be any Poultry Xtra pretty boy. It'd be me and whoever I decide to take down with me. So this is gonna get fixed, and you two are gonna pay your share."

The Deacon's face turned a sort of mottled Thousand Island pink. His lettuce wedge was untouched. Tuber stopped chewing.

The waitress arrived with her pad, popping a wad of gum. "You boys want this together or separate?"

TWENTY-NINE

Smock tails flying, Mert was in full-tilt toad-eating mode on her way to laundry and supply to deal with the latest blip in her operations.

She hit the laundry room door so hard, it rebounded off a laundry trolley, rattling the window glass and Lamentatia, who had been busy scanning supplies for a line of Posse Members arriving for second shift.

Mert ignored Lamentatia's lurch and scream, walking hurriedly into a small storage area that enjoyed a glass brick window to the outside and the best cell phone reception around. She fingered through her contacts and settled on the phone number she'd given Quickie Ricky for emergencies.

"Rich," Mert said when her cousin answered on the first ring, "Can you talk?"

"Not right now, ma'am. Can I call you back in a sec?"

"Sure, but make it soon." Mert slapped her phone closed.

Mert couldn't remember when such shit had hit her fan all in one load.

The plant's employee news wire, which most days could make CNN look like the Pony Express, was zinging with news of a bust in progress at Quickie Ricky's. It had something to do with one of Ricky's dicey side deals, something about pirated CDs. Mert vaguely remembered Rick saying something about CDs but she was so distracted lately with one thing and another, one being Fano, she hadn't been paying proper attention to her cousin's little convenience store and his various swindles.

Now, because he fronted for her micro-loan business, any law-enforcement light shining in Ricky's direction was too damn bright for Mert. She would kick his ass if this cocked up her installment income.

Lamentatia stuck her head around back of the industrial dryer. "Miss Mert, are you OK?"

"Tatia, you have any customers left out there? Can you step back here a minute?"

"Yes ma'am, folks have cleared out and Mr. Clarence is back with a load of dirty smocks, so he can help out."

"Tatia, you know anything about what's happening at Ricky's?"

"Well, Miss Mert, I know that Lovey says the deputies was down there because they saw such a line of people and arrested some guy for selling fake CDs."

"Line of people. On a Tuesday?"

"Yeah, some guy they say come down from Slapsassee set up down there this morning, copying them right there, whatever you want, with a computer and everything, selling 'em two for $7."

"Thanks, Tatia. That's all."

"Ma'am, you fix my hours like you said this week?"

"Yes, Tatia. Like always. That's all now."

Mert could kick herself. What was Ricky thinking? Letting someone counterfeit CDs right there three days before pay day. It was asking for trouble to draw more than a half-dozen at a time any day but payday Friday at Quickie Ricky's. It sat smack on the main highway between Paola and Malapee, right where all the cops and troopers traveled back and forth filling their quotas by stopping Posse Members for expired inspection stickers or busted tail lights. People tended to stay clear unless they were flush.

Mert's phone vibrated. "You busted, Ricky?" she asked.

"No, Mert, I..."

"Not now," Mert instructed. "Come by the house right after you close up."

BIG CHICKEN

* * * * *

Mert swung her feet up on her oversized couch and popped a tallboy, something she did rarely. But damn, she needed a drink. It looked like she might dodge a bullet, but she wasn't sure about Ricky, and if Ricky went down, she could be exposed.

Jesus, how could Ricky be so stupid. Not only did he let some fast-talking stranger con him into setting up what was obviously a pirate operation, right out in the open, he looked like the world's biggest accessory when the CD guy lied to the deputies who came in curious about the gathering crowd outside so early in the week.

The idiot said he was giving the CDs away. What a moron. When the Deputy went outside and told the crowd the CDs were free, people who'd paid good money stampeded the store and tipped over two drink machines and the candy counter before the cops could settle their hash, arrest the pirate for conspiracy and inciting a riot and cart his ass to jail.

When they came back for Ricky, the cops said the guy had been indicted for copyright piracy over in Sunsweet, GA, and that the case was being turned over to the Georgia State Attorney General's office at his request.

They told Ricky not to run off since he might need to testify.

That could be a disaster. Mert took a long pull on her Colt 45. She had some thinking to do.

* * * * *

Among the unintended employee benefits piggybacked on the growth of factory farm juggernauts such as Poultry Xtra are the many convenient hook-up spots created by capital expansion: boiler and switch rooms, closets and blocked stairwells that once upon a time were everyday destinations off the main production interstate. Post-build-out, they sit as forlorn – if frequently and briefly occupied – as teepee motels on Route 66.

The second floor "New Box Room," an assembly hub with tentacles that looped in a welter of downspouts to disgorge all manner of cardboard containers into a half-dozen packout areas, at the same time freed up "The Old Box Room" much to the delight of many. To be sure, no one had anticipated the benefits of so much fallow space for "storage, etc." as the original capital improvement request stated.

The Old Box Room had all the earmarks of a place where people up to no good went to do it. Plenty of ways in and out, all on a path to or from somewhere plausible for anyone whose presence wanted explaining. It was used mainly to store inactive employee files in a long cage against an interior wall and kept up by a materials management supervisor during infrequent visits. Eulie appeared even less often and only to unearth the file of some ex-Posse Member with a cheap lawyer and case to flog.

The remaining square footage held crushed Christmas decorations and the variety of junk that piles up in open spaces because somebody wants it but not much. In the most isolated corner was a mountain of files that someone once said could not be shredded by order of Sgt. Doom until some lingering class-action case held over from the Banty Roaster days ground to a conclusion.

No one knew how these files arrived in the Old Box Room or where they were before. So when the order to destroy finally came, no one who touched it knew what it meant and immediately passed it on to the next likely person. Ultimately, the shred order was shoved with a batch of papers belonging to a long-dead plant engineer into an unmarked banker's box that was sitting not all that far from the forgotten class-action files

And so they all remained in The Old Box Room, in shoulder-high ranks, forming an accommodating cul-de-sac with one double row of boxes offering a corrugated fainting couch for the overworked, stoned, drunk or horny. There were several other trysting places in the plant, but none quite so uptown.

Anyone approaching within a dozen feet of this spot, otherwise blocked by the room-length file cage, would be able to hear tell-tale slap of sons d'lamour and beat a retreat, sparing everyone involved embarrassment or a quick ride to the unemployment office.

The Old Box Room was frequented mostly by a few brazen regulars, maintenance and refrigeration techs and a number of supervisors, male and female, who had the latitude to wander the plant and who considered the availability of easily charmed ass one of the few perks of wearing uniform grays. Hailed by a management wag as the Order of the OBR, every member knew even chicken plant livery could be swoon bait in the right light.

Mert certainly did, but had always steered clear of the OBR. She had no real need of it, since she rarely sat, and certainly didn't nap at work. She didn't drink much or dope and she had always avoided any workplace dalliance as too risky. But that was before she lost her head. Fano was so worth it, not the least because it really clanged her bell to stick it to Betina for going to the EEOC and putting Mert on a radar she couldn't control.

So here she sat after Fano summoned, taking another chance, totally out of character. She'd been doing that a lot, lately. What was wrong with her? What happened to the old Mert, all business, all the time?

Shit needed fixing. Keeping things running at the plant, smoothing speed bumps in the drive to produce pounds was harder every day. She needed to delegate some of her most effective sleight-of-hand tactics, but Mert had had no likely successor to Betina. Honoria was loyal but short on brains when something or somebody like USDA or QC held up production on some lame-brained pretext, when you needed to pull a fix out of your ass in a hurry then be able to sell it. Mert would have to get more involved in hiring the next batch of supervisor trainees, start from scratch building a right hand. Or maybe find a shorter-term solution.

Quickie Ricky's CD fiasco put her in a terrible spot. She needed another layer of protection, somebody she already had in mind to handle the small loan business, for a cut of course. She'd have to pay if she wanted to keep that enterprise in play.

Naturally, Old Mert was telling her that a plan that mixed business with pleasure was a real bad idea. New Mert was not listening.

"Hey, baby."

Mert jumped a little. "Hey, yourself. So, it's baby now, is it?"

Fano sat next to Mert, his tool belt digging her in the side. She scooted over.

"Here, let me move that," he said. He stood up to unstrap his tool belt, unbuttoned and shed his smock, then sat again, pulled off her hairnet and put his hand at the back of her neck.

"What should I take off next?"

"Whoa, boy. I'm not sure about this place. I hear there's a lot of traffic in and out," Mert protested but didn't move away.

"I've got my people on it," Fano smiled. "We've got a good half-hour, no interruptions."

"Yeah, right. Like I can go two minutes without getting paged," Mert said.

"Babe, just set your channel. You can answer 'em or not. That's what I do. It's what everybody does," Fano said, starting to nuzzle her ear.

"Is that what you did when Betina was here? This where she was when I couldn't raise her?" Mert was only half joking.

Fano stopped nuzzling and looked at Mert. She thought for a second he was pissed. But when he kissed her full-on, she knew it had been a trick of the dim cage lights far overhead.

When he finished, Mert was out of breath and Fano was smiling that smile. "Babe. I was done with her a long time ago. I thought you knew that."

"Why would I know that?" Mert touched her bottom lip. It was still there.

"Well, you and me, babe. What game we been playing for all this time? You've been circling me since I got here and I been watching you back."

"Fano, I don't know about any game. You're a prize, all right and, hey, everybody knows I'm a winner. I saw this day coming, but it's no game with me."

Fano frowned. "You mean you didn't set Betina up to make it easier for us to hook up?"

"Didn't anybody set up anybody. Betina fucked up all on her own. I just wasn't willing to cover up for her screw-ups any more. Didn't have a thing to do with you."

"Well I'm hurt. I thought you were willing to sacrifice one of your best people all 'cause you wanted to jump me. Damn," Fano laughed.

"Oh, no," Mert said. "I wanted to jump you either way, Betina or no Betina. Want to jump you."

Fano leaned back, locked eyes with Mert and spread his arms wide. "Jump away, chica. Jump away."

* * * * *

Mert slipped her hairnet back on, wondering if Fano felt the same, post-grapple glow, taking a minute for a lingering look. "Fano, you sweet man…but enough fooling around. We have business to discuss."

"Ah, babe, and I thought you loved me for my body. And here you want me for my brains." Fano was busy with numerous buttons. "I don't know that I have time for anything extra. You know I work with BF."

"Yeah, but don't say no just yet. I'm having some issues with Quickie Ricky. I need a top guy to manage his business, someone who doesn't report to me here. Honoria's helping out, but she's no Betina. Honestly I wish Betina was still here. She was the best. I think being pregnant ruined her. She got so damn careless and distracted."

Mert stopped. "Hey, no offense, if you're the baby daddy."

Fano was hitching his tool belt, his back to Mert.

"No," he said. "She tried to play it off it was mine, though."

"No big surprise, I guess, knowing Betina," Mert said. She reached to touch Fano's hip. "And knowing you like I do now."

"Better go, babe," Fano said over his shoulder, then turned.

"I'll think about it, your proposition. Give me a page in a day or two, when you get some free time and we can meet back here. And talk," he bent to give her a quick last kiss. "And stuff."

PipeSnark.com
What's backed up in the 'Burgh by Resaca Toomey, pipefitter and investigative blogger
ON SEPT. 30, 20XX, 4:08 AM
Hacked off

We're back and we're mad and we're not gonna take it anymore. We learned last week that PipeSnark was being hacked. Tex Webster my IT guy hasn't nailed it down completely, but he figures it's the Chinese trying to steal my pipe laying secrets (no, you potty minds, not that kind). The Chinese have the biggest outflow issues in the world, so who else could it be? Did you ever see that Tiananmen Square full of people and not a chemical toilet in sight? Where there's hordes, there's pipes.

What else? Oh, yeah. The Pirates still suck big time and the Steelers started the season acting like they were taking suck lessons. The Pens – playing like honey boys, every last one. Oh, yeah, there was this:

I'm driving over to the North Side for League Nite at the Elk Lodge Lanes, dressed nice, you know, hot. So anyway, here comes a couple of yahoos in an Escalade dogging my bumper all the way from LarryVille. They pull up alongside me just as I'm coming across the 31st Street bridge. Well anyway, they're pointing at me and hollering at each other, and snapping pictures and then they peel off and I nearly buy the front bumper of a Yuengling Truck. WTF? Can't a girl get her Aquanet on and go bowling in peace? And, hey, if those photos end up on somebody's World Wide Interlude I'ma be extra pissed. Five Plungers for thugs in thug trucks, right up their thug truck tail pipes, with two Plungers off in case they were just looking to hook up, for a total of three Plungers.

Today's horoscope

If it's your birthday today, show a little common sense. Stop funding Chinese espionage. Make your own damn pot stickers. And don't skip target practice; with the moon in retrograde and GM in the toilet, people in Cadillacs are channeling the assholes who normally would drive BMWs.

THIRTY

Deputy Chumley Bucket had it bad. He was in deep from the minute Sharay Townsend had dropped in a dead faint at his feet when he was on random search duty at the Poultry Xtra plant the day after her daddy was killed. When he checked her pulse and his fingertips felt the warm flutter along her neck and he saw how the tears in her long eyelashes looked like little cubic zirconia against her freckledy brown cheek, it was like he'd been heart punched by Stone Cold Steve Austin in his WWF prime.

Luckily, Chumley found that at the time of her father's death, Sharay had been living the single life in Biloxi and had no current shoulder to lean on, with the possible exception of Deacon Maitland Dovey who volunteered every which way he could. But the Deacon, in all his pouter pigeon, talced and peachy windiness, was not the type Sharay would ever consider clinging to when the lights were out. For one thing, the Deacon just plain never stopped talking, which would have interfered with Sharay's near constant discourse into her Bluetooth bud.

Deputy Bucket was a tall, beefy, smitten man of action rather than words. A perfect squeeze in Sharay's hour of need. And Sharay's boy Danny liked him, too. The only downside from Sharay's point of view was the Deputy's hatred of all things drug-related, so she was having a little difficulty keeping her weed indulgence under wraps. If she were honest with herself, she would admit that the side effects of Deputy Bucket were making any other buzz unnecessary.

The lawman had been spending as much time with Sharay and Danny as he could wedge in around his hours on shift for

Beauswamp County, his extra turns on the Poultry Xtra gate each week and the DEA seminars he attended in Quantico and Georgia he hoped would prepare him for a future with the Feds.

This afternoon, he had dropped by shortly after Sharay had picked up Danny at school. Deacon Dovey had invited himself over to discuss Sharay's plan to spread Lowdes' cremains over the offal trailers at the plant. The Deacon told Sharay that the company was on the verge of giving the OK, but had a few more stipulations he wanted to cover with her. The Deputy made it a point these days to keep an eye on the Deacon's involvement with Sharay.

The three were seated on Sharay's big, new cushiony couch in front of the 52-inch flat screen waiting for the Deacon to show. Sharay was talking to one of her friends about the upcoming ash scattering, gesturing absently at the box holding her father that sat on a huge speaker next to the TV. The Deputy, cozied up to Sharay, watched Danny playing a round of Wii bowling.

The boy played with abandon, brandishing the wand under his upraised leg for a strike, over his shoulder without a glance. No Wii purist, Danny smoked his best big-league fast ball overhand. The wand strap slipped over Danny's small hand and crashed off the edge of the flat screen, caromed away to make a direct hit on the ash box, which flew sideways and upended on the floor, strewing a pile of Lowndes out the dislocated box top.

Sharay jumped up with a screech. Danny looked at the box and then his mom, wide-eyed. Deputy Bucket rose slowly from his seat, put a calming hand on Sharay's back. "Danny, just stay still, son. Not a big problem. Let me have a look."

The Deputy stepped around Sharay, who was vocalizing somewhere between whimper and full-out whine. He picked up a copy of Field and Stream he'd brought over for bathroom sojourns, flipped back the cover to use as a scoop and dropped to his haunches over the spill. He paused there a second, then leaned forward on his knees and took a closer look. When he dipped a finger in the pile of powder and raised it to his tongue, Sharay clamped her mouth shut and stared.

"Some kinda pie," the Deputy said, and scooped up another finger full. "Custard mixed with.

Sharay, who had snapped out of it when the Deputy went back for seconds, grabbed a magazine of her own and whacked him square in the mouth.

"What you think you're doing to my daddy? That's gross. It's sinful! Get away!" Sharay screamed and whaled Deputy Bucket about the head. Danny ran to help; pounding his fists on the Deputy's back, not saying a word to distract from the turn of events that had taken him off the hook.

Deputy Bucket rose and pulled both Sharay and Danny to him. "Calm down, now, both of you," he said, in a voice that caused Sharay and Danny to do just that.

"Sharay, now don't go off again, but honey, this ain't your daddy's ashes. I'm not sure exactly what this stuff is, but I mean to find out. Stop crying. Just hang on while I head off the Deacon and make a couple more calls."

THIRTY-ONE

Greta shifted uncomfortably in her seat. It was her third week pretending to work for Lock & Load Security, the rent-a-cop contractor for the Poultry Xtra southern division. Tonight, to maintain the fiction that she was a security guard, she was working the entry gate at Malapee, which consisted of a converted metal one-car garage sitting at the fork of two driveways leading to the front parking lot and rear loading areas. Cars and chicken haulers went one way, tractor trailers delivering or loading out cruised the other. It was her responsibility to check workers' IDs and halfway monitor trucks entering and leaving the property.

Greta thought she fit right in. Her fellow guards pretty much pretended to work, too. They barely glanced at the ID cards of arriving workers and would rather throw down in a rat pit than leave the tiny gatehouse pod, with AC and basic cable, to verify that some random truck wasn't carrying a fertilizer bomb to blow Malapee off the map.

On her first approach to the plant, Greta had pulled up behind a beater tricked up in 20-inch rims that was stopped at the gate, revving, waiting for security to appear. And waiting. Finally, the car flew into reverse, power swerving back, something the driver no doubt learned on You Tube spin fails. He barely missed the front end of Greta's rental, peeled around the gate house, and stomped it through the truck entrance with its barrier raised in a Day-Glo striped salute. Greta could make out three passengers in the car, rapidly retreating unchecked on the allegedly secure road to the back of the plant.

Greta nosed her rental up to the barrier, expecting to see a guard rush out to identify the gate crasher. After a solid five minutes, she laid on the horn. A head appeared above the windowsill and after another slight delay, a young man rushed out clapping his uniform hat on his head.

"I was on a call from Officer Hardy," he called, coming toward Greta. "I wasn't asleep or nothing."

"Did you see the car that drove through the other side?" Greta asked.

The guard's face, a perfect blank for a split second, wised up rapidly. "Oh, yeah, I know those guys. They're contractors. They're OK. Are you here to see somebody?"

"Lock & Load, my foot," she said under her breath. "Lick 'n Promise is more like it." She shifted again, trying to get comfortable, wondering why in the name of good sense the security gods thought a 4-inch wide fake leather belt improved performance. She'd be lucky if she got back to Skiatook with a partial gall bladder.

Ratting out the lousy security operation wasn't her brief at Malapee, but the lack of control over the comings and goings of a couple of thousand people would make her search for the terrible thumb phantom almost impossible.

* * * * *

Access to the Malapee plant was such a sieve, Greta was tempted to call Andy and tell him it was a lost cause. They just needed to get ahead of the story with the food Nazis and press and tell them what was going on, and give up this misbegotten mission to smoke out the crook responsible for throwing appendages into the chicken.

For the better part of two weeks, she spent her time moving around the plant, inside and outside, watching the processing, gauging people's routines, surreptitiously evaluating the QC supervisors and techs, talking a little bit, listening a lot trying to find a single crook. And that was her problem.

There were plenty of crooks at Malapee, Greta had seen for herself. But putting her finger on the right one was the trick. Damn, the way this place ran, it could be anybody from the plant manager to the nurse. So far she'd seen – and heard – about the brisk traffic in drugs and booze that was abetted if not entirely controlled by people employed by Poultry Xtra. She'd witnessed the supervisors and industrial health nurses rigging the substance testing procedures for people who were caught with drugs or alcohol at random gate searches or people who were involved in accidents in the plant.

Time clock scams were routine. Tipped off by some of the security guards, she watched people clock in, leave for the shift, sometimes only going as far as their cars where they promptly went to sleep, then returned in time to join the crowds clocking out at the end of shift. The guards didn't tell the Company mainly because their hourly rate was even less that the Poultry Xtra start rate, so rather than ride herd, they identified with the Posse Members and kept quiet, except among themselves.

Greta figured the supervisors must know what was going on, at least until she had made several trips to the production floor, camouflaged in smock and hairnet, where there was less chance of sighting a supervisor than spotting deer in a high wind under a full moon. They, the supers, were either colluding in the clocking fixes or didn't know that Posse Members who showed up on their time sheets were AWOL because they weren't on the production floor often enough to check. To be fair, they might be holed up in cubicles working on mounds of paperwork. For sure, some of them were in places they shouldn't be, doing things that could get them and the Company in serious trouble.

Greta eventually sent reports in regular e-mails to Andy, adding that she thought she was seeing just the tip of the funny-business iceberg at Malapee. Andy's response was to focus on the thumbs. She agreed that the thumbs were the priority, but telling her to ignore everything else did not sit well. But she didn't have a choice while she was starring in Andy's crazy-assed costume drama. She planned to do her share of foot-stomping when she was back on the job in Skiatook dressed in her own clothes.

Greta watched a car turn off the county road and prowl up the drive. If it was an employee, they were either way late for second-shift or way early for clean-up crew. She looked at her fellow officer for the evening, a pissy fireplug named Cherry whose magenta hair under her official ball cap matched the candy coat cell phone permanently fused to her right ear. Catching Greta's gaze, Cherry pointed to the phone, and swiveled in her chair, indicating that she would not be checking IDs in the approaching car.

"Oh," Greta said to Cherry's back, "I guess it's my turn. Again."

* * * * *

Greta raised the barrier and motioned the car through, not sure the IDs matched the people in the car. The light was so bad at the gate, and with the people wearing hairnets flashing ID pictures of bareheaded people, it was odds on that some who weren't employed slipped through. Greta was resigned to the convention that nobody in his right mind would show up to work at a chicken plant if they didn't have to, so the likelihood of party-crashers was small.

Greta stuck her head in the gatehouse door and told Cherry she was taking a bathroom break. Cherry kept talking into her shiny phone, but nodded. Greta could only hope that Cherry would keep an eye on things; she planned to turn the break into another opportunity to snoop.

Her useless belt chafing, Greta strolled along the walk that fronted the plant. It gave a hillside view across the sweeping parking lot, where a big percentage of the second-shift debone department's 600-plus Posse Members congregated in groups around cars with popped trunks, doors ajar and sub-woofers cracking the pavement. It was late, a mild, Saturday night, people still flush with pay. Good for the drug business, Greta supposed.

Here and there, other security guards and a couple of off-duty county deputies wandered among the groups, hired to do random car searches at the entry gate and keep the dealers on their toes. Waste of time, Greta huffed. You're looking for deals to go down in the wrong place at the wrong time. It was no big secret that the

Posse Members were transacting their illegal purchases inside the plant. On the other hand, the random searches did turn up the odd handgun and automatic rifle each week, so she guessed they weren't a complete waste of time.

Not as big a waste as her "investigation" had been. Three weeks of nothing but pain in her side from the dominatrix harness, nothing but platitudes from Andy and nothing to show for shit. So, nothing to do but blunder ahead. When Greta stopped grousing and looked around, she found herself wandering down a line of massive freezers looking for something, anything that would get her closer to winding up her predicament so she could go home.

She walked the length of the freezer corridor. The giant cubes normally churned thousands of pounds of product – injected, marinated, fried, baked or otherwise modified - over their elements and out a belt to be dumped, bagged, weighed, boxed and shipped. Now, they stood open, belts lying where the sanitation crew had dropped them, in haphazard coils like tank treads. Everything was clean, polished and dry and looked like a tornado had ripped the bejesus out of the whole place. Just as it should when further processing wasn't running.

All pretty normal until Greta turned into a narrow cul-de-sac formed between the packout bulkhead and the wall of the No. 10 Freezer in the hangar-sized room. Unlike the others, it was locked offline, a large zip tie running through the hasp of the maintenance hatch. She flipped the tag up in the dim light. The freezer was scheduled to be dismantled and removed.

Greta turned out of the passageway and mounted the steps of a catwalk that would take her through the bulkhead and into packout. As she crested the platform, she froze. Voices headed her way.

Greta wasn't a wuss, but a big damn chicken plant was kinda creepy, especially in the middle of a weekend night in the middle of a search for spare body parts, in a place where there shouldn't be too many voices.

The acoustics were playing tricks on her. She saw them now, there below, through the stainless steel mesh: Three people in hard hats squeezed into the shadowy walkway by the offline freezer, pushing a hand-truck loaded with what looked like 10-pound wing boxes. Greta watched as one hardhat used a set of channel locks to twist and pop the zip tie. They opened the hatch and disappeared into the freezer.

Surely they're not taking it apart now. Greta wondered if this undercover nonsense was about to amount to something.

"Ey-ull be ba-aack," Greta heard herself mimic the Governator as she stepped lightly across the catwalk. "Jeez, somebody just shoot me."

THIRTY-TWO

Fano was the head hardhat that night, and not exactly gung-ho about so much activity around the freezers. He was glad BF agreed with consolidating their inventory, but would have preferred to let sales empty out existing stashes around the plant as they gradually moved their new merchandise into the offline freezer.

Moving in one fell swoop seemed needlessly risky. But, it was BF's operation, and he wanted it squared away before a stream of visits set to start next week increased the number of clueless customers and corporate tag-alongs who might stumble into the wrong place at the wrong time.

So when he told Fano and Beebe to gather up the boxes, baggies, bindles, vials and pint bottles and then get all of it moved this weekend at the latest, they did what they were told. Fano stood in the center of the freezer box and checked the inventory file in BF's Blackberry to mark their progress. They might just make it.

He looked up at the freezer belt that wound from the fry line entrance around a gradual incline that ended 20 feet up at the outflow into packout. Boxes of glass containers – pints of vodka and meth vials - were stacked in a layer on the freezer floor in the smallish well created by the spiraling belt. No sense risking the breakables. Everything else – boxes of weed, bulk powders, pills and capsules twisted into Wal-Mart bags – was stacked up along the coiling conveyor.

Fano watched Hoopdy clamber up and down a telescoping ladder, lugging boxes to Beebe who sat astride the conveyor sorting them.

Fano wondered for the umpteenth time why BF and Beebe put up with Hoopdy. The little guy worked like the devil. But he was so mental, having him around seemed like another unacceptable risk. The longer he worked with these guys, saw the way they conducted business, the more certain Fano became that his homeland was not part of North America.

* * * * *

Greta didn't see anyone else on her tour through the plant, gradually retracing her route to the freezer catwalk. She crept alongside No. 10 Freezer as far as the stairs and looked down. One of the hardhats grabbed the last two wing boxes and entered the door. She hurried back to the wall by packout. She couldn't see them from that vantage, but she would know immediately if they took the stairs. She strained, hoping to hear footsteps or voices, anything that would give her a head start if she needed to beat it. She heard the freezer door chunk shut.

"OK, so we're close," one hardhat said. "Just the one load left on the debone roof and we'll be good. Beebe, can you guys finish it? BF's scheduled a connection tonight."

"Sure thing, Fano. Me and Hoop'll handle it."

"OK. Don't forget to lock it all up."

The first voice receded from the stairs. Greta started to suck in a deep breath then settled for a shorter, quieter one.

"Hoop, we need to get over to the farm. Why don't we split up. I'll get goin' and you finish up the load from the roof and then meet me as soon as you're done. How's that?"

"By myself?"

"Yeah, you can do it, can'tcha?"

" 'Course I can. I was just checkin'."

"Sure you can. They ain't that many left. Just sit 'em on the floor with the pints. We can come back later 'n I'll help you stack 'em."

"Beebe, I'm awful hungry."

"Jeez, Hoop, you got a straight gut 'n a one track mind. All right. Let's get a bite. But then I gotta go and you gotta get them last boxes in here. Where'd you put the lockout tag?"

Greta listened to the pair engage the freezer lock and heard the bump of the hand-truck as they walked off, presumably in the direction of the vending machines. She was hungry herself. She considered making a quick trip to pick up her Hello Kitty lunch bag, but rejected the notion in favor of hunkering down with her back to the packout door. She wanted to talk to this Hoop when he came back with the last load, whatever it might be.

She was happy to discover that the blasted uniform belt made balancing on her haunches easier, readier to move. She bounced a little to keep the circulation going. Crouching Greta, Hidden Brain Cells, she mused, wondering how in the hell she let them rope her into this nonsense and why real gumshoes would actually choose the crappy working conditions and boredom that went with snooping.

Occupied with these happy thoughts, she was mildly surprised when she heard the hand-truck trundling back and the freezer door open.

Greta stood and inched closer to see the littlest of the three hardhats carry a couple of wing boxes into the freezer. He was wearing supervisor grays. She watched him return to retrieve another armload of boxes. Now or never, she told herself. She watched until there was a single layer of boxes on the pallet.

"C'mon," she chided. "Get a move on. You've got a date with a guy called Hoop." Jeez. She was losing it. Talking to herself was bad enough. Talking like some idiot in a soap opera was too much. Greta ran down the catwalk stairs and ducked into the freezer.

The supervisor they called Hoop was balancing a box on each arm and trying to take a step up a 30-foot ladder slanted against the freezer belt. When Greta tapped him on the shoulder and said, "Mr. Hoop?" it was a good thing he was still on the ground. At her touch, he launched the boxes overhead.

"Beebe, fer Chrissake, don't go sneakin' up on me like that," he screamed and turned, then screamed again, scuttling back when he saw Greta. Google-eyed at her uniform, he tripped on the ladder shoe and sat butt first through the second and third rungs. Greta, startled, tried to break his fall but he ended up bent double, knees to chest, stuffed through the ladder, a flailing bouquet of head, hands and clodhoppers. She thought she heard a sob.

"Mr. Hoop, calm down. Let me help you out," Greta said. Hoop didn't seem to hear, mostly because he was sucking in great gobs of air, revving up for a full-blown fit. He reminded Greta of her boy Mikey when he was grounded from getting Happy Meals for a month because he spit in Rudy's fries.

"Hoop!" Greta used her righteous mom voice. "Stop right this minute! I mean it!"

He stopped mid-suck, shuddered and managed to look up at Greta.

"Now be still and I'll help you up," Greta commanded. He immediately grew limp and looked at her with something like adoration.

"Please, ma'am. I'm sorry. I didn't mean no harm. This is all for Bad Fruit 'n Fano. Me and Beebe ain't got nothin to do with it."

"OK, Mr. Hoop. Hang on just a minute."

Greta took his hands, braced her boot against the rung between his bent knees and pulled. She eventually managed to get him unstuck and upright but couldn't seem to get him to shut up. So she stood back and listened, nodding, trying to look guard-like.

Poor guy. He had to be masquerading as a supervisor. He wasn't even close to the crispiest nugget in the bucket because he obviously thought a security guard could arrest him. What a noodle.

He called himself Hoopdy while he ran on about the drugs and liquor, his bosses Baby and The Deacon, some dove eating rotten fruit, Greta took a look around. That's when she spotted the six-pack cooler sitting on the conveyor, its handle sticking up from behind a box. When she looked closer, she could see water puddle on the belt like melted ice.

"What's that," she asked.

"What's what ma'am? Oh, that's nothin,' ma'am," he yelped, acting even crazier. "That's my lunch bucket is all. Ma'am? I keep it in here 'cause people will take yer lunch right out of the office 'n eat it. They durn sure will. Buncha crooks around here, take a man's lunch bucket. That's all it is."

He was definitely way more nervous now. Greta saw sweat starting to bead up near his hairnet. Suddenly, his eyes brightened, and he smiled. "Yes ma'am, it's empty, except I had me a accident earlier and it's got some under shorts in it so I can take to Geneva to wash. You don't wanna to see them, a 'course.'"

He grabbed the Igloo and held it in both hands behind his back.

"Ma'am, you gonna throw me in jail? Can't we do a deal? I need my job real bad."

Greta tore her eyes from the Igloo. "What do you have in mind, Mr. Hoopdy?

"I dunno, but BF might be willin' to give you somma his money or somethin'. I'll go ask right now." Swinging the Igloo forward, grasping it to his chest for all he was worth, Hoopdy shouldered past Greta and out the door before she could react. He was out of sight by the time she made it out of the freezer.

"You forgot the zip tie, Hoop," Greta muttered. She closed the door and walked along the line of freezers, kicking herself for not being quicker, calculating her next move.

* * * * *

By Monday Greta could laugh, remembering how scared they'd both been when she first tapped Hoopdy Creavy on the shoulder. Not that she wasn't nervous now. She had expected to hear from his boss, Bad Fruit or that guy Fano he talked about, sure they would want to follow up on her "deal." But it was hard to know with Hoopdy. He probably had clammed up and was hoping it was all a bad dream, or a bad batch of drugs.

Whatever, she needed to get back in there to see that Igloo. Dinner bucket my foot. He'd just come back from dinner in the cafeteria. And why would he be blithering so about the drugs and so antsy about the cooler? It could all be something totally innocent. Greta didn't think so.

She'd called corporate to get information on the people Hoopdy had named then got Andy and the lawyer on a conference call to go over every bean Hoopdy had spilled. Andy was excited she might be on to something, but they weren't willing to call in the pros yet; didn't want to spook whoever was responsible for the thumbs. She ended up hanging up on them, closer than ever to quitting.

When she called home, Toby was his usual unruffled self. "Babe, just keep tracking the little fucker and when he's not watching, grab the cooler and haul ass like he did. If worse comes to fisticuffs, I know you can take him."

He was joking, but that was probably the best way. Stick to Hoopdy. He was not likely to notice her following, and she'd just grab and run. It wasn't a very good plan, but it was a plan. She e-mailed Andy to have Lock & Load fix her hours to coincide with Hoopdy's. She would be spending her nights parked as close to the drug-central freezer as possible.

THIRTY-THREE

Beebe and Hoopdy had been in full Metal Gear Solid mode all evening, battling Psycho Mantis. Hoopdy, Solid Snake, was especially crazed because Mantis tricked Meryl into trying to kill him. He hated Mantis, hated his buggy red-eyed stare through the gas mask.

When Psycho finally croaked after opening the REX secret passage and turning all nice, which Hoopdy didn't believe for a second, Beebe jumped up. Brandishing his controller, making crowd roaring sounds.

"That's it Hoop. We got 'er done, didn't we? Cool as hell!"

"Yep, we got 'er done. Cool," Hoopdy agreed.

"That just shows we can do it. If we do it like it was Metal Gear."

"Do what like Metal Gear? I can't play any more right now. I gotta take Geneva to Wal-Mart."

"No, talk to my daddy, I mean."

Hoopdy set his jaw. He did not want to go against the Deacon, messin' with the wrath of God and lightnin' bolts and stuff. "Aw, Beebe, I told you I can't go off on yer daddy. He's my friend."

"Friend, hell. I don't see how you can say that. He's my own daddy, but he sure ain't my friend. Would a friend leave us hanging out there getting buried in bodies and chicken shit? Hoopdy, you hafta stay with me on this. We gotta give him a ultimatum or he'll just keep runnin' us ragged."

"Well, maybe if we give him one a them mater things, he won't take it so hard."

It took a minute, but Beebe figured out what Hoopdy said.

"Yeah, we'll give him a nice big ultimater…with mayonnaise and bacon. He'll love that." Beebe sighed. "Listen, Hoop, we can do this. You Solid Snake, I'm Liquid Snake and daddy's toast."

* * * * *

"OK, now boys, run it down for me," Deacon Maitland Dovey said, seating himself behind his desk, two powder coat pink coffins shoved atop a mahogany riser and topped with a slab of tempered glass. "What is so all-fired messed up that I had to miss Rotary?"

He peered over his half-cheaters at his son and Hoopdy, wearing their Poultry Xtra grays, perched facing the Deacon on the edges of two Persian Flame Stitch wing back chairs, which pleased the Deacon because the less their filthy, nasty work clothes touched the seats, the less he'd need to spot clean when they left. He noticed that they were more jittery than usual and sweaty as ever.

The Deacon wasn't proud that Beebe worked at the chicken plant. Hell, he wasn't all that excited about working there as part-time chaplain himself. But it had its perks and opportunities. And if Beebe didn't work there, Mr. Dovey might be coerced by Mrs. Dovey into paying him more than the behind-the-curtain stuff at the Tabernacle was worth.

The Deacon hoped against hope that one day Beebe would be able to follow in his dad's Ferragamos, into the money churn at the front of the house. It seemed unlikelier with each passing year. And forget the pulpit. The boy just didn't have the all-purpose suave sincerity, much less a preacherly head of hair. Oh, my, Deacon Dovey swore silently, demon pride, get thee the fuck behind me and rub some off on my hairless boy.

Beebe took out his bandana to wipe his face and hands. Plain cotton, the Deacon noticed, curling his lip, involuntarily straightening his silk pocket square.

"Beebe, out with it. You know I got to see about Ms. Pringle's mom in Meridian this afternoon. She's failin' fast, and I gotta be there to head off her brother. Now speak up!

"OK, Daddy, but don't get crazy on me."

Thus, in a run-on of stuttering thoughts, Beebe blew through the list of failures, breakdowns, foul-ups and reverses that had deviled him and Hoopdy for weeks.

"We was backed up already goin' into Mr. Henderson's funeral with the conveyor busted and no earthly sign of the part we needed, Daddy. So, then the Bobcat kept bustin' and we really got backed up. 'Member I told you at the funeral? Plus we had to come up with something to hand out for ashes. We did what you said and figgered out ever bit on our own. Honest, we done our best to stay even, but what with the Tabernacle and the farm and one thing and the other, plus us working at the plant, it just got away from us. Ain't that so, Hoop?"

Beebe glanced at Hoopdy who was staring blankly into the reflection from the Deacon's desk, his hands gripping one another like pincers on a gearbot.

"Yes, yes, Beebe. Let me see if I understand the problem," the Deacon glanced at his watch, then began counting on his fingers. "One: There's a bunch of Tabernacle clients uncremated and temporarily stored behind the retort and one of Tuber's broiler houses. Two: The litter fertilizer is piled in a couple or three other places, and what you haven't bagged for sale, you've been hauling to The Dog Yard.

"Three: We're handing out something ashy to our the bereaved families but it's not actually their loved ones' ashes, which is not surprising since their loved ones are still corpus intactus, IF SOMEWHAT PULPY RIGHT NOW!" The Deacon hated raising his voice, even at this excuse for a son and his brainless partner, so he took a moment to seek divine guidance and continued in his usual honeyed tone.

"Sorry, boys. Blessed are those who heed the redeemer to cast calm upon the waters. I only ask you this: What the bloody Christ do you aim to do about this catfuckingatastrophy?"

"Daddy, that's...well, that is, that's what we're talkin' about, we could use some help," Beebe was stuttering again.

"Stop!" the Deacon shouted, throwing a copy of his latest book "The Untold Story of the Old Testament Profits," barely missing Beebe's head.

"What am I paying you boys for? Dammit, Beebe, I don't believe you're a Dovey. Either that or you were hiding when the Good Lord favored the rest of us with brains. You'd shave your head to save parting your hair. Your mama was right about you being special."

Beebe jerked as if he'd been slapped. Slowly, as if enduring a seizure in reverse, Beebe's fidgeting stilled and the vein pumping in his forehead that had been quivering like a cut night crawler nearly disappeared. Facing the Deacon's impatient gaze with un-Beebely calm, he spoke.

"Well, Daddy, I done figgered out what to do. Here's the deal. We need help, and you're gonna give me what I need for once. If you do, I can git her all done this weekend. If you don't…"

The Deacon, fresh out of things to throw, smacked the desk, the nugget ring on his plump ring finger sending a report like a rifle shot.

"If I don't? If I don't? What, son? Be careful now…remember to whom you're addressing to," the Deacon's normally prissy syntax somewhat scattered by the turn of events.

"If you don't Daddy" Beebe said evenly, "Well I say, pork you all the way up your Tabernacle and back. Me and Hoopdy'll quit."

Hoopdy gulped audibly. The Deacon sat forward in his peach leather executive chair, marshaling ecclesiastical menace as he rose, setting his face into the mask of righteousness he reserved for revivals and political rallies.

"Beebe Dovey, how dare you spew such blasphemy in my…"

"Shove that preacher crap, too, Daddy. You help or I'm done," Beebe said.

The Deacon clapped his mouth shut.

"Liquid Snake," Hoopdy whispered.

THIRTY-FOUR

Selby Byrd, aka TwoPack Fersure, was forthrightly gay. When he swanned in to work, out to the line, through the cavernous break rooms, into office covens, he was a sinewy, catwalking cross between Kate Moss and LL Cool J. He dressed in counterpoint to what he called the working stiffies, gents who hid any hint of body definition except where boxers blooped through a shroud of denim and jersey, cupping their buns, screaming "Check my high, tight ass!"

Though he was not averse to checking, TwoPack didn't favor boxers, unless it was a Candyman Rocket Boxer. Usually he stuck to the teensiest of silk thongs, when he wore underwear at all. Still, today, in his dart-waisted pink and gray plaid summer weight lambs wool shirt layered over a ribbed lobelia blue pick-needle Henley all tucked and belted into skin tight, dark-wash button front Levis, TwoPack wore low-rise tighties.

Feeling all Castro Street in the 70s, he channeled his Bay Area cloned-self from the cafeteria cash register to a table in the break room hoping to have his afternoon pick-me-up caramel mocha latté and fried okra while catching a rerun of the Oprah interview where Terry McMillan blabbed the dirty low-down on her down-low ex-hubby. TwoPack slid into a bench table before the biggest of six flat-screen TVs that blared non-stop into the break-room din, although now it was relatively quiet. TwoPack took his break before the rest of debone so he could help during wash down when everyone else swarmed the cafeteria.

He was aware of the looks that caused heads to swivel in his wake, but then he was a centered guy: at the center of controversy over his lifestyle choices and the center of attention for his fashion superiority. Rachel Zoe would cream herself to have TwoPack's touch.

TwoPack believed putting it all out there for people to revile or revel in was a community service. Women looked to him for sisterhood and inspiration. Men looked in longing, if they would just admit it. Longing for him, to be him. Or to be so free. Whatever, he was all about supporting people's aspirations. Everyone wanted something they probably would never have.

TwoPack's secret was to want things he could have, like right now he wanted in the worst way a break and an Oprah fix. He halfway heard the usual snide chirps from a group of maintenance goons at a table nearby, but Miss O's theme was arcing, so he sucked on his latté and tuned out the noise.

Twenty minutes later, still marveling that Terry McMillan could have been so besotted she made it all the way up and down the aisle with nary a clue her hubby was a just a little bit totally gay, TwoPack didn't see Mooney Latrile follow as he trotted for the men's room. When Mooney braced him as he stood at the urinal, he was only somewhat surprised.

Most days, TwoPack had no problem with anyone, and his biggest run-in since starting work at Malapee was with a woman who became his BFF during orientation, but later became jealous when TwoPack's circle of friends began to grow to match the size of his all-embracing personality.

But the bathroom dispute had been brewing for a while now, ever since a couple of maintenance guys had gone to Mooney, a union steward, objecting to TwoPack using the men's restroom.

"Well, Mooney," TwoPack cracked. "See something you like?"

Mooney ignored the remark. "Hey, blade, you wanna be a woman, why don't you go piss with the women? What you wanna come in here with us, unless you shoppin' around for fresh meat?"

"Ooh, honey, I love it when you hetrosexshuls talk semi-queer," TwoPack drawled, hoping a little harmless banter might cool Mooney down. He shook himself, then reached in his pocket for a foil-wrapped towelette, opened it, dabbed himself, got situated, zipped and walked to the sink to wash his hands. But Mooney followed right behind, hollering over the rumble and stomp of about 500 hundred deboners coming past the john on the way to break.

"I asked you a question, faggot, and I want an answer," Mooney trailed TwoPack into the break room as the hordes flowed around them, some people starting to notice the conflict.

TwoPack turned to face Mooney. "Sir, you are a troll with track marks. If I could pee with the women, I would, but since I'm a man with all the man parts you have, only better, I can't. It's against company policy. But, honey, to keep from having to use that swamp with you bunch of filthy thugs who never heard of toilet paper or hand soap, I'd almost be willing to cut my considerable manhood off to qualify for the ladies room."

"You skinny little cocksucker, I'm puttin' in a grievance," Mooney yelled and started after TwoPack, who had turned once again toward debone. "You look like a woman and dress like one. Damn, you look like your blind grandma dressed you half-off at the Dollar Store. You need to walk your dressy little Mary-Janes into the women's bathroom and sit down to piss like the pussy you are."

TwoPack stopped walking, and was nearly rear-ended by Mooney. TwoPack would not be caught drugged and left for dead wearing Mary-Janes. The strap and buckle so totally spoiled the long slim line of a girl's leg. Smack talk about his sexual preferences was one thing. Slighting his fashion savvy was just not to be borne. Shitfire, TwoPack reasoned, I'm not fucking Ghandi.

He whirled, yanked off his hairnet and pink-and-gray-print do-rag that exactly matched his plaid shirt, wrapped it around his knuckles and French tips and hauled back intending to coldcock Mooney.

"Fight, fight," people screamed, and within seconds, like 5-year-olds on a soccer ball, two-hundred Posse Members had TwoPack and Mooney walled in, hoping to see which of them won the pissin' contest.

THIRTY-FIVE

Mert rarely got involved in such knuck-ups. In fact, most managers were reluctant to physically intervene when Posse Members went at it. You just never knew when one of them had picked up a stray length of pipe and was jonesing to use it. Better to let them whale on each other then haul them off to HR. Or just go ahead and call the cops.

People could be counted on to watch workplace violence. Depending on where the fights erupted, Posse Members would walk off the line, leave their lunches or hook-ups, or stop mid-pee to get in on the spectacle. It gave people a break in the work day, and something to analyze and debate for days, until the next near-riot occurred.

Right now it was giving Mert a free pass through the break room relatively unseen. She was warming in all possible ways to her plan to install Fano as go-between for her deal with Quickie Ricky, but she thought Mr. Chips needed a more experienced SOB to keep him in line. As it turned out, she didn't need muscle today. Mr. Chips had finished restocking the vending machines and bagging the money. His routine was to lock the take in his little closet near the cafeteria until he finished with his favorite cashier and could head to the bank.

Mert used her master key to open the closet and slip inside. Mr. Chips had Mert's vending skim bag ready, but she took a few extra minutes to dip into the other containers, just some extra cash for the taking whenever the opportunity presented itself. Like right now, when Mr. Chips was busy hauling his honey's ashes in the kitchen and everybody else was watching a brawl in the break room. Mooney and TwoPack couldn't have timed it better.

If they didn't kill each other, Mert might have to buy them lunch.

* * * * *

Elvis didn't think of himself as a stalker and certainly not a voyeur, but he made it his business to trail some people because they hardly ever did the right thing. Comeuppance was in their future.

Mert, as Pinky might say, was riding for a fall. It might not equal the toppling and desecration of Saddam's monument back in '03, or the despot's lurch through the rotten floor of his murderous reign. But it would be a big come down in her universe.

Elvis was aware that Fano's plan for Mert was in play, not precisely sure what he had in mind, but Elvis was astute enough to know that Mert was being played. Since he prided himself on certainty, he thought he might add an extra, condemning twist to whatever payback was coming her way.

Normally, he didn't take a pointed interest in petty miscreants. There were too confounded many. But he sincerely liked Fano and had enjoyed their camaraderie here at Malapee. Elvis would disappear soon, leaving behind his young friend, one of so few whose memories he carried with him as he soldiered on. So, it was the least he could do to deliver Mert up beyond doubt and the reach of her normally fail-safe bribes.

First, he planned to co-opt one of her top money pimps. However, when he walked into Mr. Chips' Vendi, Vidi, Vici storage room and found him stomping to dust a whole platoon-pack of RPG Brand Cheesy Fire Crisps, Elvis was confused. He had expected Mr. Chips to be in a pretty decent humor, having just had a salad toss on the prep table in the Poultry Xtra canteen kitchen with chief line server, Abby "Double Dip" Spooner, known for her extra helpings and fair market hookups.

Elvis had witnessed it all, right down to the liberal application of banana pudding by Ms. Spooner to Mr. Chips, and Mr. Chips' strategic placement of sugar cones filled with mounds of Sloppy Joe loaf, creating a sweet and savory push-up bra that kept Mr. Chips as busy as Double Dip was with Chips' nether portions among the custard, overripe tropical fruit and Nilla Vanilla Wafers.

With the food fight that marked their twin epiphanies, Elvis left the pair to prepare the kitchen for the next authorized meal, and waited for Mr. Chips to return to his cubbyhole.

By now, Chips was attacking a bundle of sponge cakes, smashing the pink foam and meringue demi-globes one at a time into his forehead, spewing threats to kill Mert along with gouts of chocolate cake, coconut shreds and residual Sloppy Joe grease.

Even as he registered that he was being watched, Chips started kicking again, aiming at a row of empty vending cash boxes. He did not falter in his harangue against Mert and her spawn, whom he fantasized dumping into the chute of the biggest coin sorter in Mississippi and shoving her a slice at a time into penny rolls, then loading Mert rolls into a kicked-in change machine in the skuzziest laundrymat in the most crackhead zip code in downtown Jackson. A final stomp tipped Chips back over a stack of Yoo Hoo cases and sideways onto his desk chair. "You ain't allowed in here," he greeted Elvis. "What in fuck you want, anyhow?"

A reformed smoker, Elvis understood the soothing properties of a massive drag in a crisis. He lit one for Chips from a carton upended in the recent spree.

"Here, Chips, catch your breath, suck on this for a minute and hear me out."

"I got nothin' to say to you 'er anyone else in this dadblasted sinkhole. A body works his ass off to take care of the customers, and what'd I get? Robbed is what. Do you know what that excuse for my partner did? Mr. Chips slowed for a drag strong enough to make his eyes bulge and the ash flare like magma.

"She ripped you off," Elvis said.

"Ripped me off? Ripped me the fuck off? I'll say she did. Her cut plus every bit of foldin' money and half my coin stock. I'll have to drive home through the wrong side of Jackson and hope somebody jacks me up and takes the little bit I got left. They'll probably cut me wide open for bein' such a low-baller, but at least maimed 'er dead, I'm off the hook for this. How could she do it?"

"No need to overreact, sir. What if I found a way to help you clear this up, make you whole for the money you're missing. How does that sound?"

"Sounds like a 'nother friggin' con, is how. Do I look like I got a hook in my mouth? I trusted Mert and look where it got me. Why don't you just go out the way you came. The last thing I need is somebody to offer me more help."

"Fair enough. But the way I see it, you can help me help you or I can report you and Double Dip for bouncing your nasties all over the kitchen. Nope, don't argue, you been doing it for weeks. If you get hauled up for that, the health department will be the least of your troubles. Double's part-time pimp, the ex-felon, will make you wish you just got your train pulled by a shower full of his former punk boy roommates."

Mr. Chips gave Elvis a look of hatred that was at once lethal and beseeching.

"What do I hafta do?"

"It's simple really. I just need a couple of minutes with the vending machines down at Quickie Ricky's, no questions asked."

"So you can clean them out, too?"

"Oh, no," said Elvis. "I want to help you add stock, just a few items."

"So you're gonna poison something." For a man who got laid with such frequency, Mr. Chips had an oddly dyspeptic outlook.

"No, nothing like that, I promise," Elvis said.

"Anything else?" Mr. Chips seemed resigned.

"Yeah. Got any Vienna Sausages?"

THIRTY-SIX

It seemed like a decent plan, hanging out in the shadows under the catwalk next to No. 10 Freezer, waiting for Hoopdy to appear. Now Greta was having waking nightmares about all the ways she may have screwed up.

The first night tucked behind a concrete bulkhead at the back of the freezer, Hoopdy had showed up twice, both times accompanied by his friend Beebe, both times without carrying a cooler in or out. She didn't know what they might have hidden under their smocks, but there was no way either one was carrying the Igloo cooler, which was about the size of Greta's granny's two-loaf bread box.

She needed to talk to Hoopdy alone. If he was hauling around a bunch of severed thumbs and if she had really spooked him and if he had a lick of sense, he would have dumped the thumbs first thing. Her instincts told her he had thumbs in that ghoulish carryall, that he was obviously spooked shitless and had not a lick of sense. She was sure if she could sneak up on him again, she would be able to bully him into handing over whatever he was hiding.

So Greta was back tonight, trying to figure how to isolate the little numbskull. If he showed up with Beebe, she would simply follow him when they left and corner him somewhere. It was time to cut bait, with Beebe or without.

If he showed up alone, no problem. Either way, when she talked to him, she would be filming with the new camera phone Toby gave her last Christmas. She might not be Gil Grissom, but she'd seen enough CSI to know that she'd have to be able to prove how the thumbs got wherever they were or these weasels would just say they had never seen them before, that they were planted or some other stinking lie.

Greta's QC self told her to hold her horses. Hoopdy might be hiding shorts with track marks like he said. Her new sleuth side, however reluctant, said he was hiding sawed-off thumbs.

About 4 a.m., Greta decided that Hoopdy wasn't coming at all. She'd watched a couple of maintenance workers go in No. 10 an hour ago. They emerged a half-hour later arguing over a chess game and forgot to attach a new zip tie. Hungry, cramped and cold, Greta decided it wouldn't hurt to take a peek. Slip in, slip back out, see what she could see.

She listened for sounds of anyone approaching and walked quickly from her niche by the bulkhead to the untagged door and ducked in. Illuminated by a dim amber emergency bulb, everything looked the same as it had during her first visit with Hoopdy: ladder leaning against the freezer belt spiral, scores of 10-pound wing boxes stacked up the belt, a layer of boxes on the freezer floor.

Greta stooped to push back the flap of one box. Pint bottles full of what she suspected was some clear liquor. She quickly checked the several other boxes she could reach. Pint bottles, bags of pills and white powder. Boxes full of little black-lidded vials or sandwich bags and twist ties.

"No thumbs," she said, immediately flashed on one of hers and Toby's favorite bedroom games, when she played Madeline Kahn and he was Gene Wilder. Well, this whole rotten deal was kinda within six degrees of "The Young Frankenstein." Greta shook herself.

She grabbed the ladder, set the foot grips and climbed up, craning to see the sweep of freezer belt as she climbed. About eight feet up, pay dirt. The Igloo sat just beyond her reach. Greta nearly slid down the ladder in her haste to move it around the center of the spiraling belt, hurriedly glancing up to gauge the path that would put the cooler in her hands.

Greta was breathing fast, eager to get back up the ladder to the bottom of things. She forced herself to stop short of hyperventilating. She thought about pulling out her camera, but she didn't really want to record this visit. She'd get Hoopdy back here later to bully him into implicating himself and whoever else was in on this. But right now, she had to look.

She climbed back up the ladder and saw her internal GPS was perfect. Igloo dead ahead. She leaned into the ladder and reached around the rails to grasp the handle and put her finger on the latch button. Taking a calming breath, not sure what she hoped to see, Greta pressed the button and tilted the top open. She shrieked. Then purposely bit down on her lower lip to inhibit her desperate urge to keep on screaming.

There they were, nestled in a layer of crushed ice, looking for all the world like chicken wing drumettes. Without thinking, she nudged one wizened specimen.

"Thumbettes," Greta gasped. "No, Jesus, I mean thumbs, human thumbs."

Definitely flesh, without the blood, but definitely not rubber. Greta wondered what hysteria felt like. She might be getting close, looking at the shriveled thumbs in different shades of gray, but all the same shade of dead. Six or eight of them, no two a pair it seemed at first glance, which was enough for Greta.

She snapped the lid closed and hurried down the ladder, shoved it back where she got it. Heart thrumming like her classic GTO glass packs, Greta was horrified to feel laughter start to bubble up and know she was powerless to stop. Yep, it was hysteria. She hoped the coming outburst didn't turn to non-stop, heaving giggles. It didn't, contained by Greta's hand clamped over her nose and mouth. It was all over in just the one soprano spasm.

Recovered, Greta ducked under the belt and ran slap into a brick wall she didn't remember being there. She felt her knees lose their stuffing, the rest of her sink to the floor and had the vague notion she must have smashed into the emergency bulb and busted it, because it got dark so fast.

THIRTY-SEVEN

A screaming drive fouled off the bat of a scrawny little All Star from Okay, Oklahoma, missed pole-axing Greta, coaching at first, by a hair. It was the funny bone of the first-base bruiser racing to snag the rocket that knocked her flat. The ER doctor, shining an extremely irritating light in her eyes, told her that fast-pitch softball was an oxymoron that could get you killed in some leagues.

The whole front half of Greta's head cried out in agreement. No, wait. It couldn't be. That was ... when was it? Summer before last. You couldn't have a relapse of a concussion, dislocated jaw and broken nose. Not all at once. She reached to touch her swollen face and found she couldn't. Her arms weren't where she remembered. Her hands must be at the end of wherever they had gone.

She indulged a slight moan, muffled by a patch of tape over her mouth. Greta cracked open her eyes and tried to locate all her parts but closed them when her head began to swim. Well, she didn't need to see to know her butt was on cold concrete. Eyes still closed, she hunched her shoulders hoping the signal would get to her hands. There they were, pulled behind her back clamped at the wrists. She shifted her knees and could tell they were bent up by her chin. Trying to wiggle her feet pulled at her wrists.

She forced eyes open again, forced the nausea down. Son of a bitch, she was hog tied. All of her parts were present but she was hog tied, sitting in the semi-dark among mountains of what? It hurt like hell to turn her head. Sacks everywhere, like bulk dog food. It hurt like hell to look up. She glimpsed pipes, conduits and cage lights. Familiar in a strange way.

Her mind was having a hard time coming to grips with anything other than pain that radiated across her face from her hairline to her stuffed up nose. She turned her head a fraction, trying to focus on the sacks. The smell finally told her she was sitting in a well formed by 40-pound bags of Chili-lime marinating spice, piled five feet high on pallets. She leaned back and hit what she thought was a cinder block wall, that blasted belt gouging into her waist and bound hands. That blasted belt.

The instant she felt it, Greta's head cleared and she remembered. Everything from her fight with Andy over this cockamamie assignment to the horrible collection of thumbs in the ice chest. Shit, this predicament had nothing to do with soft-ball playoffs. She was in Malapee, still in a get-up she wouldn't wear for Halloween, apparently beat up, tied up, pissed off and scared. More pissed off than scared right now, but the scared not too far beneath the surface.

Knowing the dizzy, pukey feeling was one jostle away, Greta sucked air. It felt like mashing hamburger through a wool sock but helped focus her energy when she twisted her wrists hard in opposite directions, trying to loosen what felt like a whole roll of tape.

"It's not going to do you any good to struggle so," someone said. "I'll probably let you go in a little bit, anyway. Or maybe not."

Eyes wide open, Greta stopped pulling, homing on the voice, a man talking. She heard the stacks shift and flinched when two bags of marinade landed a couple of feet from her, salting dust into the air. The man sat down on the sacks and stared at Greta. She stared back. In the shadows of the surrounding dry goods she could make out that he was wearing a the green button front smock and gold hard hat that marked him as a Poultry Xtra QC technician. Eyes glinted from the space between the edge of his hair net and a beard net that stretched from his Adam's apple over his nose. His hands, in pale green surgical gloves, were folded in his lap.

"You're off the main box room," the man gestured at the walls of sacks. "Nobody will be up here for awhile. They're running all lines for fresh frozen, no further processing today. Nobody will be in here to load ingredients or hear if you start yelling. You won't be here long, and I figure you want the answers to your questions. I'm happy to talk if you don't start yelling. If you do, I'll have to quiet you down, OK?"

Greta looked at him. She didn't much hold with yelling herself, except when Mikey or Rudy was at bat. Or when she saw Toby Keith at Fan Fair. But she had no idea where the guy ranked on the lunatic scale. This guy, not Toby. Not her Toby, the other Toby. The star. Everybody knows that Toby's loco. Hunky but insane. Crazy good.

For pity sake, had she been knocked completely senseless? Willing herself to stop blithering and pay attention, and reserving the right to yell like the little league country music mom fan she was, Greta finally nodded. Apparently satisfied, the man reached to strip the patch of tape covering her mouth.

"Why did you laugh?" he asked.

It took her a minute to remember. "Oh, in the freezer...I didn't mean to, it was just so, well, gross, really. I saw those thumbs... I don't know, it just got to me. It just came out. I wasn't funny. Honest. Anything but." Greta realized she was rattling and stopped. Damned if this maniac deserved an apology.

He sat watching. "Yeah, I couldn't help it either," he said.

"Help what? Collecting body parts?" Damn, Greta, cool it.

"No, knocking you cold. You moved the wrong way when I moved the ladder," he said. "Honestly, that wasn't the plan. "

He seemed totally calm, his voice kind of childlike but expressionless in a creepy way. Greta kept still.

"So how many got out?" he asked.

"I'm sorry?"

"How many thumbs did people find? I know you know; don't tell me you don't. You Poultry Xtra people have a tendency to lie. For instance, you're no more a security guard than I'm John Wayne."

John Wayne Gacy, maybe. Greta was through playing pretend. "You mean you don't know?"

"I know how many shipped out but I don't know how many have been found or are still out in some freezer. Or how many have been eaten and digested. That's the real scary number, huh?" His seemed to be smiling behind the beard net.

"Can I ask your name? I'm Greta. Greta Greenberry from Skiatook, Oklahoma," she nodded.

"You can call me Tubby," he said.

"Ok, Tubby. How many thumbs did you ship?"

"Didn't say I shipped any. Nice try, Ms. Greenberry, corporate QC big shot. Whose brilliant idea was it to make you a corporate spy? I bet it's some Poultry Xtra big gun laughing his comfortable ass off at your foolishness. I know, I been there."

Been where? Greta thought her head injury must be making her unusually slow on the uptake.

"What tipped you off?" Greta wanted to keep him talking. That's what hostage negotiators on TV cop dramas always said to do.

"I've seen you watching me and the other techs and data collectors, spending so much time wandering around inside the plant. Everybody knows the only reason security guards come inside the plant is if HR calls, or to pick up drugs or screw somebody or sell band candy for their kids."

Well, fuck me running, Greta thought, vindicated and seriously pissed. Hadn't she told that nimrod Andy she would be a shitty spy. "OK. So how many thumbs did somebody ship out, Tubby?"

"I let you find 'em you know. Hoopdy told me you spotted the beer cooler and I knew we were finished here."

"Tubby, where do the thumbs come from?"

"I stumbled onto one, you could say. It looked like a novel way to stir things up. I've been doing that for quite awhile, screwing with product. It wasn't hard you know. I just looked for the people who were already ignoring all the rules – pulling hold tags, fudging on specs, hiding contamination, hooking up with USDA for favors, faking paperwork – and that's just day shift," Tubby laughed. "Your own people do the dirty work, and I do my part so they don't get caught"

"But Tubby, if they don't get caught and the company never knows about it, what does that gain? If we don't know, neither does anyone else," Greta wasn't sure questioning Tubby's logic was a good idea, but she thought if she got out of this someday, she would need to understand.

"Greta, I'm surprised. You should know your own propaganda better. Eventually, if you send out enough crap, short weights, whatever, you lose customers, you lose business. If that's all true, then you don't massacre as many chickens." Tubby, who had been droning like a demented third-grade teacher, briefly seemed more cheerful. "You know, eating one of those thumbs won't kill anybody. But I bet it kills some business and saves tons of helpless victims. They're living creatures, you know."

"Customers will just buy from somebody else. Chickens will still die," Greta wondered if this guy would get tired of her arguments and let her go.

"I'll go work for somebody else awhile," he said, back to his eerie calm voice. "I'm tired of talking. You need to take a nap while I figure out what to do with you. Maybe I'll let you go. Probably not, though."

"So, are you working for PETA or some animal welfare group?" Greta said quickly. She did not want to take a nap.

"No. I did for awhile, but they're too partial to attention. I don't much go for the spotlight. I prefer action, and I like to work alone."

"Are you after Poultry Xtra or the whole industry?"

"You think there's a difference? he shook his head. "It's all messed up. E-coli in the ground sirloin, hormones in the corn chips, listeria in your cheese ball. Take your pick."

"Tubby, I've worked in a bunch of plants. Obviously, I don't think it's like that. We work really hard to do the right thing, produce good products." Greta didn't think he'd believe her if she said she agreed with him.

"Good products like chicken wings with a side of thumbs? Give me a break. The evil stuff, you people do on purpose. Other stuff, you have no control over, just an illusion of control. You're all fooling yourselves," Tubby said, looking down at his hands, clasped and rocking gently side to side. "Like you fooled me."

Greta had no idea where this was headed. "Who fooled you, Tubby?"

"SWABBY," Tubby said, looking back at Greta. "The name of my group is SWABBY."

It sounded like something he made up on the spot. "I haven't heard of them," Greta said. "Do the letters stand for something?"

"Doesn't matter. I know what they mean," Tubby said. "Now it's nap time."

"Tubby, please," Greta said, willing herself to match his calmness. "I thought you said you were going to let me go. I have two little boys, you know? I need to get home to them."

"Probably I will. Let you go. I'll think about it. I think there's some right in you somewhere mixed in with all the company Kool-Aid. But, you've put me out of business here. The last thing I need is to get hung up in some food tampering charge, although technically, I didn't tamper with any food. You'll find that Hoopdy was a big help. Anyway, I'm ready to move on."

"Hey," Tubby nearly smiled. "Maybe hog slaughter next, though I never had a pig. They're smarter than dogs, you know, Greta. If you were using dogs like you meat packers use pigs and chickens, there would be way more people picking you folks off with pipe bombs."

"But people do slaughter and eat dogs, Tubby. The same people who eat our chicken paws. And house cats." This is not a good argument, Greta told herself, but she was feeling the desperate, now familiar tickling of hysteria.

"Yeah? So, Ms. QC, what does dog taste like? Do you know, I never had a dog either."

"I'm not sure I follow, Tubby."

"No matter. It'll be alright. I promise. We'll take good care of you," Tubby said, rising from his seat.

Greta shut her eyes, bracing for another blow. Instead, Tubby slipped on and tightened a blind fold, then clamped her head against his hip. She was screaming for all she was worth when he shoved a wad of something sweet back to her molars, then taped over her mouth. Struggling not to choke, Greta was forced to swallow. She slumped over on her side, shaking, panting into the blindfold, trying not to vomit.

Tubby, aka Elvis Ridenour, waited about 20 minutes, listening to Greta try to make herself heard, fighting the drug. After she passed out, he untaped her mouth, made sure she was breathing OK, propped her side down against a pallet of marination salt, so she wouldn't upchuck and choke. Elvis didn't have a homicidal bone in his body. The nice QC lady would know soon enough. His jarhead ethic, never strong, was smothered under rubble in Beirut. He'd get Hoopdy to set her loose later.

It was time for him to hit the road, after one quick detour.

* * * * *

Greta was shaking uncontrollably, shoved bound into an alcove off one side of the ice room, hidden behind jumbled stacks of empty orange chicken tubs. It could be worse. She could be sitting in the middle of the ice or even in the blast freezer.

When she came to, she had trouble focusing. She had no idea how long it had been since Tubby drugged her. Whatever he used, it didn't affect her memory. She remembered every bizarre thing he said. Eventually, her eyes steadied and she realized someone was sitting in front of her.

It was Hoopdy, looking about as hangdog as a body could. He jumped when he saw her looking at him.

"I'm sorry ma'am," he sputtered. "I just come by to check on ya.' I ain't able to stay long, I gotta go help Beebe tonight. We got a lot goin' on."

Greta tried to talk through the tape over her mouth, but managed only an incoherent gasp. Hoopdy looked more confused than usual.

"Now don't you worry, ma'am. Elvis told me to check on you tonight, make sure you was OK. He said he wasn't aimin' to hurt you none. He says you're a big boss from Oklahoma and you want to go home to yer kids and all."

Elvis? Oh my God, they're all completely batshit. Greta gasped again, tried to plead with her eyes. Hoopdy looked like he might cry.

"Ma'am, I can't letcha loose yet. It'll git me in so much trouble. I gotta go, now. I'm sure sorry."

Greta dismissed Hoopdy as soon as he walked out. She needed to concentrate. She had been knocked senseless on Friday night. She had no idea if hours or days had passed while she was in the spice room or when she had been moved here to the cooler. If it was still the weekend and the plant wasn't running and no one happened by to rescue her, she was afraid they might find her Monday morning, cold and glazed as a box of IQF chicken. Individually Quick Frozen was no way to go. She had to get out of this herself.

Her mouth was taped, her hands were bound at the wrist, her feet at the ankles, and wrists stretched between bent knees to be bound again to her ankles with tape, zip ties and the fucking belt from her security uniform. Still hog tied, but at least with her hands in front. The only thing struggling achieved was a slightly increased heart rate that combined with her shivering provided some body heat. But it wouldn't take long for the cold to kill her.

She looked around the tiny space in the weak yellow glow from the light in the main ice room. In between spasms, she tried to see any option, some way out. What she saw instead, near her right hip, almost cured the shakes. A parting shot from Tubby: a plastic tub liner pulled tight around its contents and knotted. A bag half full. That would make it about 35 pounds give or take of dismembered human thumbs.

If she weren't so exquisitely pissed at finding herself sitting in a stupid security uniform, tied up and left for dead for something she had no business doing for a company that had the gall to ask her to do it, landing her in such a hopeless, freezing-assed mess next to a big pile of contraband body parts, Greta might be really scared.

She needed to get out of here and back to her boys.

THIRTY-EIGHT

Hoopdy backed the Bobcat down the Penske ramp, braking as he reached Beebe's side. Beebe, covered in bits of particle board and chunks of chicken litter, mopped his face with the now filthy bandana that had started out yesterday cottony clean and Downy smelling, fresh from Rachel's ironing board. It was a gentility that Beebe adopted from his granddaddy that he thought set him apart from his daddy's high falootin' preference for silk snotrags. He shoved the dirty cloth in his hip pocket.

"Beebe, can't we put off haulin' the rest till tomorrow. I gotta get some rest," Hoopdy begged. "I gotta go by the plant 'n let that, uh, I mean tell BF something fer missing last night. He's gonna be pissed I didn't call ner nothing."

"Forget BF for now. He ain't gonna stay mad atcha," Beebe reasoned. "We're almost caught up. We get these last couple dozen bodies outta here before daylight and we'll be shittin' in high cotton. If we don't, well, Daddy's already fit to be tied. I mean, after we pushed him to rent us our own Penske 'n Bobcat n' all. We ain't got no excuses now. You don't want him to stay mad at us, do ya? If we don't come through now, he's gonna smash my X-box. You know what that means, dontcha?

Hoopdy winced. Beebe didn't care. He didn't normally torment Hoopdy, poor ignorant bugger. If Hoop thought somebody was mad at him, it was like he was a fly that'd pull its own wings off to return to good graces. But Beebe was determined that he and Hoopdy were not going to quit until they hauled their way out of the backlog of bodies and chicken shit.

He and Hoopdy had been juggling and shifting loads over to the Dog Yard ever chance they had. Tons of chicken litter from the Daylight and Dovey farm they had been too busy to bag and haul to the fertilizer distributor, plus a big mess of dead bodies they had temporarily stacked under a painfully hand-shoveled topping of quicklime and soil in a ravine behind the Gather at the River Home Going Tabernacle crematory. When the ravine had topped out, they started piling the overflow in an old breeder house at the farm, now numbering two dozen dear departed representing six counties in Mississippi, Alabama and Tennessee.

Beebe started the night jazzed that he finally come up with a Plan B to execute: Goin' off on the Deacon like he and Hoopdy was the Snake brothers. Go in guns blazin,' take no prisoners, or at least none of Daddy's lame excuses. Beebe had started out slow, but he'd stuck with the plan and finally stood up to the Deacon so he couldn't weasel on 'im. It was that crack about his mama that really got Beebe riled. Yer own daddy shouldn't say nothin' like that about a man's mama.

Anyway, the old man let 'em rent the big Penske and a brand new Bobcat, and the notion had been that they'd keep at it until they were caught up to the last bloated body. It turned out to be a lot more complicated than Beebe first thought. They had to get rid of a towering pile of poultry cake backed up from several grow-out cycles, all the overflow bodies from the crematory and all the unused cremation coffins they couldn't leave laying around in plain sight.

Then Beebe decided it wouldn't do to bury this many bodies at once in the coffins, which were made of glorified poster board. He was afraid that laying out that many at once would turn The Dog Yard into a swill of stink and corpse jelly overnight. So he and Hoopdy had spent half the night shoving the litter into the coffins and double-sacking the still ripening bodies along with a second helping of quick lime in Glad Draw-string Force Flex Drum Liners with Fresh Lemon Odor Shield.

They'd finally managed to ferry two Penske loads of coffins filled with chicken cake to The Yard and dozed them over. They would take the rest of the boxed litter last thing, to pile on top of this load of bagged remains. The other bodies still stacked in the ravine over at the Tabernacle would just have spend eternity there, under one final layer of quick-lime and soil when Beebe and Hoopdy could get around to it.

Beebe was about whipped. He had totally miscalculated how much there was to get done. They'd never make it by sun-up. Still, it could be worse. At least his stomping fit at the Tabernacle had moved the Deacon to personally order the part to fix the retort conveyor and even pay for FedEx delivery.

And, he was gonna fork over for a brand new Bobcat all their own. With all that comin' together, if they could just get these last bodies dozed, he and Hoopdy could get back to normal –burying junk ever once in a while, bagging up chicken shit and sawdust to sell, burning corpses as soon as they arrived the way God intended. And playing Metal Gear.

But before they got to the last bloated body, there were 23 others to get into the Penske.

"I think we can do the bodies in one run, Hoop," he said. "There's room in the truck, and it ain't like they're gonna complain about bein' crowded. Maybe we can even get a couple more coffins of litter loaded. Then we can rest up and come get the last of the litter boxes later on."

"You promise this is the last?" Hoopdy pleaded. "I feel bad they don't get no real burial ner coffin."

"Hey, Hoop, they wasn't gonna be buried in the first place…they was gonna be burned, remember? And since when you been worryin' about the poor souls?" Beebe was losing his patience, but couldn't afford for Hoopdy to get all crybaby on him now.

"I promise, Hoop. You heard Daddy order the conveyor part and swear to God he'd get you a new Bobcat, so we don't ever get so behind again. He swore to God, Hoop. So this'll be the very last time."

"OK," Hoopdy said. "But this is gonna be the nastiest bunch yet. I hope I don't puke in the truck. I can't stand the smell of puke."

"Yeah, me neither." Beebe pulled a can of lighter fluid he kept in his hip pocket and gave his bandana a good squirt. It made him kinda high, but it cut the smell of putrefying flesh pretty good.

Beebe soaked Hoopdy's rag then helped him tie it across his face.

"Hoop, I swear, you look like one of them sidewindin' bank robbers on "Gunsmoke." Just don't ferget and light up no smokes like you did last time. You pert near blew us both up."

THIRTY-NINE

DEA Special Agent Steve Morales watched the two backwoods traffickers begin to load what appeared to be badly wrapped sofa pillows onto the rental truck. Even with night vision goggles, he was hard pressed to discern what they were loading this trip.

The DEA task force along with deputies from Beauswamp County and a few other local law enforcement yokels, obviously in serious awe of the DEA special agents, had been watching the unlikely pair of purported drug kingpins all night. They had trucked two loads of what appeared to be ammunition containers from the back of an abandoned commercial chicken house to a dump site off an old logging road about a half-mile from the farm as the crow flies, but more like six miles through the national forest that covered this part of Mississippi.

Supposedly the two acre site was used by the original owners to dispose of old equipment, tires and other outmoded manufacturing junk in the days before landfills were regulated. The deputy said that as far as he knew, it hadn't been used for years. Somebody was using it now, that much was obvious. But for what?

The tip from Deputy Bucket was that the suspects were running large amounts of crystal meth, some of which had turned up in the cremated remains of the Deputy's girlfriend's father. Luckily, Chumley Bucket was an ambitious young man with a hard-on for nabbing drug thugs, and had aced the DEA's Operation Pipeline/ Convoy course on highway interdiction, ditto Clandestine Lab First Responder Awareness, earning the right to wear the strike team jumpsuit and red filter pack gas mask.

The oblong containers these boys were hauling started Morales thinking. Was it possible the crack heads were moving weapons? Morales has spent a couple of years in the Ozarks rousting survivalists who funded their wing nut agendas by cultivating huge stands of marijuana in wooded mountains so remote that the nearest pig trail was a couple days' hike away.

If you meant to hike in, you better be packing, just like the Ozark wing nuts, whose second biggest cash crop was stainless steel automatic weapons that could be drop shipped to cult enclaves worldwide and buried with no ill effects. Meanwhile, all the camo-wrapped head cases tramped around, communed with dead Aryans, reared ringwormy kids as recruits and waited for the revolution.

Maybe these two yahoos were up to the same thing. Drugs and weapons. Or maybe something worse. He watched the Bobcat trundle from behind the building toward the Penske carrying a load of…what? The misshapen mound in the loader bucket rocked slightly, almost quivered. Special Agent Morales squinted. The smell coming off the loading site was ripe, a combination of piss, dust and…wait a minute. He tapped Deputy Bucket on the shoulder and motioned for him to follow.

* * * * *

"I can't agree to go in now. There's no telling what those guys are up to, what's in those boxes or bundles they're packing now," Morales' Special Agent in Charge, John Kay, said from his office in New Orleans.

"With all due respect, sir, I think we have a pretty good idea what they're packing," said Morales.

"Yes, but we can't go off half-cocked because we imagine Tim McVeigh behind every truck rental," Kay's disembodied voice argued. "We don't want to get carried away, lose sight of the big picture. Think about it, you've been watching these guys for less than a week. How likely is it that a couple of cracker chicken plant supervisors are in charge of something that looks this big? We need the people at the top.

"Besides, just between you and me, I promised my brother-in-law we wouldn't do anything to draw extra attention to those Mississippi plants. You know how touchy those ICE boys get if you fuck with 'em when they're fixing to round up illegals...you still there, Steve?"

"Yes, sir. I see what you mean, sir. Naturally, I wouldn't be aware of any planned ICE raids. I just wanted to float the possibility that we might be dealing with something far more dangerous than drugs and small arms," Morales chose his words carefully.

"I just would never want to be the one who saw something disturbing but failed to act before Mr. McVeigh headed down Turner Turnpike for the trip to Oklahoma City. I would not ever want to be the one to have to explain my inaction to all those grieving families, because I didn't think..."

"Steve..."

"... some burr-headed piece of trailer-trash was capable..."

"OK, Steve..."

"...of something so big and so very terrible..."

"Steve! I gotcha. It's a go. Sic 'em, son."

"Thank you, sir," Special Agent Morales said.

"Son, I hope you're wrong, but you better be right."

FOURTY

Eulie sat slumped over her desk, forehead pressed into folded forearms, listening to vitriol pour through the ventilation panel in her office door. HR Clerk Pantasia Glass was into it as usual with a Posse Member who had the bad judgment to ask Taser a question during one of her numerous daily personal phone calls.

It was a typical response from Taser, a smart young woman with an extremely high opinion of herself, whose idea of customer service was to hover in a miasma of moodiness apparently on the theory that giving people a load of shit along with her response would get them out of her hair, allowing her to resume gossiping, scheming and just plain conniving with a handful of other likeminded Posse Members who condescended to consider one another friends.

Eulie knew it was hopeless to call Taser out on her abysmal attitude, since she had a long-standing serious hugging relationship with the Group HR manager, Roger Fricker. He joked to Eulie when she first arrived at Malapee that he was a "hands-on" guy who didn't enjoy grappling with problems he encountered traveling plant to plant nearly as much as he did "hugging everybody and having lunch."

He had gone on to make it clear that Taser and the other Malapee clerks were among his favorite hugees and that he wouldn't mind including Eulie in the all-round squeeziness. Eulie told him she would consider it if he meant to hug all the guys as well. That won no points with Fricker, but at least had kept her off the cringing end of his lingering bear hugs.

Even without that worry, Fricker's periodic visits coincided with an uptick in Taser's tendency to be a witch, although it didn't seem possible since she was routinely as nasty as humanly possible. And, Eulie discovered that when Fricker was at Malapee, Taser's habit of shredding backlogs of paperwork went into overdrive.

Unfortunately, Fricker would be here today with the corporate visitors, which explained why Taser was on such a dyspeptic roll this morning in anticipation of a big, validating public cuddle with Fricker. Eulie had read between the lines months ago, and all she could do today was try to ignore Taser's harangue reverberating through her door. Besides, Eulie had bigger worries than the clerk's outbursts and penchant for ditching work.

Eulie had to handle the festivities for the visiting South Group managers and Poultry Xtra corporate honchos who made a sweep through one division every three months just to keep everyone on their toes and half-crazed. Today, it was Malapee on parade.

She might pull her head off the desk for that, but the plaintiff's attorney in Leary v. Poultry Xtra, Mr. Braswell Boone Hockentrump, would arrive later this morning to prospect through years of personnel files looking for more ammo in Leary v. Poultry Xtra. Just the thing to start the week. In between walking the big dogs, it would be her responsibility to pull and copy anything and everything the lawyer wanted from the mountains of bankers' boxes crammed with inactive files in the Old Box Room.

It had been bad enough during his earlier visit when he went through the 25 four-drawer cabinets full of files for current employees. Eulie and two of her clerks were running all day everyday for a week catering to his every request, all at the behest of the corporate legal department, which naturally provided no help at all.

Junior, if possible, was even less useful than usual, acting like a complete nincompoop because Truly was in such a blither about the corporate visit and because the sales and quality people from Dairy Daisy were here to scrutinize a new product test. Eulie actually felt a little bit sorry for Truly. Customer visits were bad enough, but at least you expected customers to make niggling demands. Having company head cheeses hover at the same time was too much.

Corporate visits were pitched as an opportunity for the HQ crowd to keep in touch with the lesser folk in the field. But they mostly turned into photo-ops with a handful of locals to maintain the Poultry Xtra image as a good corporate neighbor.

And they were useful to managers a few notches up the food chain from Truly, so they could immediately exhibit surprise, embrace deniability and lower the boom on Malapee underlings if the COO and Group VP saw something they didn't like during the tour.

And, oh yeah, Eulie remembered. A bunch of regulators from the EPA were supposed to be here with the folks from Malapee-Paola Consolidated Water and Sewer district to re-test the re-tests of the water treatment operation. Apparently the plant had been dumping some kind of toxins into the groundwater, but nobody could figure out where or how.

No wonder Junior was in such a snit. Truly had actually told him he had to stay at the plant to help herd visitors. Junior was not pleased and was calling Eulie every five minutes to delegate something else he didn't want to do.

Her phone buzzed again. Speak of the dipstick, Eulie groaned, choosing not to answer. She needed to get her head off the desk and into the day. Right off the bat she had to investigate a near punch-out and minor uprising in the break room last week between a union steward and his entourage and a gay Posse Member who called himself TwoPack Fersure and dressed every day head-to-toe in a different Easter-egg tint.

Nearly as she could tell from the first snitch reports, TwoPack had put up with a bunch of smack talk from Mooney Latrile and his friends about TP's sexual preference, but drew a line when Mooney trashed his fashion choices. TwoPack went for Mooney and was stopped just short of gross misconduct and automatic termination when one of his BFFs from debone wrestled him away.

Now, witnesses were lining up and taking sides. Eulie was going to have to handle most of the interviews herself. This on top of all the other crap. Making it through days like today was the same as trying to decide where to stand in a dog pound earthquake. Whichever way Eulie stepped she was liable to land in flaming shit.

* * * * *

Operation Desert Shield Force Recon vet Deiter Biggs loved the new ICE. Ever since 2003 when Dubya repurposed the Immigration and Naturalization Service and the Border Patrol into something rightfully more akin to black ops, Dieter felt as if he had been sexually pleasured in glorious hand-to-hand combat, died from the rapture and gone to Soldier of Fortune heaven.

No more chasing illegals in Blue Bird school buses with some side-saddle-riding INS goober worried more about processing I-9 employment verification forms than rousting stinking, border-crashing low-lifes who came to this country to take American jobs and clog up our schools with numberless spawn.

No more going in the front door, hat in hand, only to watch the enemy run for every available exit and into the surrounding countryside at the first hint the federales were on the move. No more listening to HR crybabies insist they were arresting people who weren't even foreign. Yeah, so what? If strays were sucked into the net, they needed to do something about their appearance. Anyway, they got to leave after a night at the local armory. No harm, no foul.

In the glory of ICE today, Deiter was authorized to send troops by the hundreds to surround the target, backed up by a half-dozen armored buses with blacked-out windows, moving vans to haul away bogus documents, some custom-fitted assault Hummers, an EMT vehicle for show, and two helicopters, one of which was his personal ride. And as many and varied weapons as could ever impel this soldier's sweetest nocturnal emissions.

His men were on the move right now, staging at the Beauswamp County fairgrounds where HQ had leased the cow-barn for enemy processing, coordinating the raid with the state police, who would add wheels and a show of fire power. Operation Mess Tent at the

Malapee Poultry Xtra manufacturing plant would commence at 0900 hours. Deiter expected to capture from 400 to 600 enemy for deportation to their own goddamn countries. Country really. Everybody and Lou Dobbs' grandmother knew they were all Mexicans.

He felt a little bit guilty about not giving Darby Dummit more of a heads up that one of her plants was on the ICE hit list. She was a good egg. Ex-Army and a solid link in the military-industrial complex of compliance and control of the unskilled labor she rode herd on. Well, she'd get over it. They'd have a cocktail or few at the next convention, and she'd forgive him. They both understood that U.S. citizens who worked for Poultry Xtra were her mission to keep in line. The illegals were all fucking his.

* * * * *

Lately, Mert was having a hard time maintaining focus – she couldn't concentrate or make a decision with her characteristic cold-eyed dispatch.

Right now, for instance. She was standing on the walkway high above the debone floor with a half dozen sales and product development nit-pickers from Corporate and Dairy Daisy, listening to Wayne Daylight explain the modifications they'd be making to each of the 15 cone lines to better trim breast tenders to meet Dairy Daisy's BREAST EVER Quick Frozen Chicken Fingers product specifications.

Mert's problem was she had a terrific view of Fano, bent at the waist, working on a small chiller pump between lines 3 and 4. So it took every ounce of concentration Mert had to keep up with Wayne's spiel about the intricacies of water jet trimmers, size tolerances and other details that, to be honest, were either hard to maintain or easily skirted in the push to run pounds down the line and out the door. But honesty rarely came in to play when the sales types were involved. They never said no, no matter how impossible the customer demand.

Damn, Fano was easy to look at, Mert mused. She wanted this tour to be over. She had heard it all so many times before and it was all so much BS. With every product, hundreds of controls and requirements were built into the process at the behest of the customer and an army of regulators, so many that no process involving people could hope to apply all of them at any given time, ever.

Despite their contentious history, Mert and Wayne agreed on a simple logical progression, like the idiot's guide to successful manufacturing. It had been Wayne's first best advice to her when she was a newly minted supervisor.

"Mert, if you listen to process Nazis, they'll tell you 'don't run it if you can't ship it'. Well, I say, if you think you can't ship it, you're just bein' a pussy. If you use your head, you can always find a way. So, no matter how screwed up the process is, keep the line running, think fast, adjust, pack the chicken and move it out. Most of the time, our customers and their customers won't have a clue that we messed up somewhere. If they do notice a problem, well, it's not yours anymore; it belongs to some tool down the line. Just remember to make sure your paperwork tells the story you want told, and you'll be running chicken 'til we roll you out of here in a wheel chair."

It got harder and harder over the years to listen to Wayne schmooze customers with his hypocritical "we do it your way" routine, knowing his actual MO. Of course, Mert's own routine of apple polishing and creative paperwork was much more subtle, not to say justified.

Blah, blah, blah, Wayne seemed to say. Mert watched Fano return tools to his tool belt and wipe his hands across his smock. She immediately had visions of his broad, smooth chest underneath and other things about him that she could so far only imagine. But that was going to change as soon as Mert could make it happen. And after their last meeting, she had no doubt that it would.

"Mert," Wayne was yelling, "What you think?"

"Sorry, Wayne," she gestured at one ear. It was the most common response to any question in the plant, since the noise level obliterated 90 percent of what people said.

"Ms. Bellard asked if you think your people can handle another flagship product."

Mert looked at Dairy Daisy's tiny R&D VP. She never got used to seeing civilians tricked out in hairnets and smocks. Over the VP's head, she saw Fano leave the floor.

"It's not a matter of if, ma'am. It's only a matter of when," Mert said. "And when will be soon. Real soon."

Mert smiled at the VP and Wayne and thought about how she would make it all happen. First things first, of course.

* * * * *

Fano saw Mert watching him from the walkover and he had to admit that the encounter he knew was coming had him worried. He didn't know how far he would have to go, but he was prepared to go all the way to take her down.

He didn't know anyone else who had hooked up with Mert. BF said she had dated people in the past, but mostly guys from the city with some trappings of power. Not the top kind of power, just the assistant kind. Like a mega-church assistant pastor she brought to the Christmas Party one year, a guy with slicked back hair and tight, preacher collar, buffed nails and a lot of opinions, BF recalled. Or the associate at the Johnny Cochran firm in Jackson, an expert in gaming law who BF said gambled on a fling with Mert and apparently lost.

She came across as the kind of woman who most men avoided as too smart, too close with her money and too much to sustain if she ever got interested. Predatory kind of, like female insects they showed on Animal Planet that would give their males a quick shot and then pop them like a diet soda and chug their insides out, soul and all.

None of that mattered, though. Today was the day Fano had been working toward, tantalizing Mert a little at a time, setting the hook in the box room last week, ready to reel her in at the first opportunity.

The way she'd been ogling him all the time she was supposed to be paying attention to those visitors in debone was a sure sign he should pull the trigger. He just had to pick his place and get the radio ready. Timing would be everything.

* * * * *

Wastewater Manager Kris Kirchoff, her boss from corporate, Mona Belloc, QC head Roy McKnight and Maynard Travis stood in awkward silence at the front entryway of the Malapee Plant, waiting for the big government Suburban just flagged in at the gate to disgorge the group of inspectors from the state, the EPA and USDA who were here to run tests on her operation.

As location wastewater wrangler, Kris was in charge of the visit, and had no problem with Dr. Belloc here, or with the inclusion of Roy McKnight in the group. The USDA veterinarian, Doc Ryder, would join them as well. No big deal. It was Maynard Travis she could have done without. He was an unstable variable in any situation, a weird combination of good brain, big mouth and the judgment of a 14-year-old on nitrous oxide.

Maybe not the end of the world day-to-day, but dealing with the Feds and other regulators called for a deft touch, diplomacy and quiet confidence in your process and procedures. Not Maynard's strutting bombast. But Truly told her she needed a production manager on her team, and he, Mert and Wayne Daylight were busy with the visitors from corporate and Dairy Daisy.

As the group made its way up the walk, Kris was surprised to see a U.S. Marshal in the lead. Poultry Xtra had consented to the visit, so the show of force was unsettling.

"Well, hey now…" Maynard shouldered Kris to one side.

"What's this about?" he said to the Marshal when she reached the top step.

"Maynard, wait." Kris attempted to take his elbow, but he shook her off.

"Well, Marshal, ma'am, what's going on? We weren't expecting an armed escort, cute as that escort might be." Maynard grinned. The Marshal didn't.

"Sir, are you the owner or person in charge of this facility?"

Maynard started to answer, but Kris cut him off. "Marshal, I'm Kris Kirchoff and this is my supervisor Dr. Mona Belloc. We'll be helping you all make your inspection. I am a bit curious, though, why you're here. We're on record as having consented to the visit."

"United States Marshal Suze Ludeman," the Marshal said. "I'm just here to serve the warrant. Mr. Van Husen might be able to give you more information."

"Yes, ma'am, I'm Vaness Van Husen with the EPA. We certainly appreciate your cooperation, but we sometimes obtain warrants just to minimize any potential entry problems and to help establish the parameters of the inspection."

"OK, well sure, that's fine," Kris said. "Why don't we go in? We have a conference room reserved. We can hammer out the details and make sure you have everything you need. Please, right this way."

Kris held the door as Maynard fell in beside the young U.S. Marshal. "Well, Marshal, hon, tell me. Do they let the guys wear sweet little ponytails like that?"

Kris glared, trying to signal Maynard to shut his trap. He didn't even glance her way. So she tried telepathy, boring into the back of his thick skull with her eyes. "Maynard, shut the fuck up! She's armed, you dumbass."

* * * * *

"Fano's radio crackled. "Fano Alcides, Fano."

"Copy, copy" Fano answered. It was Mert.

"Where you at?"

"Heading for break."

"I need you to take a look at that unit again, its acting up."

"Same one? Now?"

"The very one. Right now."

"Copy, copy." Fano supposed it was good fortune. His plan for the day was forming up and so far all he'd had to do was look good and wait for Mert's unit to act up. He laughed, a little nervous. He slipped his radio from the collar holster and used the prong he'd broken from a cafeteria fork to wedge the talk button down, set it to intercom channel 1, reclipped it to his collar and headed to meet Mert.

FOURTY-ONE

While Beebe lashed the rented Bobcat to its trailer, Hoopdy hauled the ramp into the Penske box floor, grabbed the overhead handle and hopped to the ground, pulling the door closed on the last load of suppurating bodies in scented leaf bags. Together they fixed the trailer hitch, unwrapped the naphtha-soaked bandanas from their faces, shoved them in their hip pockets and stopped to suck in the comparatively unfusty morning air outside the truck box full of rising corruption.

"I could use some pancakes and eggs, Beebe, and coffee. Maybe some gravy and grits too. Boy howdy, I could sure use one a them double shot cans they got at the Gas & Git," Hoopdy croaked, running his pasty tongue over chapped lips. "Couldn't we swing by there?

Beebe looked at his partner and rolled his eyes. Only Hoop would think of food at a time like this. Beebe held one nostril closed, aimed and shot a missile of phlegm, solvent and putrefaction into the dust at Hoopdy's feet. He wiped his nose on his sleeve.

"We ain't got time for that. The sun's almost up, dammit, and we ain't gonna git done," Beebe looked wasted. "We gotta get the truck back. After the way I laid into 'im, when Daddy finds out we ain't finished moving all the litter, he's gonna rip off our heads and shit down our necks. Take a swig outta the thermos and we'll get some breakfast later. Let's git goin'."

Hoopdy watched Beebe stomp off mumbling. He slumped, scuffing his toes on the way around the side of the truck to climb wearily to his perch behind the wheel, worried all over again that

Beebe was done with him and that the Deacon would fire him. He couldn't think what to do to fix it.

Exhausted and bleak, he didn't see when Beebe unscrewed the thermos of day-old coffee and offered it to his friend across the bench seat. Hoopdy, started the engine, popped the break and eased forward to get the Bobcat trailer in line, giving a quick glance at the side mirror, where he saw a couple of black-suited terrorists wearing breather packs with big red filter caps glowing like alien eyeballs, carrying machine guns and trying to sneak up on him and Beebe.

"Fuckin' A," he whispered, eyes locked on the mirror that now reflected a big black SUV swerving around the old breeder house, headed straight for the Penske.

"Psycho Mantis…right here in Malapee."

Hoopdy gripped the wheel, gunned the big diesel and shot headlong across the brush-hogged donut of land that surrounded the broiler houses and into the surrounding forest, lurching over a mound of plow dirt where the bodies now sluicing around the truck box had been buried.

The impact jack-knifed the Bobcat trailer, snapping the hitch and sending the mini-loader and trailer cart-wheeling into the path of the SUV. The back of Beebe's head popped against the cab and then the whole front of Beebe's head slammed into the windshield, smashing his nose and mouth to pulp and rendering him bloody, speechless and barely conscious. He would not remember later Hoopdy's valor as he plowed the Penske onward in his fight to the death against the terrorist threat to Mississippi and getting the Deacon anymore pissed off than he already was.

* * * * *

"Sonovabitch," Special Agent Morales yelled, scrambling from the once pristine Escalade, its grille impaled on the neck of the Bobcat trailer. The passenger side was demolished when the Bobcat landed by the right headlight then fantailed dirt and gravel to a stop ten feet later, taking a neat, six-inch tuck in the SUV side panel as it slid the length of the vehicle, past seven astonished lawmen, six of whom were now straggling out the rear door to join their commander.

"Where's my radio?" Agent Morales barked, forgetting his headset, straining to see the Penske, lost in the stand of trees. "Deputy Bucket, where they headed?"

Chumley Bucket, one of the two officers whose approach had set Hoopdy off, stepped toward Agent Morales but stayed a touch to his rear. "Sir," he answered smartly through the mask filter of his brand-new self-contained breathing apparatus. "Chicken plant's that way. Sir."

Morales nodded. Those two guys were either smarter or way dumber than he had suspected. He flipped his shades to rub his eyes. The smell in the clearing was ungodly. Fertilizer layered over something more noxious.

Well, that's more like it, thought Special Agent Morales. It was a shame about the vehicle, but no casualties so far. And now he knew his hunch had been right. No crack cooking here. This had the stink of treason. Time for reinforcements.

* * * * *

As soon as she walked into Junior's office, Eulie could see that he had turned back-slappy and grinning trying to bond with the attorney from Pylon, Foche, Takim and Goetz.

As if anyone representing big business could get on the good side of Braswell Boone Hockentrump, Esq. He reminded Eulie of a Tasmanian Devil, sleek, watchful, ready to bite your leg off as soon as you gave up the ghost. If you believed the lawyer's tidy smile, Junior's impersonation of a Delta good-ol'-boy amused him. In her experience, you had to look past Hockentrump's smile to the eyes. His eyes told her he hadn't been amused by anything a defendant had to say probably ever. Gleeful, perhaps, but never honestly amused.

"Well, Eulie, I guess you know Braswell, here...you don't mind if I call you Braswell, do you?" Junior checked with Braswell, forgetting to invite Eulie to sit. She shook hands with the attorney and started to speak but Junior was in a hurry.

"Eulie, I think the best thing would be for you two to set up in the Old Box Room. Get maintenance to hook you up some extra lights and a copier. We can get the cafeteria to send up refreshments to keep you going."

"Junior, it's awfully dusty..."

"Now, then, a little dust isn't going to discourage Hock. Do you mind if I call you Hock?" Junior looked at the lawyer. "We have nothing to hide and wouldn't want Hock to think so, would we? No, certainly not."

Eulie looked at Hock and couldn't imagine it was OK for anyone to call him that. He maintained his tidy smile but raised his eyebrows slightly.

"Well, good, then, Hock, I'll leave you in Eulie's very capable hands. She's the best HR hand I've got around here but you've worked with her before so I'm not telling you anything you didn't already know, right? Anyway, go with her and make yourself at home. Glad to see you and you just let me know if there's anything else you need and Eulie will see to it."

Junior stood and walked around his desk to pump Braswell Boone Hockentrump's hand, moving the lawyer and Eulie toward the door. "Now I've got a conference call I'm a little late for, so you two are free to tackle those files."

Eulie and Hockentrump found themselves on the hallway side of Junior's closed door.

"Is he always so rude?" Hockentrump asked, his face wiped free of the tidy smile.

"Um, as I stand here today, you're asking me if my boss is always so rude?" Eulie mimicked in her most overwrought lawyerese. "Well, let's see. Not that I can recall, as I stand here today." She only wished she could tell Mr. Hockentrump Junior wasn't at work often enough to be really rude. "Let's go to my office. I'll get you a smock and hairnet."

Hockentrump grinned at her. She wouldn't swear to it, but she thought she glimpsed a shade of honest amusement in the lawyer's dark glance.

"Ms. LaCrosse, I'm not interested in spending all day in a poorly lighted, dirty box room," Hockentrump said, back to business. "I suggest that I accompany you for a look at the venue, a look at the volume of work I will have. We may be able to tag some likely documents and you could have them delivered to me in a more, shall we say, commodious location. How does that sound? Oh, and you may call me Braswell."

"Mr. Hockentrump, whatever I can do to help. Let's go get your smock and hairnet."

Twenty minutes later, Eulie and Hockentrump were standing before the enormous cage that ran the length of the Old Box Room and housed the plant's inactive files with a narrow path allowing access inside the cage.

"They're organized by year. Where would you like to begin?" Eulie asked.

"Most recent," Hockentrump answered.

Eulie walked to the gate at one end of the cage, unlocked it and ushered the attorney inside.

Hockentrump began looking at the box labels, typed furiously in his Blackberry then looked some more. He pulled a few of the bankers' boxes out, took a quick look inside, typed more furiously. Eulie stayed at his side, taking her own notes just in case. Hockentrump seemed to focus on particular years, but not in any pattern that Eulie could determine. Probably basing his selections on information he gleaned from his stake- out at Beeler's BBQ to pump information from newly fired Posse Members.

The lawyer had been moving steadily down the towers of files for about twenty minutes when he stopped short and looked with something like alarm at Eulie.

"What is that?" he whispered. "Hear that?"

Eulie listened. She didn't hear anything, and shook her head.

"There...listen."

Eulie held her breath. Something like tree branches rustling a little, then more. And the wind. Just a breeze at first but picking up. Then a wet sound, rain lightly pelting a pie tin. It seemed to be coming from two directions. Oh, my land, no! Eulie reached beneath her smock to pull her radio from the belt clip.

Eulie looked at Hockentrump who was looking at the radio, his burnished eyes aglitter. She'd seen that look before during Dwight's deposition. He was smiling again, but it wasn't the tidy one. It was his positively gleeful smile.

"Mr. Hockentrump," Eulie said, but he slipped past her and was gone, fiddling with his Blackberry. Eulie considered yelling after him. Maybe it would warn whoever he was about to roust. On the other hand, Junior said there was nothing to hide. So be it. Eulie tucked her notebook under her arm and followed, feeling a little guilty. Her radio moaned and panted loudly in her hand, the same sounds of satisfaction she could hear coming from the intercom overhead. Eulie finally relaxed. There was nothing she could do to stop a train wreck.

* * * * *

Ardel Patrick had his mental fingers crossed. Everyone up his food chain was occupied with customers, VPs from corporate or assorted regulators, none of whom were paying particular attention to plant safety for a change. He might actually be able to unfold out of his usual defensive posture and get some work done.

First, he'd been completely strung out with damage control after the scalping, then the blowup about the thumbs and the edict from corporate that clamped the lid on that had fueled all sorts of speculation and for Ardel, soaring blood pressure and spurts of stomach acid.

Anyway, it had been weeks since he had been able to look at the backlog of accident investigations, to make sure the OSHA logs were up to speed. Some of the supervisors were notorious for sending reports late and full of holes. He was just warming up, pecking furiously at his keypad, composing a flaming e-mail to Mert and Maynard, naming names of the biggest foot draggers, when his phone buzzed. The readout showed the guard post. He grabbed it.

"Ardel, here."

"Uh, Mr. Patrick, this is Officer Posie. I just wanted to alert you that a couple of guys from OSHA are on their way up."

"Holy crap, you're kidding."

"No sir, I showed them where to park. They'll be at the front in a few minutes."

Ardel replaced the receiver, trying not to panic. No way was he ready for OSHA today. The logs were in terrible shape, and no telling what else was going on out in the plant with all the visitors. Things generally were spruced up in advance of a corporate flyby, but sometimes sprucing up meant quick fixes that didn't actually include anyone taking a gander at the regulations. Damn, he needed time. Ardel grabbed the phone and dialed the operator.

"Yes, Ardel, I was just going to…"

"Cece, don't say anything, just listen…I know OSHA is here. First off, tell them I'm not here, I'm away from the plant. Then have them take a seat in the employment office and tell them you'll contact me and get back to them. Then wait 20 minutes and call me on my cell phone. Can you do that for me Cece?"

"Yessir," the operator agreed. "Park them in employment to cool their heels, then call you in 20. Will do." Ardel hung up and closed his laptop, turned off the light and put on a spare blue smock he kept for visitors and his hairnet. He left his safety green hardhat on the rack. He cracked the door and looked up and down the hallway of offices. No one in sight.

OSHA couldn't inspect anything without the location safety chief being alerted. If he left now, it would give him a couple of hours at the least, maybe a full day, if he didn't answer when Cece called. Then they'd have to contact the next highest safety manager, and that meant rousting a corporate dupe to give the go-ahead for someone else at the plant to sit down with OSHA and organize an inspection.

Ardel was going to do the smart thing and leave through the plant and out the back. With one quick stop on the way, he'd make certain he didn't end up on the spot with the watch dogs, at least not today.

* * * * *

Sharay Townsend hoped she was making her next-to-last trip to the Poultry Xtra plant where her daddy had spent her lifetime and the last of his. She and Danny had come to the plant to pick up the check from her daddy's accidental death and dismemberment policy. She was waiting for Taser to call her into the Benefits Office to begin signing the paperwork. She had been here so many times, thanks to her daddy's death benefits, she was getting friendly with all the clerks.

She had not been a very good daughter to Lowndes Henderson, she knew. But she wanted to be a better daughter to his memory, by being a better mama to Danny. And her daddy had made it possible for both of them to have better prospects than Sharay had ever hoped. And there was Chumley.

Sharay wanted to make things work with Deputy Chumley Bucket. He said he loved her and wanted to take care of her and Danny, and she was trying hard to believe she and Danny could have a stable, settled life. But the whole idea made her a little nervous. She was pretty sure she could trust Chumley. What she didn't know for sure was whether he could trust her.

Really, she didn't know if she could trust herself. She'd made her own way through life, and sometimes you did what you had to in order to have food and a place to stay. Even leave your child behind. That bothered her a lot. And then there was the weed. Even flush with her daddy's money, her go-to drug was a smoke or three a day. Chumley was not going to put up with that.

Chumley said he didn't expect miracles. He said life was hard work no matter if you had money or not. He told her as long as she recognized that they were talking about life together and not a picnic – with ups and downs and a child, or children to raise – they could make it. Together.

But the money didn't hurt, and she would be glad to get the last lump sum deposited in the bank.

"Sharay," called Taser, just as a piercing alarm sounded, making Sharay slap her hands over her ears and Danny jump up and run

194

around making machine gun noises, his fingers cocked as he swept the office with a hail of bullets.

All the clerks were getting up from behind their desks and coming out of offices. Taser came out carrying a handbag and called to Sharay. "Get Danny and come with me. It's just a fire drill. The check will have to wait."

Sharay and Danny followed the HR clerks into the break room and joined hundreds of Posse Members slowly streaming toward the exits, laughing and shouting, pointing at the ceiling for some strange reason, but obviously glad for the unscheduled break.

FOURTY-TWO

Fano looked so dang fine, lounging there on the boxes, in that low light. Mert was taking a helluva chance meeting him here. Going down on him today was her idea. He halfway objected, said it was her turn, but no guy in history would put up a real fight to avoid a blow job.

"OK, babe." Fano looked especially eager. "Let's get to it."

Really, men were so easy. But Mert wanted to take care of some other business. "And we will, sweet man. You know what's always on my mind. But let's talk a little first.

"You still want to deal me in?" Fano said.

"You know I need you to help me with some of my various interests, the money lending deals at Quickie Ricky's, the vending business."

"Mert, I thought we were about falling in love, having a relationship," Fano said, something Mert didn't remember he'd ever said before. It didn't hurt her feelings, but it surprised her.

"Fano, baby, we are about that. It's love that makes me want to get my shit together with somebody I can trust. People who love each other share everything don't they?"

"So, I understand the loan business at Ricky's. What's the deal with the vending machines?" Fano said.

"Just a little off the top for certain considerations," Mert said. "Not a lot and not complicated, but steady."

"Is that what you were doing after Mooney and TwoPack got into it…taking a little off the top? I heard you helped yourself to the money pouch from Mr. Chip's lockup. Was he ever pissed."

"No, babe, that was a little extra I took for leverage. He's been playing hardball about my cut off the machines at Ricky's and I needed to send a message. I have it put away. It's partly because of you I took it, so I'd have a good stake to offer to get you started handling my business."

"Like you're going to handle my business right now," Fano smiled that killer smile. He took his radio off, fiddled the control and laid it aside. Then he looked at Mert, gesturing at the critical buttons on his uniform coat.

"Yeah, babe, just like I'm gonna handle this, fine as it is," Mert said, already on button number three.

To Mert, it was a perfect way to seal the deal. Fano was a nice size, not pushy. And he smelled good, kind of like some herb she couldn't identify. Mert was more into this man than any sane woman should be. Of course, it was a huge risk, carrying on at the plant, something she swore she'd never do.

She'd been risking a lot, lately. At first, she'd ignored the change in herself, from rigid to a little loose about the right way to conduct business. Then, when Quickie Ricky had nearly ruined everything with the CD scam, she realized that every time she recruited someone to do something on her behalf, no matter how well she paid them to do it and keep quiet, she could never really rely on them. She couldn't really trust them, not really. She only trusted herself to control them. But even that seemed to go south when Betina went to the EEOC. Mert thought they had a deal, and Betina welched.

When the USDA saw Betina switching labels, Mert had no choice but to act like she'd just walked in on her own set-up. Betina understood what had to happen and had agreed. And Mert would have delivered on her end. But Betina got nervous about having the baby with no paycheck and had come up with that lame excuse about the baby and Fano. Well, where did that get her? Here Fano was, not with Betina, but right where Mert wanted him.

"Mert, you're drifting, babe. Watch the teeth," Fano said, then crooned, "Yeah, baby, that's it, that's right."

197

Amazing, Mert thought, curling her lips tighter, he was kind of a grunter, loud as a lone boar in a sow barn. It pleased Mert that she could give him such obvious, if deafening, pleasure.

Mert took her time, but between mouth and hands, it wasn't all that long before Fano seized up, once, twice, sucked in a deep breath, whooshed it out and relaxed. Mert sat back, wiped her smock sleeve across her mouth and looked at one fine man. Oh, honey, she thought, you're just what I need.

"You think you'll be able to walk any time soon, baby?" Mert asked.

"You mean sometime today? I don't know, Mert, mama. You wore me out." But Fano sat up and fixed his clothes. "So what now, about the loan business, I mean?"

Funny. The rush of blood must still be fogging her brain, all that rocking and bending. She thought she heard Fano's question, but more than once, echoing around her. She looked at him and saw that he was looking over her shoulder. She turned and saw a little guy in a visitor smock and too-big hairnet pointing a handheld at her, snapping pictures. Eulie was behind the guy, and she was holding up her radio.

She turned back to Fano, who was holding up his radio.

"I guess we're busted, Mert," he said several times, once from his gorgeous lips and once each from his and Eulie's radio, and from a loudspeaker fixed to a rafter overhead.

Mert scrambled to her feet, her face burning hot, searching for something to say, when the blaring pulse of the fire alarm made them all flinch. Mert recovered first.

"I gotta go see to my Posse." She turned her own radio back on and looked at Fano. "Mr. Alcides, you need to go to your designated area."

Then Mert muscled past the little man and Eulie. Fano followed, still smiling. Eulie grabbed Hockentrump at the nape of his neck and herded him through the maze of boxes for the stairs, wondering why no one had told her there would be a fire drill today of all days.

198

FOURTY-THREE

Greta didn't think she could get any colder or shake any harder than she already was, but when the fire alarm cut through her fuzzy thinking, she felt a shiver of fear.

If it was a drill, she'd be in the same fix, but when people returned after it was over, she'd have the same chance she had now that somebody, please, anybody would come in and she'd be able to make enough noise that they'd find her.

If this shit hole was on fire, well, she didn't see any upside. She would either be steam cooked or stuck here freezing until they had to carve her out like a chain saw swan sculpture.

Greta tried again to wiggle her way out of the narrow passage where Hoopdy had left her. Her butt was so cold it felt like a piece of granite. She promised herself if she got out of here alive, she would never confess to making that comparison. The alarm was enough to crack granite; it was so loud and persistent. It was enough to make you crazy if you were trapped and had to listen to it for very long, like the length of a fire drill, or as long as it took for the fire to fry the alarm.

Greta struggled and scooted, making little progress. It was so fucking hard to breathe with her mouth taped and nose crunched in and stuffed up from the freezing cold. She willed herself not to cry. She wouldn't be able to breathe at all if she started crying.

She decided to try yelling instead. "uhmmm mmmhhh!" Not very clear. She'd have to try louder. "UHMMMMM MMHHHH! UHMMMMMMMM!"

"You need help, ma'am?"

Greta looked up. Damned if she wasn't already dead and seeing an angel standing over her. He had the most purely beautiful face she'd ever seen looking out from under a huge hairnet and was dressed in the grimiest red smock over the nastiest sweat pants ever to bag between two knees. If he was an angel, his eye contact was not what it ought to be, and surely the heavenly host dressed in clean raiment. No she must be alive.

Greta started nodding for all she was worth. "UHMMMMM MMHHH!"

The angel knelt at her side and started fumbling with the zip ties around her wrists and ankles. She wished he'd hurry with the damned tape on her mouth because his body odor was so ripe she didn't know how much more punishment her smashed up nose could take.

Then, he vanished as quick as he had appeared. Greta groaned. He might be a dirty rotten smelling angel, but he was her angel. Please God, bring him back, she prayed. And there he was, armed with a box knife. Greta relaxed a bit and listened to the sound of her rescuer's voice.

"Ma'am, what happened to you? Did you make Mr. Dwight mad? He threatened to tie me up in a sack and throw me in the pond, like a runt hound pup, he said, but I didn't think he meant it. He's always telling me stuff like that. Did he ever tell you that? If he done this to you, I'll get in trouble again if I help you get loose. But I'm tired of him dogging me every day. I don't think it's right how he talks to me, and tells me he's fixin' to fire my ass every dang day. Even if he did give me a nick name and all."

When he finally pulled the tape from her face, Greta worked her sore jaw a second and croaked, "What's your name, sir, your real name."

"Why, it's Marcus, ma'am. Marcus Wynn. Mr. Dwight and them, they call me Mr. Mizzle, P-Drizzle, 'cause they said I do such good work with the sanitizer hose." Marcus looked bashful. "But I think they're really makin' fun cause I got a problem with using the bathroom a lot. Like, I need to go real bad now and when that horn went off and everybody ran out, I just stopped in here to take a quick leak. But I didn't, not after I seen you all roped up."

"Never mind, Marcus. I'm glad you're here," Greta said. "Now, while I get my bag, you go around there in the deepest part of the ice and take your leak. Write your name, your real name, every last letter. I'll wait right here until you're finished. No one will ever know."

Marcus looked even more upset. "I can't write ma'am. I just sign with an X."

"That's OK, son. You make it the biggest X you can. Or two or three X's. Go on."

Marcus smiled at Greta, and she was as sure as she was alive that heaven had a hand on this youngster.

"You sure, ma'am? I gotta go bad."

"I'm sure, Marcus. Let it rip."

FOURTY-FOUR

Playing Metal Gear Solid was the one place Hoopdy could escape the daily rites of subservience, endless penance for lousy judgment and the wicked who prayed on his simpleton's eagerness to please. Hoopdy was a loser. Solid Snake could win.

When he saw Psycho Mantis at the broiler farm, Hoopdy decided he needed to be Solid Snake. Like when they talked to the Deacon. Hoopdy Solid, Beebe Liquid, Deacon Toast. Hoopdy tried to imagine the Penske steering wheel was his Xbox 360 console and the windshield a screen playing out his mission – to finish what he started and carry his wounded brother Beebe – Liquid Snake – home.

Being Solid wasn't so easy outside a recliner, bouncing around in the big diesel cab over the ruts and tree roots. First, Solid wanted to turn and fight, but Hoopdy kept popping off, thinking they should stick with the plan. Both Solid and Hoopdy wished they could crawl in the cardboard box and decide what to do, but there would be no stopping by the house today. Psycho Mantis was too close.

Then he thought the Solid thing to do would be to take poor bashed-up Beebe out of the line-of-fire, right to the Malapee Quick Fix Clinic and show Rachel her hubby was in bad shape, if he wasn't already a goner. The blood slung off his face all over the cab was that high-def red that usually signaled a gamer wipeout. Putting off the moment of truth with the terrorists, Solid had headed toward town and got within a couple miles of Paola when Beebe started whaling like a coyote.

So, he swerved back to the original plan. Sticking with the mission was the right way. They would proceed to The Dog Yard, get rid of the bodies and chicken shit, stand and defeat the Psycho Mantis and his band of terrorists, then go on home where they could tend Beebe and Hoopdy could get something to eat.

"Beebe, I need you to pay attention. You and me's headed for The Dog Yard so we can finish up for the Deacon, y'hear?" Beebe bounced and moaned, bounced and moaned.

"You listen to me, Liquid Snake! We gonna have us a fight when we git there, and you gotta help. Wake up, dammit," Solid hollered, pounding on the Xbox. Hoopdy never yelled at anybody like that in his life. Solid had no problem with it.

"Now, I'm sorry, Beebe, but this is a dang emergency. I seen Psycho Mantis and a buncha terrorists back there. That's why I took off like I done. Hell, they tracked us to right here where we live, right to Beauswamp County. You know what that means, dontcha? Now stop bellyachin'. We got work to do."

The Xbox suddenly wrenched Solid Hoopdy sideways as the right side tires slid in and out of a trench. It took him a minute to regain control. Solid shouldn't lose focus like that, but he was just plain tired. After turning back from the road to Paola, he had plowed straight cross country, avoiding even the logging roads.

Switching tactics, he detoured a ways on the Natchez Trace to throw off Psycho and his squad. He had just turned onto a halfway beaten path that only Solid knew about, one that merged into the unpaved washboard of the Bobcat track around The Dog Yard. The Penske would be out of the trees and onto the target in a few seconds. Solid braked and stopped, leaving the engine running. He needed Liquid, right now.

Solid shoved the bandana soaked in lighter fluid under Liquid's damaged nose until he was part way awake and he could sit more or less upright. Then, sure they were heading into an ambush, Hoopdy laid on the gas pedal, his hand hovering over the hand brake. If this was a firefight, Solid hoped he could goose the big old Penske somewhere closer to light speed, seeing as how it was the only weapon they had.

* * * * *

Special Agent Morales looked at his field watch and second-guessed his decision to go with Deputy Bucket's hunch. Squeezed into the two remaining Escalades, his interdiction team was staked out in a stand of pines several yards from a cliff that formed the back wall of the so-called Dog Yard. His boys and the deputy had spent hours here on and off over the past several days and all last night, watching the pair of drug runners haul and bury boxes. They'd headed from the wreckage of the broiler farm on Bucket's assurance that the suspects were headed straight here. That was 45 minutes ago.

There was some kind of activity across the crater of the Yard on the observation dock of the wastewater holding pond, but his guy in the sky, helo pilot Duffy Mercer, told him it was a handful of plant people and tech-types in lab coats. They were standing on the small dock talking, pointing at the pond and a vee-prow jonboat tied alongside. He told Special Agent Mercer to concentrate on finding the truck if the onlookers seemed to pose no immediate problem. Just in case, he dispatched Deputy Bucket to move them out of the area.

"Boss?"

"Talk to me, Duffy."

"Am I looking for a convoy?"

"No, it's a Penske dragging part of a trailer."

"Well, there's a bus convoy about 1000 yards south on the state highway."

"No, get away from the highway, over the logging roads. It's just one truck, and it should be coming through the woods."

"OK, but, Boss, we got company at 3 o'clock."

"The people on the dock? We went over that, Duff. Pull your head out."

"No, Boss, at my 3 o'clock. Two helos."

"Friendlies?" Morales asked, knowing it couldn't be anything else in the middle of nowhere Mississippi. Maybe it was a guard exercise or some cable TV hotdog shooting a ground pursuit.

"Boss, the convoy's turning at the plant and we got armed troops on the hoof, setting up a perimeter. And on the roof. Looks like SWAT or something."

"What the fuck?" Morales said, forgetting he was live. Maybe it was a bomb threat. Maybe the suspects ditched the Penske and came in the front way. Shit.

"Pull out," Morales hollered. This action was not going in the crapper. "Pull freaking out. Circle the plant. It's going down out front," whatever "it" was. The agents dove for the SUVs, loaded in and accelerated out of the stand of pines, rolling single file toward The Dog Yard track.

"Boss, the Penske! You're fixing to get t-boned," Mercer shouted.

"Pull out at will, but easy," Morales barked. "One more scratch on a vehicle and we'll be hauling poppy farmers in Afghanistan."

Bursting from the forest edge, the Penske bore down on the Escalades, lurching and swaying, grinding over bumps and hollows, plunging in and out of deep ruts. The SUVs scattered and formed up behind the truck as it lumbered to the lip of the cliff.

Straining from his seat in the Escalade, Special Agent Morales watched the nut job in the Penske head for a 30-foot drop into the hollows of the Dog Yard, as he attempted some feinting maneuver. Morales couldn't say precisely what judging from the hellish sound from the neighborhood of the truck's oil pan. He must have pulled the handbrake, put the truck into reverse or tried to wrench the wheels backward. Maybe a combination of all three. None of it worked.

The truck pulled up and over the berm and went airborne just enough to clear the ledge to nose-dive into the loamy mounds below. It landed grille first, almost vertical, then tipped over like a face-planted turtle slamming onto its back. The Penske's accordion door, unlashed from its moorings, yawled open as the undercarriage heeled over. The trailer landed on its roof with a solid whomp, expelling the payload of garbage bags in a flume of dirt chunks.

Most of the bags landed close by with a wet slap, exploding on impact, releasing malformed goop that looked like bundles of wet rags and old lumber. A half-dozen, with the momentum of a group of fifth-grade community pool cannonballers, plunged into the wastewater lagoon, soaking and resoaking Deputy Bucket and the lab coats, plopping in then popping back up to float away half-submerged.

Two bags, in a high, balletic arc, crashed together onto the prow of the bass boat, flipping it into the air and driving the lab coats scrambling into the drink. The craft somersaulted over the dock and plowed nose first deep into a gap between two planks, twanging home like a huge tuning fork. Hanging in a tangle from the dislocated outboard, there appeared to be a headless man dressed in a tattered garbage bag and what was left of a blue chalk-striped suit.

Trying to process what he'd just seen, Special Agent Morales' jaw might never have returned to a closed position if some idiot hadn't fired the first shot.

"Hold your fire, hold your fire," he screamed, thinking it was one of his agents. "For Christ sake, hold your fire." The last of his order was drowned out by the high-pitched bleat of an alarm bell.

He looked toward the back of the plant, the source of the incessantly clanging alarm. So far, nothing but noise. He turned back to the Penske and saw his two jugheads crawling and limping from the truck toward the boat dock.

"Don't fucking kill those assholes, I want 'em alive." Special Agent Morales was usually the soul of decorum when it came to live transmissions, but here he was screaming and cussing. Well he had to scream to be heard over the alarm. And he was cussing because he was getting damn fucking pissed.

"Boss, the shooter's over behind the pond," Mercer said in his ear. "By the hut. It's not our guy. He's aiming at me and our company."

"What company, Duffy? Who the hell is it?"

"With all due respect, Boss, me and the two other helos up here, that's who. You need to get a grip, with all due respect."

"Point taken. Get your ass out of range. Now!" Morales took a deep breath to steady his nerves but sucked in a lungful of dust instead. Over a spasm of coughing and in spite of the alarm, he heard the familiar thwock of Blackhawks and looked up to see commandos rappelling from two helos hovering and blowing shit everywhere. Who the hell had Blackhawks?

The interlopers landed and set their weapons, eyeing the SUVs. Then, forming up, they turned attention to the hordes of people now stampeding around the plant toward The Dog Yard, clogging every path then spreading into waves, followed by phalanxes of commandos. All of them were about to stomp Special Agent Morales' crime scene to smithereens.

FOURTY-FIVE

Deputy U.S. Marshal Suze Ludeman reacted as soon as the incoming hit. She should have trusted her instincts and her hearing and reacted sooner. She'd been getting counseling for PTSD on the down-low because she'd spent two rotations in Fallujah heading a supply convoy. She told herself that some car backfire from the highway had triggered her hypersensitivity. But she'd been right all along.

She was sure she had heard a chopper and there it was. Then, the IEDs landed, the most un-fucking-believable roadside piece-of-shit bombs she'd ever seen. They looked like some kind of translucent play-dough and smelled like the base facilities after Tom Kah Kai Taco Night. They were dud devices, but still blew her ragtag little squad of EPA inspectors into the water.

It wouldn't have helped anybody if she got taken out, so she ran for some sandy hills near a cinderblock bunker and hunkered down to make her shots count. She fired one warning shot to head off the chopper before the enemy could draw a bead.

Now, she was sighting on two hajis slinking from the truck that launched the IEDs. They were heading toward the dock, probably thinking open water was the quickest way out of the cluster they caused. Blockheads. She watched them limp and hobble to the upended boat. The taller one shoved and twisted the boat, trying to dislodge the prow where it speared clean through the wood.

She couldn't hear much with the rotor noise and what sounded like a general quarters klaxon. But that would be the Navy. Oh well, hers not to reason why, etc. Suze shut it all out to focus on the enemy, who were about to free the boat and get away.

"No way, boys," Suze whispered. She wished she had her rifle but the Glock would have to do. She braced and sighted again and squeezed.

* * * * *

Special Agent Morales and his team were being surrounded by people dressed in some kind of loose robes and wearing hairnets. More continued to stream from the plant. They were alternately herded and stopped, then divided into smaller groups by what must be hundreds of troops in full battle gear. The backs of the troop uniform blouses read POLICE ICE. Border hounds.

"Guys, move, get to that Penske," Morales ordered. But when they started to climb out of the SUVs and move out, they were barred by some gunners from ICE.

"Sarge, give us some room, here. This is a DEA operation." Morales offered his hang tag to the nearest one.

"Well, Sarge yourself, since this here's a ICE raid, I have to decline the request for some room and ask your name," the ICE agent drawled.

"Son, where's your chief?" Morales demanded. "I need to get this cleared up fast. I got suspects on the move down there." Hearing the exchange, Morales's agents were moving up. He motioned them to stand down.

"And my name's Morales."

"Well, Mr. Morales, you need to step over this way with all the others of your Morales persuasion," the ICE agent pointed with his elbow, which allowed him to heft the butt of his rifle in a meaningful way. So, he was dealing with a nincompoop who couldn't read. Special Agent Morales shook his head, but slowly moved where the ICE agent gestured, angling toward The Dog Yard ledge.

Then he heard someone chamber check a weapon. Jesus, the last thing they needed was a shootout with this tool from Homeland Security and all these civilians milling around. "Everybody! Hold all fire," he ordered.

209

The second blast sounded from the far side of the lagoon. The ICE guys and several hundred other folks hit the dirt, but Morales stayed on his feet long enough to see a flash spark off the jonboat hull right before flames mushroomed from the ass of the tallest drug-running bomber, who screamed, grabbed his butt and ran for the pond. The runty fugitive was right on his fiery tail.

Before Morales was sacked by one of his guys in case the shooter's aim improved, the DEA Special Agent in charge got a last glimpse of his suspects splashing wildly for the far bank and presumably the deep woods beyond. Never mind. It should be easy enough to track down someone with third-degree burns over 98 percent of his ignorant ass.

Within minutes, the ICE troops were rousting everyone upright, tightening their perimeter and forcing them to move toward the plant. Morales told his guys to button up and move along. He wanted to ask the ICE agents if they wondered what the DEA was doing in the big middle of things. Or if they had any further thoughts about the sniper beyond the pond. But he decided it would be better to wait until he could locate the ICE Nimrod in Charge and land on him with both feet. Or her.

The silence that followed the shot that ignited his suspect's hind end had been short-lived. The plant workers were once again protesting, baiting the agents, promising that legions of lawyers would be dancing on the pinheads of ICE honchos, but others were laughing about some Mert woman's fanny and her hook-ups over the radio. All very confusing to Morales, except he realized they were all speaking perfectly unaccented Mississippi English. Although he didn't understand all the words he heard, for the most part they were not Spanish.

When a piercing cry rang out above the din, it brought tears to Morales eyes as much because of the pain in the voice as for the number it did on his ear drums. He saw Deputy Bucket dodging the blows of a woman totally out of control, trying to get closer to the flipped jonboat with a torso in a double breasted blazer hung up on the propeller.

"Dadeeeeeeah! Oh, lord! Oh, lord! Oh God! Help me, Jesus! What have they done? What have you done to my daddeeeeah? Daddeeee…Chumley, look. Danny, baby, cover your eyes…Chumley. My own daddy. Danny's own pawpaw. Dadeeeeeee…what have they done to your suit?"

FOURTY-SIX

Solid Snake was gone, but Hoopdy still had his camouflage cardboard box, where he was crouched, shaking and wondering if the terrorists had been able to follow him and Beebe after they made it across the pond.

They had limped along on foot for a good ways, keeping to the woods, away from SUVs and helicopters. But Beebe's heiney was hurting so bad from where the lighter fluid exploded, they had snuck onto one of the loggin' roads and flagged down an old guy in a pickup for a ride.

He'd sat in back next to Beebe, who was layin' with his busted up face buried in his arms, cryin' and moanin' that the Deacon would peel off what skin he had left when he heard about the Penske and the bodies and chicken litter flyin' all over those people at the plant. Then Beebe stopped cryin' and got really mad. He said his daddy had another think comin' if he thought he could pin it all on Beebe.

They were both banged up from the Penske heavin' over, so the old man dropped them at Rachel's work so she could look at Beebe's cooked backside and anything else that was broke. But Hoopdy didn't think he had any busted parts, so he run right on home, right past Geneva, who didn't look up from Maury Povich or her glass of beer.

Ran right to his room. He knew if he sat in the box long enough, it'd all be OK. He could stay here 'til ever body got over their mad, 'til they'd stop lookin' for him. It'd all be OK, especially if he could quit shakin'.

* * * * *

Greta's toes and fingers were tingling painfully by the time she and Marcus Wynn walked through the deserted break room. She held fast to the young man's arm on one side and to the bag of frozen thumbs, wrapped in a smock, on the other.

The fire alarm was still sounding but if there was a fire, it was not moving fast. Still, plant fire drills didn't usually last so long. So where was the fire department? Not that she should care. Greta was through. She planned to use the wireless internet at the Malapee Super 8 to send her resignation right before she checked out.

Then she was heading for an urgent care clinic. Thanks to that madman Tubby, her nose still hurt like the dickens. She might as well check for frostbite while she was there. Then straight home to Oklahoma. She probably should file some sort of police report on Tubby and the thumbs, but was afraid she'd be stuck here for days.

Marcus said she could borrow his cell phone to call Toby, but she wanted to get away from the alarm. She planned to give him an edited version of the last three days, and that would be complicated by a horn blasting in the background. No reason to get him all riled up until she was home. Then they could get riled up together and decide which flaming fuckheads to go after first. Andy was at the top of her list.

When they walked out the front doors of Malapee Poultry Xtra, Greta stopped a minute to relish being untied, outdoors and reasonably warm. She didn't really have a chance to enjoy the sensation because of the chaos churning as far as she could see, the entire length of the massive plant, across the parking lot all the way to the highway.

From the vantage at the top of the long stairway up to the plant, Greta could see six buses with blacked out windows, three helicopters, a dozen highway patrol cars and two or three ambulances mingled among the parked cars on the lot and a dozen tractor trailers and live haul chicken trucks stopped at odd angles around the driveways and grounds.

Posse Members were scattered everywhere in groups large and small, apparently all talking at once and at the tops of their lungs. If she had to guess, she'd say the couple hundred black suited storm troopers were trying to maintain control and barely succeeding.

A woman near the guard gate who ran screaming in circles was collared by one of the uniforms. She began pounding his flak vest with what looked like a short soda can and wailed about Quickie Ricky and Vienna Sausages.

Some Posse Members nearby apparently thought the cop was at fault and rushed to pull him off the hysterical woman. Greta heard a couple of loud pops, saw canisters arc toward the melee, which began another general stampede away from large blooms of tear gas that began to obscure the view. Greta stumbled against Marcus, dizzy. This wasn't a chicken plant, it was an asylum. She steadied herself and started moving down.

Greta could see the two or three storm troopers with the fanciest headgear talking to a crowd of Poultry Xtra managers in their tell-tale grays gathered at the foot of the stairs. She remembered that the quarterly road show of the big boys from Corporate was rolling through Malapee this week.

That meant Andy was somewhere in that crowd. Since Tubby had taken her Lock & Load radio and her cell phone, she had no idea if her boss had tried to find her in the last 72 hours. Somehow she doubted it. Anyway, Andy could deal with the thumbs and cops.

"C'mon, Marcus," Greta said. "This should only take a minute." She guided him down the stairs until she stood on the edge of the crowd of cops and Poultry Xtra grays. She saw uniform shirts identifying the lawmen as DEA and ICE. She recognized a few of the locals who worked off-duty for Lock & Load. Deputy Bucket was there, soaking wet for some reason.

In fact there were a few people who looked like they'd had a run in with a fire hose, including the Plant Manager Maynard Travis who was yelling but drawing no listeners. Truly Lovett was there too, listening to one of the storm troopers, looking pouty like Rudy

214

when they'd had to bury his hamster after an unfortunate encounter with Toby's shop-vac.

Greta saw the Senior VP for Operations, the South Division Ops VP, the Senior VP for HR Ops and his Division guy, two Assistant VPs for QC and R&D, the EVP for Sales and about a dozen assorted regional and plant manager types.

And there was Andy, talking to a group of people wearing visitor tags. Probably customers here to see how Poultry Xtra handled their products. What an eye opener for them.

She let go of Marcus long enough to wave at Andy then took Marcus and pushed through the crowd.

"Andy," Greta said when she reached his side. "Here are your thumbs." He looked at her briefly, as if he didn't know her, then turned back to listen to a guy she recognized as the head of product development for Dairy Daisy.

"Andy, I found the damn thumbs. We need to talk so I can get the hell out of here."

Andy looked again, seeming surprised to see her. He took her arm and edged away from the Dairy Daisy group. "Greta, great to see you. We do need to talk, but I can't right now. This whole day has been the most unbelievable series of screw-ups. You would not believe what we've been going through here. You were right; Mississippi may be the biggest mess in the Company. But just hang on while I unruffle some feathers. Dairy Daisy is ready to pull the plug, you understand. Oh, and nice uniform."

Andy patted her shoulder and walked away.

Greta followed.

"Andy. I quit."

He turned, frowned and waved his hand behind his back, shooing her.

"Andy, here're your thumbs."

No response.

Greta calmly removed the smock from the bag of mostly frozen severed thumbs. She gripped the bag by the length of excess plastic above the knot tight against the contents. Greta looked around to make sure bystanders were well away and with a quick swing up from the ground, wielding the bag of thumbs like a lassoed 35-pound frozen turkey, she laid it lightly up the back of Andy's head and let go.

Well, maybe not all that lightly. Greta didn't see him topple into the arms of Mr. Dairy Daisy. She had retrieved Marcus and disappeared into the crowd by the time Andy had recovered and was fighting to wrest the bag of thumbs back from one of the Company's biggest customers.

"C'mon Marcus, I'll give you a ride anywhere you need to go," Greta didn't know if it was her injured nose or that Marcus was just growing on her. He didn't smell all that bad really.

"Ma'am, can I ask you something? Don't get mad at me," Marcus said.

"Ask anything you want, Marcus. I won't be mad."

"Could we stop somewhere? I gotta pee again."

"Come to think of it, so do I, Marcus. Can you make it to the Wee-Stop in Paola?"

"Yes ma'am, I believe I can hold her for that long." Marcus smiled in his beatific way and clamped his hand firmly on his crotch.

Greta dug in her pocket, happy to find Tubby didn't take the keys to her rental. Screw sitting around in airports. She was going to fill up at the Wee-Stop and head for Oklahoma. She beeped the car open, climbed in and helped Marcus, one-handed as he was, fasten his seat belt. She leaned back, resting her head. She noticed that the blasted belt from her uniform was hanging around her neck. She had no idea how it ended up there.

Greta started the car and maneuvered out of the clogged lot. She planned to drive over anyone, official or otherwise, who got in her way. Driving past the guard gate, she rolled down her window to sling the belt at the feet of a young man in a Lock & Load uniform. She drove a few yards, then pulled to the side of the plant drive, near the turn onto the highway.

"Marcus, may I borrow your phone?"

Marcus fished it from his shirt pocket. She didn't for a second consider wiping it on her pant leg. She had to think a minute to remember Toby's number.

"Hello?

"It's me. Had to borrow a phone."

"What happened to yours, or do I want to know?"

"I'll tell you everything as soon as I get home, which should be sometime after midnight, give or take."

"Nice. Me and the boys will be waiting. We have a surprise for you."

"I'm kinda long on surprises, right now. Why don't you just tell me."

"OK. She's a piddly black dog named Lily."

"Oh, Toby, I thought we decided..."

"We did, but the boys should have some input, and it's about time they had something else to do besides Wii."

"Toby?"

"Hmm?"

"You just throw big old soft balls and I get to hit 'em."

"It's the least I can do."

"Toby, you the man, babe."

"Greta, you the babe, man. Drive safe."

When she turned onto the highway, Greta did something she hadn't done since she insisted she would drive her newborns home from the hospital. She laid rubber. Suddenly happy knowing that Gene Pitney wasn't in Malapee when he sang her favorite song. This armpit of Mississippi was way under 24 hours from Tulsa, which was only 10 minutes from Skiatook, Toby, Mikey and Rudy. And now, piddly little Lily.

THUMBS PROBED IN BIG CHICKEN FLAP

USDA orders Oklahoma Poultry giant to close Mississippi plant in contamination investigation involving human body parts victims claim they found in bags of chicken wings. DEA, ICE, EPA among Feds investigating raft of "outlandish" incidents; plaintiffs' attorneys express outrage in rare show of unity.

A Pittsburgh Herald Dispatch exclusive report by senior writers Amy Russell, Jory Cody and Brandy Looper.

In what may prove to be one of the most bizarre and complicated cases of food contamination in memory, involving flurries of individual and class-action lawsuits and investigations by at least five federal agencies, Oklahoma chicken processing giant Poultry Xtra today closed one of its largest manufacturing plants.

The Company also announced the recall of hundreds of thousands of pounds of frozen chicken wings because severed human thumbs were found in two restaurant service wing packs produced at the Malapee, Mississippi location, and in vending machines at a convenience store near the plant.

The Herald-Dispatch has learned that the thumbs, one originally sold, consumed and regurgitated in Tulsa, the second discovered during preparation at an East Side Pittsburgh eatery, come from corpses thought by family members of the deceased to have been cremated at the Malapee Gather at the River Funeralization and Home Going Tabernacle, a mortuary and crematory.

A number of uncremated corpses from at least six counties in Mississippi, Alabama and Tennessee have been recovered from makeshift graves in an area reportedly known as "The Dog Yard" on the processing plant grounds. Long time Malapee residents say The Dog Yard at one time was the venue for weekly gambling on dog and cock fights.

Poultry Xtra is a Fortune 500 multinational company headquartered in the northeastern Oklahoma community of Skiatook. It employs approximately 75,000 employees at 30 plants in the Americas and China. The Malapee plant employed 2300 and produced millions of pounds of fresh, frozen and further processed chicken each week, before the closing was ordered by the USDA.

Phone calls and e-mailed questions to Poultry Xtra in Skiatook as well as to Malapee plant managers, identified through LinkedIn as Truly Lovett and Maynard Travis, have been referred to corporate attorney Cletus B. Field, who said "no public statements with the exception of responses to court filings will be forthcoming until a thorough internal investigation is complete."

In a rare statement of cooperation, attorneys for scores of plaintiffs, who have come forward seeking redress from Poultry Xtra on a variety of claims, call the closing "way too little, way too late," alleging that Poultry Xtra knew about the severed thumbs weeks before a popular Pittsburgh blog, PipeSnark, reported that the amputated members were turning up as bar nibbles.

Plaintiffs claim that despite the online revelation, Poultry Xtra sought to "cover up the grisly affair." The statement further cites "a series of outlandish and indefensible incidents and circumstances at the Malapee plant that demand an immediate accounting from the very highest levels of Poultry Xtra management."

Among the incidents and circumstances, which court filings allege occurred during a period between July and October:

– Approximately 35 pounds of frozen severed human thumbs in a plastic bag was found by a Poultry Xtra manager and delivered to senior Poultry Xtra executives who were touring the Mississippi facility at the time of the discovery.

According to PHD sources inside Malapee World Poultry and Pork Workers Confederation Local 007 and Beauswamp County law enforcement officials speaking on the condition of anonymity, the thumbs reportedly were removed from corpses found in temporary graves behind the Gather at the River Tabernacle crematory retort, or furnace, as well as from a makeshift mass grave behind a Poultry Xtra contract chicken broiler farm. The farm is co-owned by Deacon Maitland Dovey, a part-time chaplain at the Malapee Poultry Xtra plant who also owns the Gather at the River crematory, and his brother-in- law, Tuber Daylight.

Mr. Daylight's brother, Wayne Daylight, was head of plant maintenance at the Malapee plant with oversight for the so-called Dog Yard, where the remains of 26 additional human corpses were found in various states of decomposition, scattered in plastic drum liner bags or floating in the plant's wastewater treatment holding pond. Remains of hundreds of reportedly petrified chicken carcasses found in the same area have complicated identification of the human remains.

– Several decomposing thumbs were discovered in two snack vending machines at "Quickie Ricky's," a convenience store located next to the Malapee plant entrance. Records show that at least three customers bought Vienna sausage packs containing thumbs with small notecards attached. Mr. Richard "Quickie Ricky" T. Bass and a cousin, Ms. Mertricious Ellis, a manager at Malapee Poultry Xtra, and Vendi, Vidi, Vici Vending route salesman Delmer "Chips" Buthod are persons of interest in the misappropriation of cadaverous thumbs.

However, authorities say no charges have been filed pending further investigation. Sheriff's officials say Mr. Bass, Ms. Ellis and two other Poultry Xtra employees, sisters Lamentatia and Levitica Taylor, also are being questioned in connection with alleged loan sharking activities throughout the county.

– An armed stand-off occurred at The Dog Yard between top field agents of the U.S. Drug Enforcement Agency and U.S. Immigration and Customs Enforcement. Representatives of both agencies say they do not discuss specifics of field operations. However ICE has confirmed that a field raid involving warrants for suspected undocumented workers occurred at the plant in October.

– Representatives of the Occupational Safety and Health Administration attempted to conduct an inspection of the plant in October, on the same date of the ICE/DEA contretemps, in the wake of an alleged altercation in the plant in August that resulted in the scalping of an employee whose hairnet and hair became entangled in operating machinery.

A source close to OSHA, who requested anonymity because she is not authorized to discuss the ongoing investigation, said that key lock data from the location alarm indicate that the plant safety manager, or someone using his PIN, initiated a fire alarm, causing the evacuation of nearly 2,000 employees and visitors, effectively preventing the inspectors from gaining access to the facility.

– In a related development, an attorney for the scalped employee says he obtained secretly recorded comments about his client made by Poultry Xtra managers during a staff meeting in September "so insensitive and offensive they constitute criminal stupidity." To a PHD e-mail inquiring what legal predicate would apply, Josie Barger of Nafud and Barger wrote in reply, "If there's not a law, there should be."

– An unused freezer inside the plant, containing hundreds of pint bottles of vodka and quantities of controlled substances including marijuana, methamphetamine, cocaine, Rohypnol, OxyContin and boxes of paraphernalia commonly used in packaging drugs for sale, was seized by local and state law enforcement authorities in a joint operation with the DEA.

– Several Poultry Xtra managers and employees are being sought as material witnesses in the DEA investigation, including Regis "Bad Fruit" Purdy, Beebe Dovey, Hoopdy Creavy, Fano Alcides and Elvis Ridenour. More warrants are said to be forthcoming. "We believe a number of employees were involved in this drug trafficking operation at this plant," said Deputy Chumley Bucket of the Beauswamp County Sheriff's office who has been attached to the DEA team investigating the alleged trafficking.

Citing his lack of authority relative to the Department of Homeland Security, Deputy Bucket declined to comment further about reports that some individuals sought in the drug investigation also were under surveillance in connection with a possible bomb plot involving large quantities of chicken litter fertilizer.

Several professionals knowledgeable about explosives told the PHD that there is no record of chicken litter fertilizer having been used to produce home-made explosive devices. However, Don

Vincent of bombwatch.com said, "Never underestimate the resourcefulness of deviant malcontents, especially in the deep South."

– Mr. Beebe Dovey, his father, Maitland Dovey, linked to the crematory and the chicken broiler farm where corpses were found, and Mr. Hoopdy Creavy also are being sought on charges relating to the corpses including theft by deception, abusing a corpse, burial-service related fraud, specifically, the substitution of a mixture of powdered methamphetamine and instant vanilla pudding to mimic the ash cremains given to grieving family members.

– These revelations follow the Superfund Site designation this week of the Malapee Poultry Xtra water treatment operation by the U.S. Environmental Protection Agency. An EPA official said agency representatives were invited to the plant in October by Poultry Xtra , coincidentally on the day of visits by ICE, DEA and OSHA, to obtain water samples, this in response to water district reports of elevated levels of lead, arsenic and nitrates in the area aquifer.

According to a representative of the Malapee-Paola water district, the poultry plant returns millions of gallons of treated water used in processing to the area's water system each week.

The EPA official, speaking on condition of anonymity because she was not authorized to speak about the Malapee case, said agents recovered evidence of the direct dumping of large quantities of the raw litter, a mixture of sawdust and chicken feces removed routinely from contractor chicken farms. While the subject of some debate, litter converted to fertilizer is widely used on field crops. However concentrated dumping of the "chicken cake" removed in cleaning poultry houses is prohibited.

The EPA official refused to comment on reports that the U.S. Marshal who accompanied agency officials to the plant opened fire on ICE and DEA agents executing field operations at the Malapee plant during the EPA visit, referring all inquiries in the matter to the U.S. Department of Justice, who had not responded to repeated calls and e-mails at press time.

IN TUESDAY'S PHD, PART 2: PLAINTIFFS SOUND OFF:

An Oklahoma woman says ingesting a dead person's thumb that came in a bucket of hot wings dashed her hopes for an American Idol audition, but she hopes to produce a reality show about the benefits of bulimia.

Pittsburgh pub sisters return to business as usual, except no more "Wing Night."

Seeing her father's un-cremated, headless and thumbless corpse so traumatized the Malapee, Mississippi single mother she resumed drug habit, causing lawman fiancé to cancel the wedding.

IN WEDNESDAY'S PHD, PART 3: THUMB RING UNCOVERED:

Former Poultry Xtra Quality Control manager kidnapped after finding stash of hacked-off thumbs at Malapee plant talks about ordeal.

Also contributing to this three-part special investigation, Pittsburgh PipeSnark blogger Resaca Toomey, freelance journalist and master pipefitter.

EPILOGUE

PipeSnark.com
What's backed up in the 'Burgh by Resaca Toomey, pipefitter and investigative blogger
ON SEPT. 23, 20XX, 9.24 AM
Disposable Digit Anniversary Update

More on the dead thumb in the chicken wings saga, but this time no sharing. Why would I? One measly mention in the PHD, plus they wouldn't run the horoscope I did for the "Special Report." Sheesh!

I tried to interest The Tulsa Daily Would in some free-lance tidbits for a second anniversary round up, but they had no interest in the story to begin with, even though it was a Tulsa girl who barfed up the first dead person's fried thumb. Said it wasn't a "family-oriented story." Well no shit.

Screw 'em all, and here you go: The little guy who turned state's evidence or amicus cretinous or whatever it's called, Hoopdy Creavy, has landed on his flat little cracker feet. After copping every kind of plea known to man and imbecile for messing with corpses, dumping chicken shit in the wrong place and generally being a flaming loser for most of his pitiful life, Hoopdy was released for time served during all his trials and six years' community service swabbing out tanks for the Malapee-Paola, Mississippi water and sewer department.

Also, he is at work full time as a janitor at the Malapee Middle School, a job his sister says her new boyfriend, middle school principal Prat Lopeter, helped little brother land.

224

Parents of Malapee Middle School Students will be glad to know that Creavy was ultimately dropped as a defendant in the federal sex harassment suit, Leary v. Poultry Xtra.

When I called to check on him, bless his heart, Hoopdy told Resaca that he's minding his p's and q's, and that the kids are great. Says they totally appreciate all the tricks his Uncle Kevin taught him. So here's two Plungers for the little creep.

Today's Horoscope
If it's your birthday today, show a little common sense. Do your darndest to avoid frauds, cowards and charlatans, but if you can't, make the best deal you can and get back to normal.

ACKNOWLEDGMENTS

Several generous readers – DJ, Bob, Karen, Kris, Kristi, Michael, Dennis, Doug and Nancy – I cannot thank enough for the frankness and expert guidance from first draft to last. My champion and publisher Tim Barger, who will always be Khamis to me, has kept me in stitches, in awe and on the writer's quest for years. Absolutely nothing bad or indifferent in these pages is their fault – it's all mine. Anything worthy here is through their good graces.

Diana and Snooze, Alan, Barb and Amber gave this hack a home in needful times, the warm environments of friendship and family where a chick of an idea could grow into a different kind of big bird amid backyard gardens, musicales and cook-outs, tornados, blizzards, honey bees, dogs, cats and acres of inspiration.

Whatever one's views on factory farming, no such list would be complete without a nod to the thousands of upstanding people in the poultry industry who work with absolute integrity harder than one can imagine, every single day.

And much love with extra sauce for wing nights everywhere.

Sijin Belle, LeFlore County, 2012

For more fine original works of fiction and non-fiction in either e-book or print format you are invited to visit the Selwa Digital web site at www.SelwaDigital.com

www.ingramcontent.com/pod-product-compliance
Lightning Source LLC
Chambersburg PA
CBHW070610130626
46556CB00001B/330